— — —

Library and Archives Canada Cataloguing in Publication

Horne, Christine, 1945-
           Tarstopping / Christine Horne.

Issued in print and electronic formats.
ISBN 978-1-926455-47-1 (pbk.)
ISBN 978-1-926455-48-8 (epub)
ISBN 978-1-926455-49-5 (mobi)

     I. Tarstopping.

PS8615.O759T37 2015   C813'.6   C2015-901821-8   C2015-901822-6

— — —

Board Editor: Kit Dobson
Cover & Interior Design: Greg Vickers
Author Photo: Lee Horne

Cover Image: "Protester, throwing a piece of paving during at riot police during clashes at Bankova str, Kiev, Ukraine. December 1, 2013." by Mstyslav Chernov/Unframe is licensed under CC BY-SA 3.0. Image has been re-coloured and cropped. © 2013 Mstyslav Chernov

NeWest Press acknowledges the financial support of the Alberta Multimedia Development Fund and the Edmonton Arts Council for our publishing program. We acknowledge the support of the Canada Council for the Arts, which last year invested $24.3 million in writing and publishing throughout Canada. This project is funded in part by the Government Of Canada.

201, 8540–109 Street
Edmonton, Alberta | T6G 1E6
780.432.9427
www.newestpress.com

NeWest Press

No bison were harmed in the making of this book.

We are committed to protecting the environment and to the responsible use of natural resources. This book was printed on 100% post-consumer recycled paper.

1 2 3 4 5 14 13 | Printed and bound in Canada

A THRILLER

TARSTOPPING

CHRISTINE REHDER HORNE

NeWest
PRESS

SUNDAY
MAY 27 2012

They should have cancelled dinner tonight, Tim thought again. But everyone had wanted to come, to get close to ground zero, as Jason was calling it, since Tim and Shannon lived only blocks from the site. If he stood on his front porch would he be able to hear the roar of the crowd to the southwest? Was it swelling even as they ate, soon to engulf his house?

"I can't believe this has happened," Jason was saying. It was what everyone kept saying. "I can't believe they could just walk into the house of the company's president and take him and his family hostage. Just walk in on a Saturday morning when everyone's home and the alarm system's off. No violence, no guns, just all those radicals who'd convoyed over the mountains chaining themselves together around the house. Who'd ever think that'd work? The hostage-takers have to be as gob-smacked as everyone else at their success."

"We're never prepared," said Shannon. "Despite history, we never believe ahead of time what can happen."

Tim smiled down the table at his wife. "None of this surprises you," he teased, her dim view of humanity something of a joke among them. He was half-expecting her to pop up and get the dessert, even though no one had eaten much of the main course yet. She'd served the meal within moments of everyone arriving, annoyed that they hadn't been able to reschedule this dinner, their turn in the regular get-togethers of the six of them.

Cole, usually the quietest of them, was red-faced with rage. "How can the government have not known about this ahead of time? Can you answer me that? Why weren't they under surveillance? It has to have been all over the Net, to have been this organized. Trust the Canadian government to be asleep at the wheel."

Already Tim hated the emotion in people's voices, either excitement like Jason or fury like Cole. He didn't want to hear any more wild rumours and predictions. All day he hadn't been able to watch any of the television coverage because of the edge of hysteria in the reporters' voices. He said now, in what he knew was his mitigating, downplaying way, "There's so much fantasy and intrigue on the Net that it's easy to see how stuff gets over-looked. These guys are probably experts at avoiding detection. This has been brewing for years. It's probably been planned for months."

"I can't believe they're getting away with it." Cole was

yelling now. "Somebody made the dumbass decision not to go in there the minute they heard. Why was that? They should have aimed guns at their heads and forced those flower-lovers to unchain and leave. Right at the beginning. Now the whole thing's out of control. Now we're in crazyland. Every looney on the continent's on their way here now." He shook his head violently from side to side. "It's fucking unbelievable."

"There were already thousands of people around the house," said Tim, "before anyone knew anything was going on. Students and Occupiers from last fall and every radical in the city had been tweeted up. No one knew what was going on until Wendy made her demand. And by then it was too late, there were too many of them." He had to laugh at himself, always the facilitator, trying to explain one side in a conflict to the other. He should just sit back and wait for this ill-advised dinner to be over.

"Why didn't they know?" Cole demanded. "How asleep is that? A crowd of thousands amasses and nobody in authority knows until that fucking Wendy woman phones a radio station? Shut down the oilsands! Who the fuck do these people think they are?"

They were all tiring of Cole's anger. He usually had so little to say. Truth be told, they were all much fonder of his wife, Lori, than of him.

Jason said, "Can't you just watch it as something fascinating going on? The whole thing's gone beyond Wendy and the ringleaders now anyway. Even if they were to release the Morrisons tonight, it wouldn't change the dynamic that's unfolding. All those environmentalists and anarchists on their way here from all over the country, from all over the continent, are going to keep coming. And it's only been — what? — not even thirty-six hours since Wendy and her boys slipped into the Morrison house. Their followers are going to take over the city. Elbow Drive's already blocked off. Coming here, we couldn't even turn off Glenmore onto Elbow. They say there's like five thousand people around the house now and more arriving every minute. They're setting up tents in parks and school grounds around the house and then joining the Wall. That's what it's being called. They'll take turns sleeping and then standing in the Wall."

Jason's voice was almost gleeful. He was consumed by the developments and theories, his iPad open on the table beside him. Tim thought Shannon just might accidently spill her wine over it.

Before he could stop himself, Tim said, "This whole thing feels like an eruption out of our collective worry about the future. We've been trying to figure out a way to live with the news about the fragility of all our systems while still going on with business as usual and it just doesn't compute. Something had to happen. The cumulative tension in our collective unconscious has to be huge and explosive." Why couldn't he just keep quiet? He hated his own propensity to jump in and sum things up from some deep vantage point.

But then Alysha, Jason's girlfriend, a good ten years younger than the rest of them, laughed and said, "I think most of us are a little more concerned with how it's going to affect our own lives and not so much with the big historical forces at play. Anyway, you all know what I think. Global warming is mostly a scam. The global temperature is actually holding steady. Global warming is one of those ideas that has a life of its own – when there's lots of gullible people around."

Alysha was the type, Tim thought, always on the lookout for something being put over on her. But she was also a lawyer who worked for a big firm dependent on the oil industry, which might explain some of her stance, although she'd indignantly deny it.

Jason, much more interested in current dynamics than debating global warming, said, "They say there's like fifty thousand people on their way up from the States. The whole environmental thing is huge down there. They have the numbers. If even a fraction of them come, we'll be swamped. They'll set up tent cities all over the place. Tarstoppers. Have you heard that? I don't know if they came up with that name themselves or the media or whoever. This is going to be the first real outbreak in the war between the right and the left."

Cole burst out again, "Fucking idiots. We should close the fucking American border. We should bring in the army. Use tear gas, rubber bullets, whatever we have to, and ignore the wusses who'll yell about police brutality. We've got to do whatever it takes to shut this down now, while we still can."

Cole's wife, Lori, distressed by his extremism, used one of the tactics from her classroom to divert attention. "What I don't get is, say they're able to get the oilsands shut down. Won't the oil then just be replaced from somewhere else? Like

Venezuela or somewhere? Is the oil from the oilsands really all that different?"

Jason, their petroleum expert, took it upon himself to instruct Lori. "They think it's dirtier because it's bitumen, not light and clean crude. And that its production causes more carbon dioxide release. But that's a myth, actually. They just need a target. We've done studies and we found that diluted bitumen – dilbit, it's called – is actually less corrosive in pipelines than regular oil. And it's certainly less explosive. But what do the facts matter? Why don't American environmentalists stay in their own country and protest the use of coal? Now there's a dirty industry. Or fracking? The whole thing's a joke. They're all such game players. They're totally fuzzy-minded."

Jason, who worked for a pipeline company, liked to say that work was a game to him, not to be taken seriously, but he gave himself away, Tim thought, when he used "we." He and Jason had become friends when they'd started out together in their first jobs after university, at entry level in an American food conglomerate. Although they'd both hated it, and Tim had soon jumped to a non-profit, Jason had stayed in the business world, switching over to oil and gas, where the money was, and keeping his irreverent attitude, or so he liked to think. Jason was his best friend, but sometimes he couldn't stand to listen to him.

Cole had his arms crossed and he gripped each arm as if holding himself down. He lunged forward. "How dare those fucking hypocrites think they can come and take over our city? How are they even getting here? It's like Al Gore or David

Suzuki flying around the world lecturing the rest of us about the dangers of oil consumption."

Lori put her hand on his arm but he shrugged it off and sat back, engulfed in his emotion and barely aware of them looking at him in concern.

It was strange, Tim sometimes thought, the people who became your friends. Cole and Lori had been neighbours at their old house. When Cole had lost his job and their daughter had been diagnosed with cancer, the four of them had skipped ahead into intimacy when his and Shannon's style of give and take had meshed with theirs. It had bonded them beyond positions and leanings. It was also odd, Tim thought, how passionately Cole believed in the system, his loyalty to the oil industry, despite having never done well in it. He'd always been on the edge of big plays, things never quite working out. As far as Tim knew, Cole wasn't taking any money out of his latest venture, a start-up oilrig servicing company, and they lived on Lori's teacher's salary.

Alysha said, "It's almost like Wendy Tsang and her hostages are getting forgotten in all this. They're like the black hole at the centre, with nothing coming out. Not a word more from them."

Jason was watching something on his iPad, the flashes of light bouncing off his face. He could barely pull his eyes away to respond to Alysha but he couldn't pass up an opportunity to hold forth. "There's nothing more to be discovered about Wendy and those two disciples of hers anyway. Within a couple of hours of the hostage-taking yesterday we knew

everything there was to know about them. We'd seen everything they'd written, every speech they ever gave. Without new
information we can't keep them in mind. They weren't all that
interesting to start with. They're the usual west coast fanatics working on limited information. And the Morrisons are
just as limited, your typical oil business elite out of Oklahoma
or wherever they're from. The people in the house aren't the
story any more. It's what's going on around them."

Lori said to Jason in her prompting teacher voice, "You're
not as furious as Cole and yet you work for a pipeline company.
Are you really as objective as you seem?"

"Well, I actually get that there's a lot wrong in the world. I
get it about pollution and having to be more careful with what
we dump and emit. No argument. I get that corporations have
become so big they're beyond any government's control, an-
swerable to no one. The problem I have with the Tarstoppers
is that they want to tear the whole civilization down because
parts of it need fixing. They'll put us back into the Dark Ages,
living in tents. I happen to believe that we'll fix the environmental thing. I'm all for putting pressure on corporations to
clean up their act. Eventually we'll find better fuels. This is
just a stage, a point of transition, not an excuse to go backtracking into the past."

"The Dark Ages is right," Cole burst back in. "Do those
idiots not know what they're messing with? The economy is at
crisis point thanks to all the social spending those types have
insisted on. They'll bring civilization to a crashing halt."

Lori said brightly, "There's a huge amount of positive stuff going on in the world. I'm with Jason on that. We'll find solutions. Like they're doing in Denmark, almost totally reducing their carbon footprint. Like everybody I know is into recycling and eating stuff without pesticides and all that. Who ever thought that would become mainstream? It's coming. I'm pretty optimistic. I don't see how getting the oilsands shut down like they want is the way to go. The whole province would go into financial meltdown. As Jason says, we're in transition. It'll get cleaned up and eventually phased out anyway."

Tim kept his face still as he said, "It'd be nice to be so optimistic." But he wanted to say, oh, come off it, Lori. Recycling and eating organic food is hardly going to offset the SUV you drive to work every day. You know you'd move to a bigger house in a flash if you could afford it. He ran around his mind, trying to punch down this balloon of invective. He liked Lori. She taught high school, she was no airhead. But she'd grown up in Saskatchewan, longing for a more vital and stylish world, Paris or New York or Montreal. But here she was in Calgary, still on the prairie and without a lot of money. She still keened for that better, richer, more interesting place of her imagination, whatever the environmental consequences. He knew this much about her. He knew all their backgrounds and how old needs and deprivations invaded and compromised their beliefs. He was no better himself in the way he lived with his own contradictions. He should be more understanding.

No one was eating. The evening would never end at this rate. Shannon, her chin raised and her eyelids lowered, wasn't even pretending to listen. She would be planning her work day tomorrow or wondering when their son, Armie, would be home.

"Let's be realistic," Jason admonished Lori. "As their income rises, peasants in China and India and those Brazilians in their barrios and favelas are going to want air conditioning and cars and travel. They're human. Who are we to say they can't have them?"

"Maybe we're underestimating them," Lori replied. "Maybe they'll find better ways to live, maybe they won't want that stuff."

Alysha found this so preposterous, she said, "Oh, come on." She thought Lori far too susceptible to airy-fairy thinking. "You don't really believe that."

"Hey," said Jason to Tim, not changing the subject to cool things down but because he'd just thought of it, "I hear your brother's on his way."

"How do you know that? Though I'm not surprised."

He kept his eyes away from Shannon's. She'd have been shocked back into attention. With swelling alarm she'd be envisioning her-brother-in-law taking over the house when he arrived and inviting his new friends in.

Jason said, "I read his blog. Don't you? He's always kind of fascinated me in an appalled kind of way. So when this happened of course I went to him to get his inside view. He's the only person I know on the other side. So to speak. A real Tarstopper. He left Toronto yesterday, within a couple of hours of hearing about it. He and thousands of others. I can't believe you never read it."

"Even to imagine bringing it up on a screen gets my stomach dancing."

"I forgot about your weirdo brother," said Cole. "I should have realized he'd be on his way out here. What's his name again?"

"Deke. Derek."

"You have a brother who's one of them?" Alysha asked.

"Oh, that's right," Tim said to her, "you've never met him. Before your time. He doesn't come out here anymore because he doesn't fly, which I have to say is no big loss. He's always been a radical. You know, doesn't own a car, rides his bike in all weathers, lives on very little. And very holier-than-thou with it."

"You should check it out," Jason said to him of the blog. "He's more succinct than usual because he has limited access to power on the road. He gives you a real sense of what it's like out there. The TransCanada's apparently turned into one long pilgrimage route. It's a parade of old buses and vans and recumbent bicycles with homemade trailers. All the highways leading to the city are getting like that now. You know what they call it? Stomping the TransCanada. Get it? Stomping TransCanada pipelines and the proposed Keystone pipeline to be built across the States — to the environmentalists' horror. It's a crusade. They take turns walking, trying to be congruent, but like everybody else they end up having to compromise. I mean, there isn't time to walk the whole way from Toronto or Vancouver or Seattle all the way to Calgary and get here in time for anything. It actually even sounds kind of fun, if you were eighteen and it was like 1967. Real solidarity. Part of me even envies it. But I grew up and put away childish things, like protesting that the world's not the nice place we were led to believe it was when we were kids."

"What's his blog called?" asked Lori.

"The Wholly Green Giant. With a WH. Get it? Here, I'll bring it up."

Tim groaned. "Please please don't." He still couldn't look at Shannon.

Jason laughed at him. "Normally I can only read it until the naivety gets me so irritated I have to shut it down but now he's my source on developments."

"Is your brother going to stay with you?" Alysha asked. "I'd sure have trouble having someone like that around."

"What," said Tim in mock horror, "stay here and not be in the mud with his Comrades? Not share the burden as they wage the revolution? Sorry, my brother brings out the snarl in me. We've never been close. As most of you know, even though he's my younger brother, he dominated my childhood. He was as big and loud and in your face as a kid as he is now. So I haven't talked to him. I don't know what he's planning."

"He'll be able to pitch his tent right out front in your park," Jason crowed. "It's going to be the next to fill up with tents. You'll be right in the middle of the action. I'm surprised there's none out there yet."

Shannon stood up and left the table. After a moment Tim said to the others, "She doesn't want to talk about this or even think about any grubby greenies making themselves at home outside her house. Never mind Deke. Can I get anyone more? More wine?"

"Is she coming back?" asked Jason. "Or have we finished her for the evening?"

"Do you want me to go talk to her?" asked Lori.

"Maybe she's just in the washroom." But they all knew that wasn't it. She hadn't excused herself; she'd bolted.

"Maybe we should go," said Jason. "At the rate people are arriving, maybe we won't be able to find a way out of here, the streets will all be blocked. It's blowing up so fast."

Cole stood up. "I can't sit here any longer anyway. I'm so fucking mad I'm going to explode. I gotta get out of here." He walked through the living room and out the front door without looking back.

Jason said to Lori, "Better catch up or he'll leave you behind. What's going on with him? Nobody likes this but he's taking it way too personally."

"He's barely able to keep it under control now," she said as she stood up to follow him, "but he's always been a guy of extreme feeling. Mostly anger. You guys don't get to see the half of it."

Tim and Jason could only nod, which didn't seem to satisfy her. She twirled and ran from the house.

Jason said, after she'd gone, "It's not like we don't know it's under there. We've always had flashes of it. Remember that time he got going on immigrants? It sounds now like his usual controls have been overrun. Poor Lori."

Alysha said, "The only time I see them is when we're

together like this. They're an odd couple. You partner up with someone and you get their friends in the bargain. Let's just say I'm much more in tune with you and Shannon."

Jason teased her, "I seem to have heard some pretty nasty yelling coming out of you today when you were online."

"Most the city is outraged at the take-over. It's not just me and Cole. But I still have some grip."

Tim said, "Shannon's so furious she can't talk about it. She was so quiet tonight because she doesn't trust herself to talk about it. She's afraid she'll sound like Cole."

After Jason and Alysha had left, Tim went to find Shannon. "You've chased them all away," he called to her through the bathroom door.

"Sorry. I'll be out in a sec."

Tim stood at the big front picture window looking out into the evening. Now that it was almost June, the sun set very late. Across the street, over on the far side of the park, on the red scree of the baseball diamond, a blue light blinked on. A round plastic tent glowed blue. He could make out the shadows of the people inside as they moved around the source of light.

"You'd better see this," he called to Shannon who was now in the kitchen beginning the clean up.

"What?"

"Our first tent."

Shannon, arriving beside him, said, "Fuck." She liked to save the use of the word for impact. "I knew it was only a matter of time but still, fuck. The whole park will fill up. We'll have to move out."

"And go where? They say there are no hotel rooms left. Journalists from around the world are flying in, security forces are converging. And then there's all the people forced out of their houses, all scrambling for a place to stay."

Shannon paused, then said, "I'm sorry I broke up the party. I couldn't listen any more. I thought Cole was going to have an aneurysm or something. And the thought of Derek coming." She never called him Deke, as if by formalizing his name she could distance and contain him. "Him being here in the middle of it."

"Maybe he'll be so caught up in this he won't be around much."

She lowered her chin at him. "No. He'll be able to pitch his tent across the street and have the best of both worlds. Bliss out with his mangy communal tribe and escape over here for showers and a quiet nap." She made a face. "I can outdo Cole any day when it comes to hostility, if I let it out."

MONDAY
MAY 28 2012

THE WHOLLY GREEN GIANT

2:41 AM

What a lesson in geography this is. Middle of the night in the middle of Canada west of Lake Superior in never-ending Ontario. We're a long way from TO now. It took us like five hours just to reach the TransCanada driving straight north from Toronto. You forget that. This is the real Canada. Mother Nature in the raw. A billion spruce trees. Thousands of lakes. Ancient rounded granite rearing up like the backs of dinosaurs. & close to a billion bugs in the air on just this strip of the TransCan alone. If you stop & get out for even a sec you're so covered in black flies & mosquitoes & what-all that you look like a bear. Speaking of which — a black bear ran out of the woods earlier today. Had to slam on the brakes & send everyone topsy. This wilderness is what we're trying to appease – like calming a bear that's getting irate.

As you know I'm not one of those romantics about nature. I'm not one of those folks out canoeing & portaging all the time to be at one with nature. To me nature is brutal. It scares me witless. The idiot capitalists have lost their fear of it & think they've conquered it – that they can do what they want with it. Ha. Total delusion. Imperiling us all. Now most of us are finally waking up. Hallelujah. Thanks be to Saint Wendy & her Apostles James & Paul. This whole busload is reverential about Wendy & her boys.

As you can imagine we've got limited juice for our devices – I'm using my allocation to write this – but we try to stay current. Latest numbers – 7 thou around house & at least 50 thou on their way – maybe 100 thou – maybe a million. Tarstoppers as we've come to be called. Folks willing to leave their jobs or their schooling – whatever else – because this is a million times more important. We knew it was going to come to this in the end & some of us think it long overdue. In the end it just took someone like Wendy & the boys with the balls – so to speak – to force the issue. The revolution is at hand.

But you've probably got better info than me. I'm here to convey the feel on the ground.

We can't get over how they did it. One of the guys on the bus I'm on was in on it – one of the elect. Knew it was coming down – just not when. He'd been sitting ready to go for weeks. Elaborate elaborate security on it – best guy in the world designed it – some Chinese dude. & of course Wendy is Chinese-Canadian. The future. The planning's one thing but to carry it out & have it work is mind-blowing.

I keep visualizing it. Small ordinary Wendy Tsang & her two burly Apostles knocking on Bastard Morrison's big castle door. Excuse me, sir, but your house is surrounded. Your phone & computer access is blocked. We're coming in. The look on the poor schmuck's face. Poor my ass. I know I know – I've always promised to keep this blog profanity free – but the guy made 7 mil last year alone. Bastard & his trophy Barbie wife & their kid. With all these scruffy chained-together folks on their lawn & trampling their designer flower beds. Pressed up against their windows. The masses. Must be terrifying for them. The wife usually spends all her time shopping & jetting off to their place in Palm Springs & partying with other rich folk & is clueless about what this rabble is after.

I'm dying here. Back to you soon as I can.

●

First thing in the morning Tim received a text from Jason. *Deke now west of L Sup. Could be here as soon as tomorrow.*

Tim went to look out his front window. Overnight four more tents had popped up in the park across the street. Tim watched a group of people as they dug what he assumed would be a latrine in the lilac bushes behind the baseball diamond. By itself it just looked odd, something that should be stopped, but then he had to remember that this was the leading edge of a take-over. From all he'd heard, this park, a city block in size, would fill up with campers and then the next free space to the east, a park or a school playground, would be colonized. It was the new norm, hard as this was to take in.

His brother was coming. All day Tim would imagine Deke's steady advance towards the city. He'd picture him on his unicycle, leading a merry band of tricksters in jester hats, all of them banging cymbals and staggering around on stilts. It probably wasn't fair to them but every time that day that his attention sagged, and it was a day of boring meetings, this image clanged and whistled back into view. It was a struggle all over the city, he knew, to keep one's mind on business as the streets clogged and helicopters buzzed overhead and foreign journalists took over the downtown.

To avoid any chat or speculation about the Tarstoppers and the hostages, Tim tried to arrive at meetings a few minutes late and to leave as if overdue somewhere else, although the situation kept breaking through into even the most unrelated conversations. Phones and iPads were out on tables, new images were passed around. Some people were almost giddy with their proximity to a world-changing event, while others, the majority, were enraged. Like Cole at dinner last night, people could barely contain their fury, although in one corporate boardroom he visited in the afternoon, there was almost as much perplexity as rage. What the fuck were the Tarstoppers after? Shut down the oilsands? Were they all imbeciles?

At one point during the day he'd had to give a speech, something he was good at, a routine part of his job as head of a fundraising organization, and he could not keep his audience with him. It was a void he fell into, no cushion of attention there to hold him. He felt like an adolescent again, his magic trick failing and Deke, watching, was laughing at him.

Deke and his friends were taking over Tim's mind the way they'd once forced him out of the family room at home as a kid. Deke, younger but bigger, had always had more friends; he'd always been in the lead, talking non-stop so loudly and insistently that Tim used to fantasize about having him on the ground somehow and pressing his foot into his larynx. Or at the very least muzzling him with a whole roll of duct tape. Just shut the fuck up for a while. Now Deke was about to take over Tim's house, the park across the street, his neighbourhood, his city. Deke would soon know much more about Tim's own city: he'd talk to more people, spend more time online, get in there in the middle of things.

Although he might be able to take it, having had long experience, Shannon, he knew, would end up leaving home. She'd find a friend to stay with, no tolerance at all.

●

THE WHOLLY GREEN GIANT

11:03 AM

Way it works out here is you can get off your bus or van at any Way Station. Take a break or get some rest or food or whatever then hop on another departing vehicle. It's a pilgrimage. Even here in the endless no man's land of northern Ontario folks have set up Way Stations.

Lots of stories. Some of our vehicles are not in the best of shape. Old school buses & ancient motor homes & those big old deathtrap vans. Whatever folks could find to get them on the road & picking up pilgrims. They break down a lot. Middle of nowhere & you've rolled to a stop. Then suddenly you've got a mechanic stopping or just coming out of the woods & pretty soon everyone's on the move again. The support is amazing. We think of rural Canada as full of roughnecks & loggers — which it may well be — but — there's sure lots of our guys out here. & of course lots of Natives out here in the bush. They're totally with us, the land sacred to them, them so tired of having oil companies & mining companies & governments just tromping all over them.

I won't lie. Not everyone's with us. Some heckling. Quite a few fingers. Most truckers not too thrilled with us. They try to crowd us off the road. Blasting their horns at us. But we're careful not to stop at truck stops & mostly it's just gestures & no confrontations. We just pity those folks stuck in the old paradigm.

We're going through endless empty northern Canada where you know the towns & commerce doesn't extend much beyond the highway but even here you can't escape the ugly side of civilization. We've seen enough pulp mills & clear-cut logging and turn-offs to open-pit mines to realize the wilderness is riddled with human contamination.

All that's going to change. We're going to make it change. & meanwhile we have this wonderful camaraderie — this joy & hope. With the promised land ahead.

●

In her office Monday afternoon Shannon could pretend the

Tarstoppers had never happened. She'd stopped listening to the radio in her car, stopped reading the newspaper, and she no longer checked the Net. She wouldn't let her assistant, Madison, update her. Or her partner, Lanie. "Let's proceed as if," she said to both of them, "as if the city will be back to normal soon, for sure by July, by Stampede time."

Back to work. She had seven big corporate Stampede events in the works, more than they'd ever taken on before. And only a little over a month to go. She had to believe they would all go ahead. For inspiration, she pictured the Morrisons, who usually attended a lot of Stampede parties, making their triumphant entrance into one of her events next month. Not that she liked Baxter and Tonya very much, the kind with wine cellars and no discernment, a restaurant kitchen in which Tonya never cooked, weeks out of the year booked for cosmetic surgery. But she liked them better than the Tarstoppers and infinitely more than her brother-in-law.

She was finally concentrating again when Derek burst into her mind, just the way those hostage-takers had barged in on the Morrisons. Big sloppy motor-mouth Derek. He was laughing at her: guess who's winning now? He was crowing: you and your fat ass clients are history, better get ready, Babe. Not that he had ever called her Babe. His dislike of her was never that flip. He was earnest, God he was earnest. When he used to come to visit them, before he thankfully stopped flying, he'd wanted to argue with her all the time about the way she lived, as if she could be talked out of it, as if she was a sinner in purgatory who just needed to be told the word. He would trap her at dinner or even once as she came out of the bathroom and start in on her again like the resumed drilling at the dentist. He'd bray at her about the evil of running a business that catered to corporate grandstanding. He'd criticized everything she did and everything she owned, the car she drove, the meat she bought, the cosmetics she used, the dye in her hair. Most of all her acquiescence, as he put it, to the psychological manipulation of brands. She was such a patsy, he'd once yelled at her, to buy into that whole fraud. Didn't she see that?

She hadn't engaged with him; she'd been at her most remote, but inside she'd been defensive and hotly argumentative, which she'd hated and resented. Tim had been no help. He'd asked his brother nicely to stop harassing her, to no effect. She'd stayed away as much as she could. Since then any time she'd seen him had been in Toronto, with other people, and never for too long.

Now after something like eight years, he was coming back, with thousands of his Comrades, like an army advancing on her, and Tim would be even more helpless against him. She used to try not to be rude to her brother-in-law, to wait him out. Those days were gone.

●

THE WHOLLY GREEN GIANT
3:58 PM
Finally on the prairie – well the start of it anyways. Manitoba. It doesn't look much different than Ontario – trees & lakes & rock.

But you can see the land start to flatten & the trees thin out. I'm in a very uncomfortable van at the moment − broken seats & no heat & windows all hazy. Not really road-worthy. So I'm looking around at my fellow − sorry − know that term's sexist − passengers so I can give you a feel for who's with us. Folks from all over. We're thoroughly mixed together now with all the hopping on & off. There's a bunch of guys from Montreal who stick together. Speak English but accented. I guess there's buses that left Montreal that are all French-speaking but these guys got impatient with the stops & took what they could. Intellectual types who've never been this far west before. Never spent any time in the wild. You can tell it's sobering. They might as well be on their way to Mongolia.

Four students from various places in Ontario, all on their own − one of them a girl. They must have started out clean & ardent but now they look a little sick as they slouch all bedraggled into their seats. Maybe they're in shock from not having any juice for their music & games. An older couple who look like they've spent a lot of their lives in sit-ins around old-growth trees & the nesting sites of water birds. Implacable. Patient & enduring beyond anything the rest of us can imagine.

None of us can talk over the noise of the engine. We've all got visions in our heads. Who'd ever think Calgary would become the Promised Land? The coming together of the unbelievers in our millions. All those of us who either never bought the whole myth of progress & the domination of nature or who woke up to the danger & the absurdity of it. All of us who see the system bare-assed naked as a dangerous fairy tale.

●

By the time Tim arrived home, the park across the street had filled up. Red and blue and yellow round tents (how could plastic tents be seen in any way as earth-friendly?) shone out among old canvas jobs and tent trailers and canopied trucks and ancient motor homes that had been dug out of someone's back field. A water tower made of what looked like an old silo was under construction over by the swings. Human ingenuity at work.

From his front window he stared into the upraised front of a canvas tent. A young woman sat out front on a webbed lawn chair, watching a toddler chase a red balloon. His new neighbours. Seeing him in the window, she waved. An ordinary young woman, his daughter's age, with the same long dark hair. Except his daughter, Ardith, was doing an MBA in Vancouver and thought, like the majority of Canadians, that the police should have invaded the Morrison house at the very beginning, even if it had meant hurting, even killing, a few of the Tarstoppers. Ardith had been texting him since it started, incredulous about what was transpiring in her hometown.

Tim turned away. Waving back like they'd just moved in as permanent residents felt false but no response left him uneasy. She couldn't have expected a welcome, he told himself.

He heard someone come in the back door and then make a noisy descent into the basement. It had to be Armie, his son Armstrong, home from work — at least if it wasn't one of his new neighbours scouting out the house for a takeover.

Tim heard Armie plod back upstairs. A few minutes later, after a dip into the refrigerator for juice, he joined Tim at the front window. His son loomed over him, tall but skinny. Tim sometimes worried about drugs, to be so thin, but saw no other signs. Armie wore his hair long these days, to his shoulders, reminding Tim of a page at a medieval court. Seeing the tent city across the street in the park, Armie said, "Holy shit," which was pretty strong for him. His head moved as he studied it like it was a complete Lego or Santa village, some intricate stand-in for reality. He waved to the young woman now trying to keep her toddler off the road and then he tucked his hand under his other arm as if rescinding it.

Tim told him, "Your uncle Deke's on his way. He left Toronto Saturday afternoon, arrives tomorrow or Wednesday, I think."

"Is he staying here?"

Tim tilted his head at the park. "He'll want to be with his Comrades."

Tim could feel the indecision wafting off his son. His indecision about going back to university in the fall after a year off, his indecision about life in general. He sometimes thought of Armie as someone on a starting line, rocking back and forth, waiting for the gun to go off. Or he thought of him as a one-way system, like he was encased in a semi-permeable membrane, packing in more and more information and theory without anything much coming out, talk or action. It seemed to be an end in itself.

"At least we'll know now what's going on," Armie said.

"Uncle Deke will know it all."

Tim smiled. "And what good will that do us? Do you ever read his blog? Isn't everything he knows already there?" Armie, he knew, mostly thought the oilsands should be strictly monitored and that nobody should earn seven million a year the way Baxter Morrison did, but that was the most Tim ever got out of him.

Armie shook his head about the blog. Did he talk to anyone? He didn't have many friends, mostly just his girlfriend Katie, and as far as Tim could tell they never talked but could sit for hours intertwined on a sofa, each on their own iPad.

Tim said, "I expect him to pull up any minute on his bike with that trailer." He laughed, to share the joke of big Deke on his bike, his homemade trailer behind, the one he wheeled in all weathers to his carpentry jobs all over Toronto, his tools fitted into an elaborate cushioned box he'd made.

"What's cool," said Armie, who'd got to know his uncle better during his year at university in Toronto, "is that he's never self-conscious. No matter what kind of idiot he looks like. I don't know how he does that."

Tim had to be careful not to rush at his son now that he'd said something somewhat revealing. "He's always been like that. It's like he was born without the gene. I used to envy him that if nothing else."

Armie hummed his vague agreement and wandered away.

In the kitchen at the back of the house, Tim rummaged around in the fridge for what they might eat tonight, leftovers from last night, the makings of a salad. Out back flowers bloomed, magpies hopped across the grass, squirrels ran through the trees. The garden furniture awaited a warm day. And soon half the people in the park could follow Deke into this oasis, to sit around and drink Tim's beer and eat his food. How was he going to stop it? How was he going to keep Deke and his cohorts away from Shannon?

A call from Jason interrupted his thought. "Is your park filled up yet?"

"Pretty well. It's weird, all my new neighbours setting up home."

"It's just getting started."

"Don't sound so enthused. It's not entertainment. I can't be as detached as you. It's in my front yard." Alysha and Jason lived far away from the fray in a gated community outside the western city limits.

"Right now they say it's mostly west coast people arriving, they're getting here first. Apparently there's quite a few American Tarstoppers trapped at the border because they don't have passports. A lot do, of course: American west coast greenies tend to be from the educated travelling class. Have you seen the pictures of the line-ups at the border points? All across Washington and Montana. Thousands and thousands of people. It's going to take the Easterners, both American and Canadian, a little longer to get here. Like your brother. And then there are those types who put the cause first, ahead of their principles, and just flew in. There's stories of people flying any circuitous route to get here, dang the carbon dioxide emitted. You've got to shake your head."

"I'm trying not to follow it. I don't want it to take over my mind. Does it sometimes seem like we just live from one crisis to the next these days? We focus on it for as long as it's urgent and then we move on. I hate living in a constant state of agitation. You have a higher toleration threshold for this kind of thing than me."

"It's Deke who's got you going. He should be in Saskatchewan by now. He'll be here tomorrow."

"Tell me something else. Something totally unrelated. Distract me. It's not Deke himself so much as Shannon. It'll be the clash of civilizations right here in my own house."

"Okay, have you heard about the freedom riders and militia guys and biker types working their way north in the States? I guess they're coming to fight the godless anti-capitalist communitarian Tarstoppers from ruining civilization. It's going to be almost as big a clash as between Shannon and Deke."

"It's ironic, drug dealers and bikers as the defenders of free enterprise. But this is hardly unrelated. I said, distract me."

Jason couldn't stop. "These guys'll clean out what the government's too wimpy to do. The saving grace is going to be that most of the yahoos coming north don't have passports. Most of them wouldn't have any idea they even need one these days. Maybe the big war will erupt down there, along the border, and spare us. I hear it's a total zoo there now."

"Can't take anymore. Some of us are put off our appetite by all this. Talk to you later."

●

Armie had been at Katie's most of the weekend, in her parents' enormous house in a far northern suburb. He and Katie knew nothing about politics or what was going on in the world, deliberately. In a violent, corrupt world you had to keep yourself separate, Katie said, or you'd contaminate your soul. Katie's soul produced her art, so it had to be looked after like the soil a plant grew in. But since he was home now, he was curious about what was going on in his own front yard. It wouldn't hurt to just walk around a bit and take a look. He wouldn't tell Katie.

Out on the street, he felt like he fit right in, lots of kids his age coming and going. Everyone was wearing the badge, the black circle with the green X through it. He'd seen it on the C-train on his way to Katie's, people in sympathy with the Tarstoppers. There were all ages in the park though, everybody kind of grubby from camping. There didn't seem to be any plan to the settlement but paths almost like streets had formed around the tents and people sat around on folding lawn chairs like on a front porch and other people slept, getting ready for the night shift on the Wall, he had to guess. Even he had heard it called the Wall. Already the paths were getting muddy, the grass wearing off. He kept going.

The schoolyard was also full of tents and campers. They must have had to close the school down today. It seemed even weirder to have the schoolyard turned into a camp than the park, more out-of-bounds somehow. Elbow Drive had been closed south of 50th. For the moment the small shopping centre and the funeral home just north of the intersection were still open but he didn't think that they would be for long.

He started walking south amid a lot of people milling around on the street, some, he noticed, with bottled water, which he'd thought was a no-no for this crowd. It was like a street party, everybody looking kind of blissed out. Lots of hugging. Droopy clothes and long hair and old-time guitars, like the pictures you saw of the Sixties, the counter culture all over again, or like it never really went away. Who knew there were this many of them still around? The street got denser with people, packed so close together he could no longer move. No chance of getting any closer to the house where the oil guy and his family were being held.

He realized that he was in the Wall. It had spread this far. Like eight blocks. Would it continue to expand, suck his own house right in? It filled front yards and the surrounding streets. He couldn't think of what it looked like. A flood maybe, a substance like water that could flow into every available space.

Maybe he should go stay at Katie's until this was over. This didn't have anything to do with him. He knew his uncle would try his hardest to pull him into it, when Armie hadn't even worked out yet how he felt about closing down the oilsands.

●

THE WHOLLY GREEN GIANT
10:22 PM
Swift Current, Saskatchewan. We were on the moon today — that's what it felt like anyways out here on the bald prairie. Now

we're at a Way Station in a river valley that has actual trees — aspens & poplars & a few birch though some of them are pretty big — but if you get up top on the river cliff it feels like you could see all the way to the North Pole if it wasn't for the curvature of the earth. We're passing through something called the Palliser Triangle – an area so dry it should never have been plowed. It extends all the way to Calgary. Like everywhere else it's going to take generations to get the land back to health. There's a big movement here to reclaim the land I was glad to hear. The only way to live in a place like this is the way the Natives did – on the move. But as most of you know I think that's the way humans everywhere on this globe are meant to live. I'll say it one more time – settling – agriculture – was our big mistake ten thousand years ago. This big expedition has confirmed everything I ever thought. We're supposed to live on the move. Everything should be in the people & the sharing – food, stories, songs, warmth.

It was a shitty day today — cold & rainy. None of us were prepared for how cold it gets out here at night — like below freezing. It's almost June after all. The cops here are mostly leaving us alone – they know we'll be gone soon & more of us will arrive & the day after that & the day after that. Right from the beginning of this movement they realized they couldn't start arresting us for camping outside the designated spots. But I like to think they know deep down that this is the beginning of the end of regimentation. You can't fight it.

I've decided to stay put for the night & get some sleep. There's enough people on the Wall now that my presence is not urgent. There's a huge number of us here tonight – more & more arriving every minute – coming up from the States & talking about Montana & North Dakota & Wyoming like they've just come through a foreign country – that we're our own force right here.

Just heard about the biker types who tore up a camp somewhere in Colorado. People hurt & vans & tents set on fire & everything trashed. Took the police a suspiciously long time to get there. Everybody's talking here – it's so crowded in this valley tonight that no one's sleeping anyway. We were on such a high until we heard this bit of news. Maybe it's good to get a dose of the other side before we arrive in Calgary. How tough it's really going to be when all we've got on our side is compassion & turning the other cheek against the violence of not only the state but those who are terrified of us. Terrified of real freedom. Terrified of being seen as a sissy. Afraid of what they themselves might do without law & order to constrain them. It's the old story. Club us pacifists down but we keep coming back all through history.

TUESDAY
MAY 29 2012

As he left for work the next morning, Tim thought he should be able to hear the city's outrage and collective fury at the Tarstoppers over the top of the commuter traffic hum from MacLeod Trail. Hansen's house next door should be shaking with the emotion contained inside it. Nice mild grandmotherly Mrs. Hansen, Greta, had practically spat at him in her anger at those shirkers, those infants, those hooligans, in sounds he'd never heard from her before. Hansen himself had said to him, not kidding, "Where's Vladimir Putin when you need him? Or the Chinese army. They know how to deal with dissidents." Tim hoped the Hansens would take off to stay with their daughter in Kelowna before one of them had a heart attack. If they didn't go soon they might not be able to get out. Maybe a tent city in their front yard would do it.

The garage was in the back of the house, on the back lane in this older part of the city, otherwise Tim thought he might not be able to get out himself, the camp in the park spilling out into the street in front. Luckily Tim's office was in the opposite direction from Baxter Morrison's house. For now Tim could still get there, and Shannon could get to work downtown, unlike the people who lived around the Morrison house. Those people were now sealed in. The rich in the estates along the Morrisons' side of Elbow Drive, which all backed onto the Country Club golf course, had probably fled early, the rich having other houses to go to, penthouse hotel suites to take over. On the east side of Elbow Drive, the condo and infill dwellers had no recourse but to push through the throng every morning, working their way eastward in search of a functioning bus stop. They were probably even more furious than Hansen at this disruption to their lives.

Below Tim's house, Stanley Park, with its trees and sweeping lawns and river banks, was now pocketed with tent settlements. The road through was impeded with cars and trucks and buses but still passable. Soon he'd have to find a new route to work. Or maybe he'd no longer be able to get his car out of his garage. Once across MacLeod Trail and the railroad tracks and into industrial Calgary, he was in another city altogether, busy with routine. By the time he was at work and in his Director's parking spot, he could almost pretend it was an ordinary Tuesday.

●

THE WHOLLY GREEN GIANT
1:39 PM

Got a late start today. Couldn't wake up. Right now I'm making a pit-stop here in Medicine Hat, finally in Alberta. The promised land. Where it's going to happen. The big confrontation. The clash of civilizations. The peaceful versus the warmongering, the hippies versus the straights, the people versus the corporate, the 99% versus the 1%, the enlightened versus the establishment – however you want to put it. If we can win over a redneck corporate place like Calgary the next stop is the world.

Southern Alberta feels even flatter & less hospitable to life than Saskatchewan if that's possible. It's almost a desert. That limitless horizon gets you feeling religious. I can see how it happens. Thinking about Saint Wendy & her Apostles James & Paul – for they so loved the earth they gave themselves. As you all know I'm not formally religious in any way but I can see how religions get started. We just have to know enough this time around to keep it out of the hands of the patriarchs & oligarchs & control freaks everywhere until everyone everywhere gets it.

& hey – just in case it looks like we have no sense of humour, we call ourselves Wendy & her lost boys. Big guffaw. We can't be insulted. Pride & ego are the old paradigm. Part of the patriarchy & all that misguided crap.

On the personal front I have to tell you I'm also heading towards my brother. Yeah I have a bro in Calgary. Big brother. Older but smaller. If I can knock my brother off his fence – which he thinks of as maintaining a balance – & into our camp then I'll rejoice. I think he's afraid mostly of alienating his wife – we aren't close – but I won't get into my sis-in-law for now. & his son – my neph – who I got to know last year when he came to TO for university, is another fence-sitter like his old man. The sis-in-law is impregnable but I've got great hopes for the Bro & the neph.

●

From her car Shannon texted Tim. *Is he here yet? Still safe to come home?*

Tim responded: *Not here. Haven't heard. But check news. Our whole area cordoned off. Armed forces brought in to help. Long line-ups.*

She'd already hit the traffic stall. She hadn't moved in five minutes. If the Tarstoppers' big concern was supposed to be global warming, then turning the city into a giant parking lot of idling cars was not a big help in that direction. Her iPad said huge delays. Proof of residency was needed to enter the sealed area.

Why didn't they start asking for proof days ago, when the containment area would have been so much smaller? How had the authorities been caught so flat-footed after all the years of over-reaction to what they'd said were Muslim terrorist threats?

She tried not to panic, stalled like this. She knew the techniques to ward it off, the slow breathing, the diversion of her mind into a visualization of some satisfying progress. All her life she'd had a fear of stoppage. Without forward momentum, the forces of entropy could pull you backwards, destroy your plans. She still remembered the day in high school she'd discovered entropy and the justification she'd felt to learn that the tendency to disintegration was a fundamental law of physics. Today the force was everywhere at work. Didn't the Tarstoppers understand about entropy? Bringing this part of the world to a halt like this, no matter their intentions, could only lead to chaos. It was beyond naïve to think something spontaneous and natural would then arise.

The world was on the brink of backslide as it was without this disruption. European leaders held their breath over their Union; the amount of carbon dioxide in the atmosphere kept escalating; the American recession threatened to return; and China was trying to imagine a next act. With the supply of Canada's oil to the United States threatened, and all it had taken was a threat, the barrel price had zoomed so high that overnight whole economies were teetering and the world quaked even harder. Never mind her own event planning business, so dependent on corporate Calgary's health.

She tried to keep her mind off Derek, a dark force below her family who could pull on Tim but also on Armie. Derek was a counterweight to her upbeat message of hard work and progress. She'd saved Tim when she'd met him, as he'd readily admit. She'd rescued him from indecision and depression by steering him into nonprofit, as an out between the contradictory demands of his parents, the business success his father expected of him and his mother's hope for him to act as a leader in social change. That he'd taken her advice, that he'd recognized the urgency for action, had sealed them. The whole twenty-five years that they'd now been married, she'd had a hold of him, keeping him from slipping back into uncertainty and self-doubt. Even as she'd gone through bouts of wishing she'd married someone more dynamic, someone who didn't need her encouragement, she'd waited it out, never believing that any subsequent rebirth would be worth the destruction of her marriage. You fixed things, like the oilsands, like gross income inequalities, like marriages, you didn't bring everything down.

She feared that same passivity in Armie. Had she made it worse, jumping in too hard when he slacked off, when he didn't see the point of so many things, when he hesitated to get involved? Her panic might have only increased his fear of the world. He seemed very vulnerable at the moment, open to anyone. Right this minute Armie could be out with his newly arrived Uncle Derek, out lollygagging among people who believed that humans weren't meant to strive, to build, to impose themselves on nature. Derek was like the devil with his hand on her son's ankle.

She hadn't moved in ten minutes. But as soon as she turned off the engine a gap opened up ahead of her. Someone changed lanes and filled in the space. At least she was sitting on cemetery hill coming out of downtown and not a little further south in commercial ugliness, although she'd be stalled there too eventually. Elbow Drive, which she usually took home, had been closed south of the bridge over the Elbow River because of Tarstopper congestion, forcing her onto MacLeod Trail. Her belief in enterprise clashed here with her dislike of strip malls and used cars lots and fast food outlets.

"Forget your bottom line," Tim liked to tease her, "for

god's sake keep your enterprise stylish." Which always made her grumpy, as if finding and mocking inconsistencies was a justification for inaction. As if visual satisfaction, beauty, what redeemed the world for her, was trivial.

At last she was inching forward, never coming to a complete stop. But Derek stayed with her, as large and loud and messy in her mind as he'd be in her house.

There were soldiers ahead, dressed in camouflage, not that there were many trees on MacLeod Trail to hide among. They were stationed at intervals along the west side of the roadway, a foil against new Tarstoppers trying to enter the area on foot. Most of the intersections were blocked off on that side. At her own turn, when she finally reached it, one of the few left open, she showed her driver's license to a young woman who nodded to let her through. It was like a war zone. How could this be happening in Calgary? How could some so-called peaceful protesters be causing this chaos? Her own fucking brother-in-law one of the worst of them all.

Two blocks in, the road curved around Stanley Park, just since this morning full of tents and cars and buses and lean-tos and people. It was exactly how she imagined everyone would end up living if the Tarstoppers had their way. Why didn't the police clear them out? It was illegal to camp in a park. She hadn't understood it last autumn when the Occupiers had taken possession of a downtown park for months. The authorities were apparently only working at clearing the golf course behind the Morrison house, because it was private property, she guessed, and because so many prominent people belonged there. She felt like Cole the other night at dinner, so furious at this breakdown of order that she imagined the soldiers who were busy checking up on innocent citizens like herself instead turning their guns on all these illegals in the parks.

There were people strolling in the alley behind her house! Just moseying around enjoying her neighbourhood. All the properties were fenced or these people would be right in there picking the lilacs and reclining on the lounge chairs and making themselves right at home. The back gates were mostly unlocked which meant it could still come to that. She wanted to run one of these people over. Like those two scruffy-looking men arguing about something. She'd pin them there against the Herbertsons' garage door with her car and leave them. Her fury was acrid in her mouth. It might kill her, never mind anyone else. Rage was plugging up her whole body like lust. It hurt the top of her head like skyrocketed blood pressure.

Tim's car was in the garage. As she ran for the back door she was only peripherally aware of the green and flowery glory of her garden, usually her solace, her joy. She opened the door and screamed into the house, "Are you alone? Is that fucking brother of yours here yet?" She didn't recognize her own voice.

Tim came running. "No. I haven't heard from him. What's happened?"

"I'm surrounded by them but I don't need one in my house." She was still screaming. "He's not staying here. Understood?"

Tim never comforted her. That was how it worked, his

trust that she never needed it, that she was the tough one. When she yelled about frustrations, he would only look tolerant. And she never cried. Which was just as well. If he were to come near her now she'd probably take a swing at him, just because she wanted to hit somebody, anybody.

She was still screaming. "We can't even leave and go somewhere because then they'll take over our house. They'll break right in. I bet they're doing it already to empty houses. I'm so fucking angry I'm scaring myself." She pushed by him. "I'm going on my treadmill to try and work some of this off."

●

THE WHOLLY GREEN GIANT
11:54 PM

They've closed all the entrances to the city! Like a couple of hours before we reached the city limits. The word goes down the long lines of travellers. If you don't live here or have somewhere to stay then they're not letting you in. You have to have a hotel booking. Or you have to be driving a transport truck because after all commerce has to continue. Of course what's happening is folks are abandoning their vehicles & setting off on foot across the fields now that we're this close to the epicenter. It's total chaos here on the TransCanada. Some folks are standing in the middle of the highway to talk & vehicles are turning around any which way. The wide dividing strip — the kind where you can't even see the traffic going the opposite direction from the other side — is turning into a make-shift camp as people decide not to go any further tonight – to wait for morning. What a smozz.

We're still quite a ways out of the city in a line-up. Would you believe the TransCanada goes east west right through the middle of the city & there's no complete ring road? Everybody's saying we should go round to the west side of the city 'cause it has the easiest access on foot to the house. The problem is getting there without stepping over any city limits. Somebody on the bus I'm on takes a vote & they opt for staying put for the night. So I find a van that's keeping going.

Everybody on the van is hungry & tired & some of us are a little smelly. We expected to be welcomed into some nice settlement in a park & ladled with warm food & a few sweet spliffs. Instead we're travelling south in the half-dark – boy it gets dark out here late – from the TC in a whole cavalcade of vehicles like us who've been spurned by the city. We don't know where the hell we are. Nobody has any juice left in their devices – I'm writing this in longhand if you can believe it to enter later – so we have no maps. We're on 84 st ne & it heads due south with almost no crossroads. I guess we'll know we've gone too far when we hit the American border. The city north to south – & we were only a little north of level with downtown when on the TC – is as big as a province. Calgary's everything that's wrong with our way of life, & that's before you even talk about the tarsands & the corporate mentality. Talk about urban sprawl. I though TO was bad. You can see the subdivisions to the west – mile after mile of glow from the street lights – even though everybody's tucked into their king-sized beds in their giant houses on their own little piece of private property. We go in & out of industrial areas but mostly it's just getting dark. Overcast & no moon. We cross something called Glenmore Trail – out here everything's cowboy folksy & highways are called Trails – & I know we're nowhere near the city's southern limits. I remember that further west of here Glenmore Trail passes close to the Bro's house. I'm no Calgary expert though, I've only been here a couple of times – a long time ago & both times I flew in – apologies for that though my longtime readers know I haven't now flown in nine years – & I only saw the part of the city my Bro lives in & the mountains to the west. Anyways we know Glenmore Trail will be blocked off at the city limits so we & everybody else have to keep going. I know the whole city's on a grid system & we're approaching 84 street & 114 ave. Southeast.

Then a big flashing sign. Road closed ahead. & we come to a stop – another line-up. We can see up ahead that the line-up's mostly turning east in search of another road south. The blockade on the road going west can't be too far in from the intersection for folks to know not to go that way. I hop out. I know they're going to have to go way way south & then west practically to the mountains to get to the west side of the city. There's an Indian reserve in the way & god knows what all. There's a little bad feeling when I ditch but I know the Bro is not picking up any extras – if he's even going to agree to come & get me.

It's weird out here in the dark on my own. Up ahead there's all this giant earth-moving equipment & these huge piles of dirt. Maybe building an intersection for the nonexistent ring road. Still building roads & intersections. Out here in the middle of nowhere. How wrong is that? I'm up to my ass in mud. The blockade's not much – only a few cops & their cruisers. Anybody coming this way at this time of night has to be up to no good & easy to turn away. I guess the big jams are further west & south where Deerfoot Trail & Macleod Trail enter the city & Americans are piled up. & even more on the west side of the city where all the folks from the coast – from Vancouver & Seattle & California – are stopped – so I heard – at the entrance to the city on the TransCanada there. Apparently there'd be thousands more Americans if they didn't need passports to enter Canada. It's a real ball-up at the border I guess. They're settling around all the border towns in Montana due south of here & in Washington to the west & they're joining our protest from there.

Course they're not letting me in here. I show my fake name & ID – I'm not giving it out here because you never know who's reading this post – because I know I'm red-flagged on all their computers – but still no go. Eventually I talk some guy into letting me use his cell phone to call the Bro. 12:17 am but he says he'll come – after this long pause to make me wait & suffer. I have to warn him about using my alias – which causes this big sigh at the other end of the line. But he's coming. It takes him forever to get here. I stay out of the cops' way while I wait in case they come up with a reason to exclude me. They'd love to. I have to admit I'm not at my best – so tired I look hung-over. I'm dirty & unkempt – everything they hate.

The Bro throws open the passenger side door but doesn't get out to welcome me. He's as stiff & grim as our dad used to be picking me up as a teenager. That same straight thin mouth like he has no lips. The Bro thinks because he works in nonprofit &

he has this little goatee that he's totally different from Dad. The Bro's not going to talk to me – not even hello. I'm beyond caring. I shut the open passenger door & instead crawl in the back & I fall right to sleep & only wake up as we're pulling into his garage. I stumble down into the basement guest room & with my last gasp of energy I'm entering this report at top speed into the Bro's computer in his basement office – such a trusting guy to leave it on like this – & now I'm crashing. So much for our triumphant arrival in the city. It's tomorrow the fun begins.

WEDNESDAY
MAY 30 2012

Waking up, Armie could hear his uncle snoring from the bedroom across the hall in the basement, the door open. As he began to get ready for work, Armie tripped over a duffle bag that spilled dirty clothes in the hall and the bathroom stank of something Deke had unloaded. How had this happened? When had he arrived? Armie could sleep through anything, it seemed, if he could sleep through Deke's arrival.

He texted Katie. *gd morning. luv u. adore u. lust 4 u. uncle here in house. my moms going to be upset. all of us ll be gone to work b4 he even gets up. good thing.*

He texted Katie every morning as he soon as he woke up, although she wouldn't be up for a while. It was only six.

He hadn't seen Deke in a year, not since he left Toronto. Deke had long ago laughed him out of calling him uncle, so now it was just Deke. He'd seen quite a bit of him that year, more than he'd often wanted. In the year since, he sometimes checked out Deke's Facebook, mostly for the links, some of them pretty unique and interesting. Either Deke spent a lot of time online or he had a wide circle of friends who fed him sites. Armie had never gotten into his blog.

Deke would try and drag him into getting involved. He'd think his cause so obvious and non-debatable he'd just assume everyone felt as strongly as he did. Armie tried to get his head around the issue, to have a hold of something when Deke started on him. He had a vague sense that there were pretty strong arguments on both sides, shutting the oilsands down because of global warming or going ahead full tilt because the Canadian economy depended on them. And there were likely more than two sides, too. He didn't want to think about it. He was much happier in the deep past, his pet subject, paleo-anthropology, figuring out how humans evolved, or else in the imaginary futures of science fiction. Now Deke was going to press his nose into the confusing present. Between work at the brewery and being with Katie, he hoped to avoid his uncle as much as possible.

●

Tim might be at work, in his grown-up life, but he felt right back in his childhood, a kid again and tied in a sack with his younger bigger brother. Come and get me. Twelve o'clock at night. Like when Tim was sixteen and had his license. I need you to pick me up and what I'm doing is more important than anything you've got to do, like sleep. But once he was awake last night there'd been no point in not going. If he'd resisted, he'd have only thrashed around in distress and woken Shannon up.

From behind a police barricade, Deke had lurched out of the dark like a monster suddenly looming into view. Enormous, dirty, his hair like a kid's after a day of taking on and off toques and helmets. Seeing Tim at the steering wheel Deke had rocked back and Tim had felt his disappointment in him for still being the small uptight guy with no open arms. Deke had slammed the door and instead crawled into the back. He hadn't said a word and Tim had soon realized he was asleep.

Tim himself hadn't slept again once home. Getting back into bed he'd woken Shannon.

"You went and got him? He's here? Downstairs? Are you crazy?"

"Just for tonight. I promise he'll be gone tomorrow. He'll want to join his Comrades."

He didn't think she'd slept again either. At six-thirty she'd gotten up and showered. There was no point in saying anything more.

Now as Tim tried to work, he knew everyone in the building was keeping up on the Tarstoppers on line, talking about them, speculating, exchanging rumours. The worst was Connor, head of fundraising, who was now settling a cheek on the edge of Tim's desk and saying, "You're right in the action where you live. I hear you have a brother who's some kind of voice in the thing."

Was Connor reading Deke's blog, did he know all about Tim and his brother? "How did you hear that?"

Connor was a problematic employee, brilliant at fundraising but hell on the people who worked for him. At some point, a tilt in the balance between the amount of money he raised and what he cost the agency in terms of lost staff would require Tim to let him go. Tim had been hoping for months that Connor would be lured away by a bigger organization so he wouldn't have to fire him. With his talents, why was Connor still here at this small agency? Knowing he was irreplaceable at the salary they paid had made him almost as insufferable as Deke with his swagger and his dominance.

"Word gets around. Is he staying with you?"

"I'm hoping he'll be so involved in the Tarstoppers I'll hardly see him. I'd really rather not talk about this. Here at work I like to pretend the whole thing's not happening."

Connor took his time getting off his desk. He gave Tim a look that said he knew all kinds of things about him now. Tim would not ask him if he was reading Deke's blog. He didn't want to know. Instead he went back to his computer screen and tried to focus on work.

A few minutes later, when his phone rang, he read the name GARTH MADDOX on the display. He'd asked his dad not to call him at work but he was not the listening type. Tim closed his eyes before picking up and saying hello.

"What the hell's going on out there?" his dad barked. "I can't believe what I'm seeing on the news. This is nuts. Why don't they bring in the water cannons or stink bombs or attack dogs? I'd clean it up fast enough. You can't let a bunch of naïve children take over like this. Next thing you know your brother'll show up."

"Actually he's already here. He arrived last night."

"Shit. Figures. How did I raise a son capable of taking part in something like this? I hate to say it again but it's your mother's fault. She filled his head with such cockamamie ideas. I really don't get it. So the planet warms up? We adapt. We find opportunity. That's what us humans do. I get fucking furious. It's like he's spitting in the eye of everything I've accomplished. But meanwhile he'll just use what of it he needs. And no thanks for his straight teeth and excellent education and getting practically everything he ever wanted. Christ, he's forty-something years old. He's not a kid anymore. I always thought he'd grow out of this. Shut down the oilsands. Jesus. The world runs on oil. It's a fact. There is nothing, nothing, that goes anywhere near replacing it. That's a fact. I've done the research. But will your brother listen to reason? I'm sick of trying to get through to him."

"Okay, Dad. Calm down. If you were here you'd see that this thing has a life of its own. It's going to have to play out. It's too big to control."

"I can't calm down. I don't want to calm down. This is a catastrophe. Our oil is going to be seen to be as unpredictable as Nigeria's. Do they really have any idea what they're doing? What they're wrecking? The consequences? How did it ever get to this? It's only been a couple of days. Who would ever have believed it?"

"Nobody realized how many people felt this strongly."

"Don't give me that. I bet half the people there just have nothing better to do. They want to poke a stick in the eye of the powers-that-be just because they're all still basically adolescents."

"Okay, Dad. I'm surrounded by angry people. Shannon. Most of the people I know or run up against."

"You're not angry?"

"Annoyed by the inconvenience. Otherwise fascinated to see how it's going to play out."

"You've always been a sidelines kind of guy. I have to say I blame your mother for that as well. She made you afraid of yourself."

"Okay, Dad. That's enough. Say hi to Eva. Try to calm down a bit, if only for your health. I'll talk to you later." Tim jabbed the button to silence him.

Didn't his dad hear himself? Even as a kid, Tim used to ask himself that. If this call was all you had to go on, you'd think him a boor. You'd never guess him a connoisseur of wines and tailoring and rare books. Garth thought of himself as smooth and it had worked on a lot of women over the years, until the anger showed up too often.

It was ancient, his dad yelling at Tim about Deke. Old emotion, usually kept at a distance, clogged Tim's throat, almost gagging him. Being over-looked, being a receptacle for his father's obsession with Deke's short-comings. And then afterwards falling back on analysis as a way to cope, wondering what it was in his dad that was triggered to rage by Deke, right from the beginning. Deke standing up in his crib and bellowing, and Garth knocking him down with a blow, making Tim want to throw up with the sound of it. And none of it had had much effect on keeping Deke down. His dad would never acknowledge that his responses to Deke had always been extreme. No, it was always Deke's fault and he'd always needed to convince Tim that his anger was justified.

Deke could be in Tim's house right now, making himself at home, eating through anything in the fridge he could find. He'd probably by now toured the park across the street and invited all his new friends back to the house. They'd be sitting around now in their filthy clothes, eating his food and using his bathroom. Was this fair to Deke? Was he exaggerating his boorishness? He hoped so. But he'd leave work early today to make sure everyone was out long before Shannon arrived home. He'd clean up and make dinner. Basically suck up, which Shannon hated, but what choice did she give him?

●

THE WHOLLY GREEN GIANT
2:24 PM

I've been wandering around all day in a dream. This is how life's supposed to be lived — in camps — everybody working towards the same thing. We know we've got to keep the whole thing organized but it's amazing how it works mostly on its own. There's a need & folks figure out how to fill it. They share what they have.

Right now I'm in the park across from the Bro's house finding out how it all works – talking to all kinds of folks. This park's only been going for like three days but already they've set up a system to deal with all the petty stuff like theft & drugs & the mentally ill folks wandering around. A lot of this was worked out by the Occupy camps last fall – the whole horizontal organizing thing. There's manuals about it on the Net. Everybody's intent on making this whole movement about compassionate & inclusive ways of dealing with life. We're living it as a demonstration – not just existing here & taking our turns on the human Wall around Wendy & the house. We deal with everything that comes up – then & there. Every night each area or park or whatever holds a general meeting. I'm thrilled beyond words by how it's working. We have a problem with dogs at loose or barking too much? We vote on muzzles. Just for this park. Too much partying too late into the night? Curfews. 'Cause what matters is getting enough sleep to get back to the Wall. That's why we're here. The real anarchists among us complain about all the rules & we listen – we get their point. Majority rules in the end though so some of them have moved on. For me – for most of us – we have to have rules – I'm no anarchist – but it's a real debate. Let's totally rethink how we should all live.

One neat thing – there's these people – mostly women – making these badges we all wear. It gives the sewing types among us something to do as they take their turn in the Wall. They're a black circle with a green X through it. Kind of like the red badges the student protesters in Quebec are wearing. Get one & wear it all the time.

& one more thing I'm a little embarrassed to mention. I'm blown right away by how everybody knows me here. Everybody follows me online. Total strangers clapping me on the back, even hugging me. I'm like some kind of hero. People are even looking to me for leadership, even though we don't believe in leaders. Weird, weird, weird.

●

Shannon didn't want to go home. Tim had let Derek stay last night, knowing how upset she'd be. Once Derek was settled into the house there was no way he was going to abandon a comfy bed and a shower and a full fridge to forage in a camp. Derek had always been an easy-way-out kind of guy. This morning she'd known Tim was awake when she got up but she hadn't spoken to him. He knew what he'd done. He hadn't phoned or texted her all day. She'd have ignored him anyway, which he knew.

Coming into the house, the aroma of something Tim had in the oven, lasagna by the smell of it, overpowered any un-washed stink of Derek that might have been sucked up the stairs from the basement. Tim would have made a salad, chilled the wine, set the table in the dining room. Derek wouldn't be here now. If he were, Shannon would turn around and leave, as Tim well knew. Her friend Gizelle, who had a condo down-town, had said she could come and stay any time she needed an out.

"Hi," Tim said, coming into the kitchen. "All clear. Let me

get you a glass of wine."

He was more afraid of her than he was of his brother, but only just. She hated that. Tim liked to think of himself as considerate, sensitive to the feelings of others, but she knew it was fear a lot of the time. She didn't think she'd be able to watch him twist between her and Derek, unable to stand up to his brother. They had to get this conflict out in the open now, so they wouldn't sit in silence through dinner, which she resented, stressed as she was and only hoping for peace.

"Is he gone for good?" she asked, taking the first long sip of wine, the best one, when she could feel it travel through her body, lighting her brain with a sudden expansion of possibility.

"I had to let him stay last night. It was the middle of the night. I couldn't just pitch him out into the park in the dark. I didn't talk to him this morning. I'm sure he'll want to be with his Comrades from here on out."

"You hope. Is his stuff still here?"

That sideways look she hated. "He'll come back for it."

Was she being a bitch about this? How generous were you supposed to be with someone you didn't like, someone you thought would have a negative effect on your family? Just because he was related?

Tim took the lasagna out of the oven. "I've shut all the blinds on the street side. For now we can pretend nothing's going on out there. You go get changed. I'll put Deke's stuff out on the front porch so he won't interrupt us if he comes looking for it. How's that? It'll be okay."

"Armie's at Katie's?"

"Where else?" He gave her their look of complicity over Katie. He'd try to pull them back together with their mutual search for signs that their son was moving on from Katie.

Over dinner Tim did all the talking, trying too hard, floundering for subjects, the Tarstoppers off-limits. He talked about staffing problems at work, their shared difficulties in running a business, although he knew not to talk about the agency clients directly. She didn't want to be reminded of the poverty and distress in the city on a daily basis, although she was well aware of it and gave substantially to charity both personally and through her company. Not that Tim had that much to do with the clients of his agency himself, although he liked to talk statistics, which she didn't want to hear. So, the old fallback, talking about the kids.

"Ardith's been texting her outrage over the Tarstoppers," Tim said. He smiled. "She's your daughter. She's as outraged as you and she's not even living here."

Ardith might be her mother's daughter, as organized, as good at business, as pragmatic, but Shannon knew it was Tim she was closest to; he was the one she texted a number of times a day, even when nothing much was going on.

And of course they could talk about Armie and the small changes that might indicate he was getting ready to move on from what seemed a dead stop, working at the brewery and hiding out with Katie. Tim was much more patient and understanding with this than she was.

She listened for Derek on the porch. He wouldn't just take his bags and disappear into the night. She knew Derek. He'd ring the door bell when he found the door locked, holler out for them, loom like a moose on their doorstep.

She made it through dinner and then escaped outside into her back garden where she could detangle the clematis, the early small ones, now full of perfect green buds showing the pink and blue colour beneath their calyxes. She snipped out the dead vines, up on a ladder, her nose in the greenery, the music through her earbuds like cloister walls.

●

THE WHOLLY GREEN GIANT
7:31 PM

I'm here taking my turn in the Wall – packed in with folks from all over. I'm so high on this I may never sleep again. Lots of talk all around me. Guy from Oregon's been here a couple of days says he's in touch with friends in the big camps setting up on the city limits now that it's tough to get into the city. Lots of folks are getting through on foot though 'cause the city's big footprint means the cops can't possibly patrol the whole circumference. Ironic or what? This whole thing is way too big now for anybody to put down except maybe the whole of the American armed forces. Maybe they'll be invited in next. The guy puts me off though. For him it's all about the defiance of authority – not a thought about what we're trying to do here. He's an anarchist. Couldn't care less about the tarsands. I know folks are here for all kinds of reasons but this guy's pretty snarly. Full of hate actually.

I move away & get talking to a woman 65 years old who was

at the original Woodstock. We practically bow down to her. 43 years later & she's still at it. She says a lot of what the counterculture wanted back then has actually happened but that's only because corporations realized that social movements didn't threaten them. They could co-opt anything as another consumer lure – health food, gays out of the closet, women working, sexual freedom, whatever. & meanwhile the military-corporate juggernaut kept growing – unaffected. But this – she says looking around grinning – is a real threat they can't subsume. She really makes us see how long this has been going on & what we're up against.

Next I'm talking to a clean cut kid who says he's 16 – if that, I say – who left class in Red Deer, Alberta – a small city an hour & a half north of here – soon as he heard. Says all earnest: at school they tell us all the stuff wrong with the world like the environment & individuals with billions of dollars & people starving but then all you hear about from adults is keeping the economy growing & creating more jobs no matter what. This kid is in shock at the double-face of the world. We can only hope he'll stay that way & not get sucked into making a living & compromising & tuning out on video games.

Another guy – a young laid-off environmentalist from Vancouver – says he was sent over the edge by the Harper government cutting back funding on environmental protection & monitoring. This guy says he's been up on the roof. You have to be patient to get a turn up there. Helicopters buzz you up there. Can't land though because Bastard Morrison had to build a house that looks like a European castle with steep roofs & turrets & there's nowhere for a helicopter to land – never mind all the people in the way. I guess it's not that comfy up there clinging for dear life to the slope on slippery slate tiles & hoping not to fall asleep & fall off – but it's still the place to be though you're really no closer to what's going on. Who knows what's going on inside with Wendy & the boys & Bastard Morrison & his wife & kid. None of it gets out. The police or the army or whoever have got the house fire-walled no matter how our techies try to puncture it. A real battle going on there – our hackers versus their experts. Maybe nothing's going on & nobody's talking. For all we know Wendy & the boys slipped out into the crowd days ago.

One thing we do know for sure – we've been infiltrated. The most perfect protester standing next to you proudly wearing the black & green could easily be undercover. No way of stopping that. Maybe in the end there'll be more of them than us in the Wall. It's making us all paranoid though. I have to really work at getting people to talk to me. They think me a cop? The local cops and the RCMP have really got talent if they can replicate me.

Lots of talk of course about what's going on at the border. Stories about the dumb American rednecks who think they can just drive their semi-automatic weapons on over into Canada. Those guys usually never leave Alabama or Virginia or wherever they're from. This is their first big trip away from home a lot of them I bet. Even the militia types coming north from Montana barely know there's even a place called Canada.

●

Tim again stood at the front window, wanting to close the

blinds on the park across the street but instead standing trans-fixed, unable to shut it out. Smoke from campfires hazed the air. A large bus, an old decommissioned Greyhound, sat at the opposite curb, blocking a lot of his view. Inside the bus, a woman was getting changed, down to her bra, not a pretty sight, her flesh bulging around its restraint. The young woman in the tent sat on her lawn chair to the right of the bus in a small circle of people, her toddler asleep in her arms, both of them wrapped up in a sleeping bag. The temperature was not much above freezing. East of the bus, someone had set up a kiosk selling brightly knit hats and mitts. Further down the street a man was throwing up into a storm grate. People of a variety of ages walked his street, gathering and talking, wander-ing, no one sticking to the sidewalk.

Deke was in there somewhere, a part of it after being in the city less than twenty-four hours. If Tim was to walk around in his own park right now, he'd want to take this window with him. Then there'd be solid glass between him and participa-tion, never mind any camaraderie. Deke would have dived into the throng across the street, to be borne along like a rock star surfing his audience. Deke the blogger. Deke the Wholly Green Giant, the minor celebrity in environmental circles.

When Lori stepped out from the tangle of people and commerce and vehicles onto his street, for a second Tim couldn't place her. Lori, Cole's wife, here for dinner three nights ago. She had to be coming to visit him but first her attention was diverted by the kiosk. Did she think that this was something like a village fair? That there would be handicrafts and artisanal cheeses and pony rides? That if an object was handmade then buying it would somehow not be the same as consuming?

He didn't want to listen to her enthusiasm. He ducked out of the window but he couldn't know if she'd seen him or not. So when the doorbell finally rang, he had to open up.

Lori was aglow with stimulation. Quickly, to forestall her ebullience, Tim said, "I thought we were sealed off from all new visitors now. How'd you get in here?" His bonhomie sounded forced in his own ears. He had a practiced smoothness that often deserted him outside of work, like an actor offstage.

"I said I was coming to visit you. Isn't this amazing? There was nothing three nights ago. I have to say that there's a really good feel to it when you walk through."

It was something happening. For Lori, raised in what she thought was a backwater, any quickening or gathering or momentum had to be a good thing. He understood her, although it made him want to back away. So instead he slipped into the old wry humour. "Are you bringing your tent next time? Cole would probably see it as grounds for divorce."

Lori was so sharp she could quickly push him into inarticulateness. She cocked her eye at him the way his mother used to, vigilant about sarcasm. That was what it was about Lori. He rushed to ask, "What are your grade elevens saying about all this? You must be having pretty lively discussions these days. A giant civics lesson."

They were still standing in the front hall. Lori smiled and

nodded and looked around him, ignoring his prodding. "Is your brother here?"

So that was what she was after. "I picked him up at the edge of the city last night and brought him here but I haven't seen him since. Shannon's gone to bed. I think she's putting off any chance of running into him." He unfolded his arms, trying to loosen up a bit, although he couldn't make himself extend an arm to invite her to sit down in the living room. "Has Cole calmed down from the other night? It's a good thing you don't live around here, where it would be in his face all the time. It's funny: usually he's the kind of guy you don't know what he's feeling. But when it comes to this, he can't keep it in. It's like they're attacking everything he holds sacred. It's so personal to him."

"I'm mostly just avoiding him right now." She wasn't really there to talk about Cole, much as he was an aggravation to her. "I've been reading Deke's blog, so I know about you picking him up last night. I haven't had a chance to look yet today. I've turned some of my kids onto it. I like him. No big ego gets in the way unlike some other sites."

"A celebrity. Even though he's against the whole celebrity culture." Tim said this while gulping on his outrage. Deke had written on his blog about him picking him up? That was out of bounds, much too personal. He didn't want to be any part of Deke's blog. But it was very familiar, Deke using him, exposing him, blowing any cover he had.

She peered at him, evaluating his irony. "He really gets to you."

"Yeah. Well. Look, I'd invite you in but it's been a long day and I didn't get much sleep last night. Deke was asleep as soon as he hit the backseat of my car but I never closed my eyes again. I'll let him know you wanted to see him. If he ever shows up. Shannon doesn't want him staying here."

She put her hand on his arm. "We're all a little unhinged by this. It's so dynamic. It feels so alive and out of control. It's both scary and thrilling. And you get it all wrapped up in one overpowering person. With the history and all. He's as tied up in you as you are in him."

"He writes about our relationship? Oh great, though somehow I'm not surprised. I don't want to know. I'm sorry. Even if I wanted to, I can't talk about my brother." The emotion from the night before, with Deke asleep in the backseat of his car, then beneath him in the basement of his house, still seemed too big to begin to analyze, or even to circle to get the size of it. Not now, Lori. Maybe not for years. He leaned forward just a bit as he imagined nudging her out the door.

She went back to searching his eyes, trying to read him. "Okay," she ceded. "Say hi to Shannon. Tell your brother I'd like to meet up with him sometime. Maybe he can come and talk to a class." She gave him a quick hug but he was too slow to respond.

When she was gone, heading back across the park like a tourist in an Arab souk or an African bazaar, he leaned back against the wall, knocking the mirror askew. He was just tired, dazed from lack of sleep, which was making him jumble the personal with the political. He prided himself on being able to keep the two separate, at least in his mind if not in his actions, but he had slowly become aware that this divide was much less under his control than he wished. He was full of dread and he knew it was not just because of the chaos around him.

Connor. Shit. That's what all the smugness had been about. Connor was indeed reading Deke's blog. He knew all about how Tim had picked Deke up. What in God's name had Deke written? Should he look? If thousands of people now knew about him and Shannon: shouldn't he know what was being said? Was it better to know or not? If Connor was reading the blog, then so were the rest of the staff at work. Connor wouldn't keep something that juicy to himself. Tim was too tired to think. He'd have to find a way tomorrow to deal with everyone at work looking at him like a character in a soap opera. He couldn't think now. How dare Deke do this to him?

●

THE WHOLLY GREEN GIANT
11:29 PM

It's dark – it's cold – I'm sitting on a piece of pavement bareass – or at least it feels like that. Not so much fun. All day I've been sorting through the info I'm receiving. The place is awash in rumour – some of it planted by undercover – wild stuff like St. Wendy & the boys & the Morrisons are all dead. People say somebody heard shots inside at one point. Bastard would be the type to have a gun collection. Here's what we can safely say. The army's doing a pretty good job of keeping folks out of this area of town but a lousy one keeping them from getting into the city. They don't have the manpower – even with the army & the RCMP brought in – to patrol the whole periphery of this gigantic spread out city. Consequence – there's a whole new Wall now around this part of the city. Folks just camping down where they get stopped. Right on MacLeod Trail & on Glenmore Trail to the south. Crowchild Trail to the west. Love it. Stopping the flow on traffic routes. What better message. Then there's another ring of people on the edge of the city – folks who can't or don't want to abandon vehicles on the edge & hike across the city. Campers & tent trailers & such. & there's the big problem at the border. Big camps of our guys have formed at the border towns now that the whole border is mostly shut down. I guess there's an underground railway kind of thing setting up where folks walk across the border in some god-forsaken untended stretch of prairie-nowhere & get picked up somewhere on this side. Course lots of folks don't want to do that – leave vehicles behind or walk as far as you have to. It's mostly young people doing it. & then there's all the yahoo types with their guns & pick-ups & the extremists of all kinds who are mixing it up & attacking the Tarstoppers.

What else am I hearing? Wendy & the boys are not negotiating. For all we know they play video games all day waiting for the cops to figure out what to do with them. The authorities sure don't want to make martyrs of them. We've got a rule that no one talks to the cops or to the media. We have no leaders. Course there's always dudes who think they're the anointed ones but they get shut up pretty fast. Our demand is simple. Close down the tarsands. A moratorium. No negotiations.

So what else is going on around here? Okay no hiding stuff like the regular media does. We have some problems. I'm not talking about the human stuff like drugs & scuffles & theft. We've got a grip on that mostly. Deeper than that. Like major philosophic splits. Like the anarchists on one side & us greenies on the other & no common path from here. This whole thing is about global warming & the rape of the earth but the anarchists & old Occupiers want to use it for their own nihilistic agenda. We have to be very careful to not let this revolution be taken over by extremists. Then you end up with somebody like Pol Pot or Stalin. Second, we have a problem with the hordes — mostly idealistic kids — who've just hopped on a plane or a bus or put out their thumb & landed here without a tent or a pot to pee in or a penny to their name most of them. Huge amounts of our time & resources are taken up looking after them. They're not getting enough sleep or enough to eat — making them a pretty unpredictable rabble. We're all committed to just letting this whole revolution evolve but there are forces within us that could turn the whole thing ugly — there's already been quite a bit of vandalism from the more unruly or frustrated among us which plays into the hands of the nightly news.

& we won't even get into the bikers & vigilantes & law & order types prowling around among us in greater & greater number. Somebody's dubbed them the Wildcatters & the name seems to be sticking. Maybe the cops are even encouraging them — letting them in to the sacred centre if they look evil enough. Like the way the cops dropped off released prisoners at Zuccotti Park in New York last fall.

THURSDAY
MAY 31 2012

THE WHOLLY GREEN GIANT
1:04 AM

I'm here on the Wall. I can't help it – I know it's weak – but I want to know what's being said out there in the world. Not that I can't guess. So I find the national news on my iPad. All around me bent faces are lit up by phones & tablets on laps or knees. Nobody can sleep. There's a little hum from all the music coming into people's ears on their white earbuds. They glow in the dark, all you can see of people sometimes. Keeping powered is a big issue with all of us. Luckily I got to use the Bro's electricity last night. I might need to go back for a top-up. I'll take as many devices with me as I can from other folks & hope the Bro will not mind contributing a little electricity to the cause.

So I pull up Stephen fucking Harper on the news. The Right

Honourable Prime fucking Minister bursts right through any re-solve I have to keep this profanity free. That stupid corporate helmet of hair of his & those studious little glasses & his grim thin mouth like my dad's or the Bro's. I hate the guy. I really hate him. He sincerely believes that corporate facilitation is the role of government. On the news he's saying what you'd expect. The policy in this country will not be set by hooligans & drifters & disaffected Americans. I shut it down. The temptation to see what's being said internationally & by celebrities & heroes like Bill McKibben is tempting but dangerous. Don't start admiring ourselves in the mirror.

4:52 AM

First hint of dawn. Everybody in pain. Couple next to me talk about there not being a need for the Wall anymore. This might be their last night. Let them arrest Wendy & the boys & release the Morrisons. How to disperse all us Tarstoppers is a much much bigger issue. But then we have to wonder if we're just looking for a way out of sitting here in dark cold painful misery. Too bad we got turfed off the golf course on the other side of the house with all that plush golf course grass. (Don't let me get started on the evil of golf courses.) That'd've been cool to have lived on the golf course – desecrating it – shitting all over it in fact. But it's forced us out onto the parks & school grounds.

So I'm stuck on the pavement & I have to think it may not be necessary to sit here all night in discomfort. Just our presence in the city now is pressure enough on the government & the oil companies. Same way I have to think about the Bro. If I go back to his place now & get some comfy shut-eye am I in some way betraying the cause? I'm still here in the city & what counts here is mass – bodies. I'll be back on my rounds out here soon enough. Suffering doesn't have to be part of something to make it valid. That's part of the old mindset we're trying to dislodge.

Now for a little rant about hypocrisy. That's the charge that's aimed at us the most. If we use an electronic device or hop on the subway or borrow a car then that's us taking advantage of the modern world while we're at the same time trying to disable it. Or if I go to the Bro's for some shut-eye that's me having it both ways somehow. I can't tell you how often I hear it. David Suzuki spends half his time in the air flying to conferences or Al Gore has a monster house & that somehow negates the message. All those fat burghers can get indignant about the hypocrisy & stop listening to the message as they sit behind their wall of self-satis-faction because at least they aren't hypocrites. They know we're on a bus heading for a cliff but they have the comfort as they careen towards the abyss of knowing they've been consistent & stayed with the bus. Didn't stand up & start yelling at the top of their lungs. They think it was their choice to get on the bus in the first place so they have to hang on. & at least they're not being hypocrites. You have to laugh.

●

It scared the shit out of him. Armie was deep in sleep and he came to in a panic. Someone was throwing stones at him. He was still in his dream, now tied to a post in a square in Pakistan, ringed by accusers. But nothing was hitting him. It was the window above his bed that was getting it. Were those guys across the street trying to get in? He sat up and then hesitantly lifted up the folding blind on the window. Whoever he was, the guy outside was huge. Knees like basketballs. Then the guy shifted and Armie recognized his uncle from a glimpse of the side of his face. He raised the window a bit.

"Let me in, okay? Come unlock the back door."

Five thirty in the morning. He had to get up for work soon anyway. Armie trudged upstairs and opened the back door to the bulk of his uncle. It was surprisingly light outside this early in the morning. It was getting close to the summer solstice before there'd even been much of a spring. Once inside, Deke surrounded him with a rank hug. He said in a sort of a whisper, "Hey, kid. Have you grown again? We need to put some meat on you."

Armie shrugged, said, "Later," and went back downstairs.

Deke lumbered after him. Armie thought his parents had to hear him. His mom would be giving his dad an ultimatum. Downstairs, Deke took a shower, he flushed the toilet, he didn't care about the noise. He probably didn't ever think of anybody else.

●

"I'm going to stay at Gizelle's tonight," Shannon told Tim over the phone late in the afternoon, her office to his.

"Okay. I understand that."

This morning, waking up, she'd known just from Tim's hangdog apologetic hesitancy that Derek was back in the basement. "I didn't let him in," he'd rushed to say. "I heard him in the night. Somehow he got Armie's attention and he let him in."

He asked her now, "What about your stuff, your toothbrush and everything?"

"I took enough with me this morning. I'll have to come back on the weekend for more, if this goes on."

"Can I ask you something?" Tim said after a pause. "Why has this got to you the way it has? I understand you're worried about your business suffering and you don't like strangers in your park, but there's something more going on. Something deeper. Deke should not be getting to you quite like this."

"Now? You want to talk about this now?" This was pure Tim, Shannon thought. He only talked like this on the phone, or by e-mail. Those dreaded e-mails where he went on for pages after carrying around some displeasure with her for days or even weeks. It was the only way things ever got talked about between them. It frustrated her that she could cut through guff and demand satisfaction from suppliers and venues and staff but she had a hard time being as straightforward with Tim. Was it something in her or something in him that after all these years they still shied away from direct interaction? Life would be so much easier without the carefulness.

"It's important. I feel like you're far away. Almost like

you've left."

"I'm at work. I'm busy. Can't this wait till later?"

"That's just it. I feel like there might not be a chance to talk again. Tell me what's going on with you. Please."

"I'm really scared, okay? Everyone should be. It's not something personal. Don't do that. Don't make it my psychological problem. You complain I don't talk to you enough but then you won't take my word for what I'm feeling and you start probing and analyzing. This is really scary stuff all on its own."

"Okay, I won't do that. Just tell me what you're thinking."

"Okay, I'll tell you what I think. I think people in a crowd, in a mob, are really unpredictable. This can't end well. I'm scared Armie's going to get caught up in it and maybe even you too because you can both be passive and too open-minded. But mostly I'm terrified of anything out of control. I have zero faith that people on the loose will result in anything but chaos and destruction. I don't care what their good intentions are. Like the French Revolution. Like the Russian. I shouldn't have studied history in university. Your brother's so naïve he's dangerous. But it's the whole thing, not just him. All the people like him who feel so passionately. I'm much more afraid of people with passionate convictions, whatever they are, than I am of global warming."

It was a relief to get this out. Who else could she tell how terrified she was? Gizelle might be a close friend but like everyone else Shannon knew, she was too caught up in the drama to think ahead. Anyway, Gizelle wasn't much of a thinker: she was Shannon's fun friend.

"I've always been the one to see the best in people," Tim said in his thoughtful slow voice. "I have more trust in people's better natures than you but I'm almost as unnerved now as you. Not so much by the Tarstoppers, because I really think they can't win in the end, but by the reaction to them. Hansen has his front lawn spiked with all these signs. I don't want to go out and see what they say but I can bet it's something like, set foot on my property and I'll blow your head off. I was talking to Mike on the other side. He's says these people are beyond the law now, there's so many of them. He says nothing legal will work. You know his solution? Round them up and force them all onto buses and take them to the Arctic and dump them there. See how they like the simple life they're trying to take us all back to. I joked, said, yeah, we could set up work camps in gulags. But he wasn't laughing. It's stupefying how many people want to bring in the army to clear everyone out by force if necessary. Bring in the Americans if the Canadian forces can't handle it. Tanks, landmines in the parks. A few bombs to get people moving. I'm kind of sickened, and horrified."

"We're afraid of opposite things, me anarchy, you the extremes people will go to for law and order. Sometimes I think the only solution is force. It's a stalemate. Nobody's going to shut down the oilsands and there's no one to negotiate with. I just want to get on a plane to anywhere else but here. Is Armie coming home after work? Have you heard from him?"

"Haven't heard. He must be coming home. Maybe there's trouble in lovebird land. We can always hope."

"Okay. I'll talk to you tomorrow. If the phones still work. You probably think that sounds hysterical. Me taking it all too personally."

●

When he reached home, Armie found the kitchen startlingly full of people. On his way home from work he'd felt he was wading through people, the streets full, and now it seemed to continue right into his own kitchen. His dad and Jason were standing talking, his dad leaning against the counter. Liam, Jason's son, who was a year younger than Armie and just finished his first year of engineering, hung around looking like he'd been dragged here as part of his education and wished he could be anywhere else. Armie had spent his childhood on camping trips and at ice rinks and arenas with Liam, mostly being shown up. Liam wore his hair short and kept what opinions he had conventional, maybe too worn out from strenuous sport and exercise to think. He and Liam nodded at one another. Jason would have brought him along as an audience to the debate he hoped for with Deke.

Jason, in mid-sentence, was flinging his arms around. He only stopped talking when he followed Tim's eyes and saw Armie in the doorway. Then he smiled and said, "Our brewer."

They all watched him as he got the juice out of the fridge. The others were drinking beer. Armie would probably never drink beer again in his life, or even want to smell the least trace of it. Liam was looking out the kitchen window.

"I heard the noise last night," his dad said to him. "Did you talk to Deke at all?"

Armie shook his head. But then because he knew his dad would want more, he said, "It was still night."

Jason asked him, "So what's your take on what's going on?"

Armie couldn't think. He didn't have a little capsule of his views ready to hand out. When he watched experts on TV come up with short smooth answers to huge questions, he was always amazed, watching it like a card or magic trick. He might be able to write a thousand words on the topic but it would take him a couple of days. And in front of Liam, he probably wouldn't even be able to read it out loud without stammering. Anyway, Jason didn't really want to know what he thought, it was just a way to get back to expounding his own views.

His dad came to his rescue. "Give the guy a chance to recover from work."

Jason said to him, probably repeating what he'd already told his dad, "I had to bring Liam so we could see for ourselves what's going on. Your whole area is like a fortress now. It's like getting into a prison. I had to prove we live in the city, prove we were visiting friends. I had to say your dad was ill. So they phone here and of course your dad answers sounding chipper as hell. We had to leave my car south of Glenmore and walk in. There's no room for cars on the streets anymore anyways." He said to Tim, "You're socked in here, you know. You'll never get your car out."

His dad said, "Coming home, I had to take a very circu- itous route and even then the last few blocks were impossible.

People in the street just staring me down. Inch by inch. I was even a little scared, like they were going to start rocking my car or something. But then I had to remember they're all pacifists."

Armie asked him, "Where's Mom? Is she home yet? It'll freak her out to have to go through that."

His dad sort of laughed. "She's staying at Gizelle's. Maybe we won't see her again until this thing's over."

Jason said, "It's getting harder to see how it's going to end. They're talking about a million people here now or on their way. The saving grace is that so many of them are stopped at the border. Course not all of those are supporters. A lot of strange types around. It must be a temptation for some ultra right-wing neo-Nazi types to decimate a whole lot of what they would see as the enemy in one fell swoop. Like that guy in Norway last year. The Net is full of that stuff. Scare the pants off you. Have you ever looked at any of it?" he asked Armie, shaking his head at it and adding, "Wild wild derangement out there."

"Never go there. Too much hate for me."

Jason said to Tim, "You could have Armageddon in your own front yard. You get the feeling something like that's the only way it's going to end."

His dad caught Armie's eye. "A little relish there? It's not a video game." His dad was always putting Jason right, pinpricks to deflate him a little. They'd been friends like forever but they got on each other's nerves. Jason was not fooled by the humour his dad inflected his downplays with. But his dad was probably right, that Jason had just come over because he wanted to view the action, maybe even hoping for a little jousting. And because of Deke. Deke was almost as good as if he was their very own resident neo-Nazi.

Armie nodded to the room generally and set off downstairs. This was rude but he had nothing to say to Liam, they'd never been real friends, and he didn't want to listen to Jason right now. He didn't want any more opinion or information or rumour. The guys at work were full of it, making him keep to himself as much as he could because of it. He knew the government and the oil companies were pledging billions on oilsands clean-up and carbon solutions, to no effect, and some politicians in the States were talking about taking action to ensure American oil supply. Obama was saying it was a sovereign Canadian matter but the guys at work all said you knew American security forces and the CIA and armed forces spies were thick on the ground here already. That kind of thing. His head hurt. And that was without Deke going at him.

●

THE WHOLLY GREEN GIANT
5:40 PM
You lose total track of time. The date & the hour's always in front of you on your phone or whatever but it's like info from a different world. How many days has it been? A little over five days since Wendy & the boys walked into Bastard's house & since I left TO. A lifetime ago. So where are we? Demonstrating the

way we should all be living. Co-operatively. Consensually. Focused on relationships & not things. Being careful & taking care of our Mother – though we shouldn't think of her as the calm loving type but instead as the wildly changeable one who has our survival in her hands. We know how to cater to her – what she needs. It's just the transition that'll be tough. & then there's the backlash to deal with.

We're all scared under our jubilation that we're actually pulling this off. We know there's a huge undercover police & security force among us. We know the yahoos are circling us like wolves. I need a break sometimes. I should have gone over to the Bro's earlier this aft when no one was home to get a breather. Maybe they're not home yet.

●

From the basement, Armie heard someone who had to be Deke come in the back door and then clomp on the hardwood floors upstairs. He could imagine Jason rubbing his hands together and his face lighting up at the sight of him. He could also imagine Deke's scowl on seeing Jason in turn.

As much as Armie wanted to put in his earbuds and stay downstairs and block everything out, he wasn't able to do it. Fair enough that he'd gone downstairs to clean up and everything but his dad would expect him back up.

In the kitchen, Deke and Jason and Liam, all big guys, made his dad look small. Joining them, for a moment Armie felt like one of the adults and his dad the kid. His dad was still leaning against the counter, his arms folded. It was how Armie pictured him, leaning back with a bemused and tolerant expression on his face. Deke and Jason both stood forward, wary and alert as gladiators. Liam was practically in the dining room trying to stay out of the way.

"My rescuer," Deke cried when he saw Armie and surrounded him with another stinky hug. His clothes were wrinkled like he'd slept in them a lot of times. He had on a green t-shirt – maybe that was the only colour he owned – and he had the black circle painted on it leaving a green X through it. Deke, who didn't have any kids, liked to say Armie was his once-removed son, sharing half their genes as they did. Some cultures really honoured that connection.

"You off somewhere?" his dad asked him, giving him permission, probably wishing he himself could get out.

Katie was at a class. The streets were plugged. He had nowhere to go. So Armie shrugged and stood there in the doorway, joining his dad and Liam on the sidelines. He'd be able to dash downstairs if he had to escape.

It was like Deke and Jason were going to battle over his dad, each with an arm pulling him their way across a line. Deke had once told him he thought Jason a bad influence on his dad. Deke and Jason had supposedly met in the past, although Armie didn't remember this. There was one time in Toronto when Deke had talked about his dad (Deke seemed to never get enough of talking about his brother), when Deke had said, with a lot of suggestiveness, that you knew someone by their friends. Deke had liked to yell that Jason worked for a pipeline company, for Christ's sake: what more needed to be said? In Deke's view, if you worked for a corporation or one of its tentacles, and especially in the oil industry, that in order to collect your paycheck, you had to buy the company line. Even if you thought you weren't. Otherwise you'd have to turn to drink or despair. Deke said he didn't buy Jason's detachment. It was just a stance to make him able to live with himself.

If Deke was so sure of his own viewpoint, why did he need to convince his big brother so badly? To justify himself? Like a verification or approval?. It didn't make sense. Armie was always surprised to discover again the insecurity in noisy bold people.

"So what's the latest from the front?" Jason was asking Deke, cynical and curious at the same time.

Deke stared at him deadpan. "Go out and wander around for yourself. You might learn something."

Uh, oh.

Deke turned away from Jason, rudely, and asked Tim, "Where's the sis-in-law? She's probably not taking this well."

Armie knew Deke also thought that his mom was not good for his dad, as he'd told Armie one night in a Toronto bar. In his opinion, she gave him an excuse to equivocate. It weakened him. Deke himself had only been married once, for a short time. He called himself a serial monogamist. Right now he was between women, his favourite position, as he liked to say, a joke Armie thought he should bar himself from ever saying again.

His dad said, "As you'd expect. She's staying at a friend's."

Deke was one of those dangerous people who thought everything should be out in the open. Armie never trusted him to keep any of his own confidences, if he were ever so rash as to tell him any. Which didn't mean he hadn't listened to Deke's lengthy analyses of his parents, at least in the beginning, because you never knew what you might learn. He didn't want Deke to get going on his mom now though. He couldn't stand to watch his dad have to defend her.

But Jason wasn't here to talk about Shannon. Just as Deke went to gloat over his sister-in-law being so put out – Armie could easily read his face, like a cartoon character's – Jason cut in with, "I'm serious, man. What's going on out there is huge. I really need to know where they're coming from."

None of them believed this but Jason probably knew Deke couldn't resist the chance to lecture and then Jason would be able to pick off his points. And true to form Deke started into his rant, he couldn't help himself, especially with two impressionable young people in the room. Jason would hear him out, you could tell, and then begin his argument.

Deke spoke straight to Armie, like Jason wasn't even in the room. "As the man says, there are inconvenient truths everyone keeps hoping will go away. But the facts are undeniable. Our only home is being raped by our ravaging species. I'm not exaggerating, much as you'd like to think I am. I can go on for days with the specifics. Let me tell you just one story about unintended consequences and the way the earth's been fucked, particularly by carbon in all its forms. Somebody notices that there's all these tiny pellets of polyester and nylon and the like in beach sand. Polyester and that shit, as you know, being manufactured out of oil. Where the heck is the stuff coming from? Nobody knows. So after long investigation it turns out that every time you wash a piece of clothing or a sheet or whatever with that stuff in it, tiny pieces break off and go down the drain and because they're so small they go through all the filters at the water treatment plants and then they get into the rivers and eventually onto the ocean beaches around the world. It builds up in the sand and ends up in the shellfish. And that's only one small process we didn't know was happening. How many thousands more are there?"

You could tell he loved this story, like it was one in his collection of jewels he took out to display and admire. Armie didn't have to pretend to be unsettled by this news. Was it true?

Jason said, "So? The stuff's inert. It's like sand. It's probably not hurting anything."

Deke whirled on him and did a pantomime of disbelief. "Plastic sea food is not a problem? Are you nuts?"

"So we get better filters, now that we know the problem. What's this got to do with shutting down the oilsands?"

Deke shook his head at Jason's stupidity. He went back to talking just to Armie. "It's just another horrible consequence of using oil. Don't you see? Like global warming. It's so obvious now that there's no rational person left who can deny it. The ramifications are beyond calculating. Aside from anything else – the increased weather disasters and the acidification of the oceans – it'll cause the melting of the permafrost in the Arctic, which will release methane equal to four times the amount of greenhouse gas as has been generated since the beginning of the industrial revolution. And methane is thirty times as potent as carbon dioxide. Think about it. Get your mind around it."

"Where does all that methane come from?" Armie asked, something he was curious about, forgetting for a moment how nerdy this would look in front of Liam and how he wasn't going to get involved.

"Thousands and thousands of years of death with no decay. All the plants and animals that died just got flash-frozen. They'll thaw and decay all at once, wooly mammoths, millions of birds, tons of bugs, you name it."

Jason was waiting him out for his own turn, his mouth twisted with skepticism and even mockery. Liam had sat down on a dining room chair, just out of the room, just waiting for this to be over. Deke was so obviously wacko he wasn't even entertainment.

Deke had the floor and he was not giving it up. Boy, he could talk. Smooth and urgent and uninterruptable. His deep voice was the smoothest part of him. It was such a contrast with his appearance as to be almost comical. He should have been on radio. Armie was tired of looking back at him, Deke's eyes starting to bug out with the pressure of what he had to tell him. "We've all being held hostage by the lie that it's business as usual or we'll be back in the Dark Ages. It's a scam. Don't you see?" And on and on he went. Armie stopped listening, like he'd been trudging against a current and was now just letting it sweep over him.

Deke had stopped for a moment and now waited for Armie to nod vigorously, won over, ready to go down on his knees. It was like Deke wanted to reach out and start his head nodding for him. Armie had to look away.

Jason was almost laughing now. He straightened himself up, ready to demolish Deke's arguments without even raising a sweat. Never mind that Deke wasn't paying any attention to him at all. "You and your pals are so unbelievably naïve. It's like you have no idea how the world works. You tell yourselves fairy tales about how it can be different. The truth is there are no alternatives to oil that can even begin to replace it. Not now and not for the foreseeable future. You and your Comrades are playing around with the destruction of people's lives. The whole economic edifice is rickety at the moment, with European debt and the States taking a long time to get back on its feet. Shut down the oilsands and the whole economy could topple. As it is, the markets are down like twenty per cent. It's a disaster. And that's just the threat. It really pisses me off that Americans come up here to wipe out our economy in the name of their idea. They want to close down the oilsands as some kind of signal, as a symbol. Never mind tackling coal and fracking in their own back yard. They're not even thinking of how people would suffer here. The system might have all kinds of flaws but it's all we have. You guys don't know what you're playing with. Nobody's really denying we've got environmental problems, big ones, but we have no choice but to keep going as we are, fixing what we can and adapting to the rest."

"It's too late," Deke practically screamed, lunging around at him. "We need really drastic action now." He stopped himself. "You know what? I don't have to talk you around. I don't care what another Neanderthal like you thinks. Because our side is finally winning. We've got the numbers to force change."

They were really terrified of one another. That's what Armie hadn't understood. They couldn't afford to listen to the other. They were too scared of the consequences of what the other wanted. It didn't have much to do with logic or rationality. But maybe he and his dad, both such moderate bystanders, were so busy being fair to both sides they'd missed the reality that both sides were right about the peril — those who supported both of the extremes, stopping the oilsands or keeping it going full tilt — and either way we were all doomed. And the default moderate position that somehow we'd avoid disaster if we stumbled on like always, adapting and improving as we went, was wishful hopeless ostrich thinking.

As they'd tried to convince each other that the other's plan for the world would be catastrophic, they might not have had much effect on one another, or on his dad or on Liam for sure, but they'd scared the hell out of Armie. Jason said that all kinds of new science was being developed to combat global warming: there'd be a solution. And Deke said, like what? And Jason searched his memory and came up with the idea of mimicking the cooling effects of a volcano by pumping sulfur dioxide or other reflective chemicals into the air. And even Armie could see the potential that would have for making everything infinitely worse.

There was no hope. He might throw up. They were both right. They cancelled one another out. There was no solution that didn't wreck the world one way or another. He couldn't listen to any more. He turned and ran downstairs, he didn't care who it offended.

●

Tim called Shannon at Gizelle's. "I just had the war of the worlds move into my own kitchen. Jason and Deke. Good thing you weren't here."

"It wouldn't have happened: I'd have thrown them out. Was Armie there? I worry that your brother's going to pull him over to his side. At least Jason would be a counter-balancing force."

"Liam was here as well. Jason and Deke really went at it and Armie listened for a while but then he went tearing downstairs in the middle. I don't know what was going on with him. He's kept to himself the rest of the evening. I heard him rummaging for food a little while ago."

"Jason and your brother are fighting over you, aren't you flattered?"

"No, just more confused than ever about the solutions and really tired of listening to people's opinions."

"Well, try and keep Armie out of it. You too if you can."

●

THE WHOLLY GREEN GIANT
3:41 PM

Okay this Jay guy as I'm calling him. The Bro's best friend. I'm out here wandering around trying to calm myself down but I can't stop going over the conversation I just had with the guy at the Bro's house. No, not conversation – that implies something two-way. I went to the Bro's around suppertime just for a little friendly visit. I haven't actually talked to him since getting here. But his friend's there waiting for me. He wants to take me on. I knew this guy years ago when I used to come west. & I've seen him once or twice when he's been on business in TO. I could never figure out why he called me up. We'd argue then too. He likes to argue.

Anyways he starts right in on me tonight. You'd think he'd be interested in the view from someone on the ground – but no – he just wants to argue again. He got to me because he didn't want to know. According to him we're on this track & there's no getting off & we'll deal with the shit on the track when we get to it. He says who knows what'll happen – maybe it'll never turn up or be gone by the time we get there. The guy's a joke. He admits business is a game to him. But it's the only game there is. At least the Bro knows the dangers are real – even if it just paralyses him. But this Jay dude just walls it all off. I tell him all my worst stories & examples & he just shrugs. The guy's impervious. He shrugs it all off & instead gets steamed about the threat us Tarstoppers pose to civilization as he knows it. It's not like I'm unfamiliar with the type. Hell my old man – as you all know – is a retired bank executive. I know the mentality. What got to me about Jay is his cynicism. My old man really believes that corporations & globalization & high finance are all for the good. He's banked his whole life on it – so to speak. Jay knows it's mostly a scam but he's sticking to it anyway & casting us as the destroyers. What do you do with a guy like that? He really wanted to have at me so he could counter all my arguments & not have to wake up to the reality of the danger. He doesn't believe in anything. Okay I'll stop. You can tell how much he got to me. & my nephew's there listening to everybody & I wanted to cover his ears like against evil. So for the past hour I've been wandering around talking to folks & getting my equilibrium back.

●

Katie didn't get it. Armie would have said they agreed on everything, even though they didn't talk much about serious stuff. He shouldn't have called her. But he had to call her, he always called her. He knew he was jabbering. His uncle, Jason, the threat to the world.

"Why did you listen?" she asked. "Why let it upset you? We have control over what we let through to us. Remember? This doesn't have anything to do with us."

"You don't know what it's like. This whole huge Tarstopper thing. You're so outside it where you live. You don't know. You go to class and do your art and it doesn't affect you. But we can't go on pretending this has nothing to do with us. I feel like I've been locked away in a fantasy kingdom. Don't you see that?"

But she didn't. She was just hurt that he saw their love as some kind of prison. She repeated, "It has nothing to do with us. Neither of us even drives. And if we're as doomed as you say we are no matter what happens, then that's even more reason for us to stick together and find our own happiness." Her voice quavered. She was almost in as much of a panic now as he was.

"I can't do that. I'll know I'm hiding out."

"But what can you do if the best minds in the world don't have any solutions?"

"I don't know. But I can't go back to sleep. I'm upsetting you. I'm sorry. I didn't mean to. I'm just so jazzed up right now. It's so weird with all those people camped around my house right now."

Nothing was helping. He could tell from her breathing he was making it worse. "I'm just upsetting you. I didn't mean to. I'll talk to you in the morning. I'll calm down. It's okay. I love you. I love you, I love you, I love you."

FRIDAY
JUNE 1 2012

Friday after work. Shannon and her friend Gizelle were in a bar downtown drinking martinis. It seemed a little decadent to be enjoying herself while Rome burned but it was not as if there was anything she could do. She absolutely wasn't up to going home and keeping Armie and Tim out of Derek's clutches, although she probably should. Maybe tomorrow, Saturday.

It was easy to forget the world when with Gizelle. She was divorced, still beautiful at forty-seven, and alive to men in ways Shannon no longer was used to, although she was aware that controlled flirtation was part of her own business strategy. Gizelle was excited by all the new men in town to cover the Tarstoppers. "One good thing to come out of it," she joked. The bar was crowded. There was a buzz, a little like there would be a month from now during Stampede, minus the cowboy hats and boots that everybody would wear then. What happened if the Tarstoppers were still in town for Stampede? The organizers had to be having conniptions. So far Shannon hadn't had any event cancelations, her client companies all holding their breath.

A man, older, nice-looking, not a snake, was watching her, not hiding it. She didn't know him; she was good with faces. It was hard to ignore someone in your line of vision who was staring at you, although she tried. Gizelle noticed – she was alive to every body signal in the room – and nudged her like they were in a high school cafeteria. Maybe coming here wasn't such a good idea, Shannon thought. She picked up her drink with her left hand to expose her wedding ring. He was coming over anyway. Her body pricked to him, the sensation identical to a ruff of fear. For just a second she imagined running off with him, just to get out of here, out of Calgary, away from what would be a frustrating, nerve-wracking, infuriating month leading up to what was usually her busiest time of year.

Gizelle was turned away toward a man who'd appeared at her shoulder, someone she knew, not a prospect. Which left Shannon open. The man put his arm through the gap between her and the person squished in to her left and put down his business card on the granite counter. Matt Brown, ABC News. His body, in a denim jacket, touched against her back from the press behind him. She could feel his breath in her ear, her hair up.

"Can I talk to you?"

She turned her head. "Are you on the job?"

"Off the record."

She shifted her chair closer to Gizelle's and he was able to squeeze in enough that she could see the side of his face. She was not often this close to another man except in the hugs everyone felt impelled to give these days, free gropes as Shannon thought of them. This was more sustained.

"Are you local or imported?" he asked.

"My house is surrounded. I escaped."

"I take it you're not a sympathizer."

"I'm an event planner. I have my own company. Most of my clients are connected to the oil industry in one way or another. Do I think they have a point? Of course. I just don't think they have a solution that's not worse than the problem."

"You know, one thing I'm aware of. How much more liberal your average Canadian is, even if they define themselves as conservative. You're probably all for gay marriage and open abortion."

"What do they have to do with oil? Actually, I don't get the States. Obsessed with freedom, everything wide open, except your personal life, no freedom to have an abortion or be an atheist. It doesn't add up. But then little in life does."

"What do you think is going to happen here?

"What do you?"

Gizelle put her hand on her shoulder as she slipped off her seat: she'd be back. Matt slid across Shannon's back to take Gizelle's seat. It gave her a little breathing room not to have him pressed against her but now he could watch her face. She wished she could let her hair down and shield that side of her face.

"No, I want to hear what you think."

She didn't believe him. He was busting to tell her how it would all play out. She saw a lot of men in her life. It had never happened that she met someone who made her imagine not being married. She liked stability. She would say, had said, that an attraction to someone else was caused by internal dissatisfactions, boredom, old issues, so deal with those. But this seemed pure chemistry. The last time she'd felt something like this was in grade nine. It made no sense. She hadn't even noticed him until the stare. Maybe it was just the gin and the surreal times, being out of her house. Nothing to do with her. But it was like the anarchy in the city was contagious.

She said, "I don't think we can know how this will end. Something's been released. Damned if I understand what it is. Not something I can relate to. I have to say the protesters seem to have learned a lot more from the Occupy movement than the police did. We had it here too in the fall. At a downtown park."

She wouldn't be able to sit here much longer. The skin on the side of his face was a little rough, stubble just showing. She wanted to lick it. Suck one of his thick fingers with the flat nails. "Your turn." He could put his hand on her waist, his tongue in her exposed ear.

"Could we go somewhere? I'd really like to talk to you. Somewhere a little quieter."

"I'm married."

He pulled back as if chiding her. "I'm not hitting on you. I just want to talk to you."

"Here. And not for long."

"What's your name?"

"I don't think I'm going to tell you. I want to hear how you think this is going to end."

"I'm the one trying to interview you. Okay. The Tarstoppers. What do I think? Eventually they'll dissipate. But not before it gets ugly. It won't end here though. Did you know that there are improvements we could make right now to the engines of cars that would make them way more efficient and reduce fuel emissions? Did you know that? But they would cost. All the things the Tarstoppers want are going to cost. Which is going to enrage even the people who are generally in favour of reducing impact, never mind the people who don't even believe in global warming. It's going to be a long war. This is only the beginning."

"As long as they move it out of my front yard. I'm as self-interested as the next person. So what's your personal position?"

He didn't seem to know what she meant. Hadn't he just told her?

"Do you believe global warning is real?" she prodded. "Do you drive an electric car? Or are you full steam ahead?"

"I don't even think about it. I use what I have to to get where I want. What does your husband do?"

"Non-profit. He's much more concerned than I am, generally." She looked around for Gizelle. "I can't stay."

"Why are you so skittish? What's going on here?"

She didn't know. Her body seemed to be paying no attention to her. She stood up, not easily from the stool she'd been perched on, and he grabbed her hand to steady her. A jolt. An electrical jolt. The body was a network of live currents. She yanked her hand back and pushed away. She didn't even look for Gizelle. She could walk to Gizelle's condo and she had a key.

She would go all the way home, to her house, if she could only get there. There were long lines of people waiting at taxi stands. No bus would go near her house now, although she couldn't imagine taking the bus anyhow. She didn't look around to see if he was following her. It didn't matter. She thought she was going to be years getting the pulse of this guy out of her system. It was stress. It was like wartime when all kinds of affairs started up. That was it. But then she had to remember how one-sided this had been, the guy really not making any overtures to her at all. What was wrong with her?

●

Armie was at Katie's house, in her bedroom, in her childhood room still with its pink walls, now plastered with her weird intricate collages and with all her totems and downloaded images and found objects that went into her art. Some might find it claustrophobic. All of it had meaning, but only to her, from her childhood or her interior life or dreams or from what she'd encountered in the run of a day. Even he didn't know what most of it meant, even with explanations, so how could anyone else get much out of it? It didn't matter though because she would never sell any of it. A storage box stood in the corner, collecting the past, the colourful representational record of her days. It would eventually join the rows of containers in the basement.

He still felt himself to be in some kind of vise, even after a day of hard labour. When he'd taken the job at the brewery he'd had some idea that hard work would purify him. It would be like yoga or meditation or something, emptying his mind so that he could then think more clearly. Mostly it just exhausted him. And he hadn't counted on the poison of his co-workers' views. He felt now like he couldn't breathe.

He'd burst into Katie's room feeling like he carried so much agitation with him that the force could blow all her painstaking creations into a blizzard of litter. Now he was scaring her with his panicked recitation of what he'd been thinking ever since he'd listened to Deke and Jason. She tried to take hold of him but he evaded her. She would smother him. He'd have to gasp for air.

Now she was rooting among her pills, all in their colour-coded, decorated little boxes, for what would either calm him down or else harden him to distraction. "I'm not taking anything now," he said and the tone of his voice, the hint of exasperation, caused her eyes to fill. Katie's emotion slopped around inside her, barely contained at any time. She started pulling him toward the bed. She was wearing one of her lace and silk slips or nightgowns or whatever they were that she made herself, that she lived in, that she wore even to art class, like she was turning herself on just to walk down a street. Sex was always their default solution to everything. Either they were on their iPads or they were fooling with each other's bodies.

He broke away. He couldn't touch her. She'd pull him right back under and he'd get entangled. The way he was always getting tied up in her hair, which she wore straight, dyed black, and hadn't cut since she was nine years old. Strands of her hair clung to his clothes, got into his mouth, caught under his body making her cry out in pain. He hated her hair. At the moment he was almost afraid of her and her drugs and her hands always on him.

He put his hands up. "It's me, it's not you. I love you. I'll always love you. I just have to get my head straight. I'll be back. I'll text you as soon as I can. I love you. Trust me." He couldn't stay. Even though he knew how much it would panic her, he couldn't stay.

But on his pell-mell dash through Katie's house, he was stopped by Katie's dad, Jim. "Hey, hey, what's the rush? Are you okay? Trouble in love land?"

Armie liked Jim well enough, even if he was a little hokey. He liked both Katie's parents, who treated him like a son, which meant they were always trying to fatten him up and needle out his future plans. Jim was an accountant at a big firm, which was beyond Armie, crunching numbers all day, but obviously well paid. Both her parents were older, like over sixty, almost like grandparents.

Armie was feeling so unhinged that he blurted out, "How do you do it? How do you put it together? I mean the whole global warming thing and having to keep the economy going and everything?"

Jim put his hand on his arm. "What's happened? What's got you so riled up? Come on, in here." He pulled Armie into his den, his office or study, which was paneled in wood and had plaques and golf pictures on the walls, dark leather furniture. Armie had never been in here before. Jim poured scotch from a glass decanter into two glasses. Armie hated hard liquor but he had no choice but to take it now that it was poured. He thought of it as medicine, which maybe Jim intended.

"Okay, tell me."

"My uncle's here. From Toronto. He's a Tarstopper. I was listening to his lists of things damaging the planet. It was kind of overwhelming, one huge danger after another like that. And my dad's friend was arguing the other side, about how fragile the whole economy is, how it can't take any more hits, and they got to me. We're doomed either way. So how do you put them together?"

Katie was at the door. She'd been crying. He wanted to go to her but not in front of her dad. He tried to communicate this with his eyes but she ran away. He couldn't look at Jim. He took a gulp of scotch, which seemed to shoot straight up through his brain and hit his skull.

Jim was going to set him straight, Armie could tell. He obviously had it all worked out and he was quite happy to have an occasion to present it. Especially to an impressionable young man like him at a crossroads. "You can't let the doomsayers get to you. There's nothing new in any of this. There are always people who think the end is near. When I was your age they were all worried about nuclear warfare and over-population and how we were going to run out of both food and oil. There was an oil embargo and shortage in the States. Sound familiar? Did any of it happen? No. We came out of it. And we will again. Rather than catastrophe, things got much much better for everyone, even in the Third World. The US has huge oil and gas reserves now accessible by new technologies. It'll refuel economic growth. And private sector ingenuity will overcome the destructive side of oil. I'm very optimistic. Sure there's going to be change and fallout. Life's like that. The Tarstoppers are causing incredible chaos on the markets — that's all doomsayers accomplish in the end — but we'll recover. We always do."

As he listened, Armie could almost see the spreadsheet in Jim's mind. He had global warming on it as an opportunity. Did all adults go around with the issues lined up in their minds like this? Knowing what they thought? Like Deke. Like Jason. Adding what fit, figuring out how to reconfigure developments that didn't seem to. Everybody but his dad, the waffler, seeing too many sides. He was no role model. Armie didn't want to live his whole life in this cage with anxiety in every direction.

Jim was still going. He was a little louder now as if Armie was not hearing him properly. He had hold of Armie here in his study and he had to pull him away from all the negativity out there. He was getting a little annoyed that Armie was not nodding and leaning towards him in gratitude. Armie didn't want to argue with Jim. He didn't want to say that he'd heard that fracking, which had to be one of the new technologies Jim was talking about, was very expensive, had the usual environmental problems, and had to be continually repeated. And still produced CO2. But what did Armie know? He was not an engineer or a geologist. Neither was Jim. And he didn't want to become one. But neither did he want to pick out his own rationale out of all the bits and pieces of the information cloud so he could sleep at night.

He was stuck here for now. He'd learned – he was grown-up enough to know – that he was not selling himself out if he appeared to go along just to make things easier. He didn't need to turn Jim against him. So when Jim looked to him after another long explication basically saying the same thing, *NOT A WORD* Armie smiled for him and said he'd made him feel better and maybe he should go up and see Katie, who was upset by his distress. And he was feeling better, which was probably the scotch, which he'd somehow sipped right to the bottom. Jim gave him this fraternal small smile about the needs of women.

Jim had his hand on his shoulder as he escorted him out of his den. Armie felt a little sick, which also might have been the scotch but more likely how catering to Jim's self-esteem had lessened him, Jim, in his eyes. He used to like Jim. He used to think him pretty solid. And there went another adult off the list of possible mentors or examples.

Katie saw his confusion as betrayal. They agreed on everything and yet he was in distress about something she'd never even thought about. How could she have never thought about it? The only thing that mattered to her was her interior world. They were going to end up breaking up. He could see it. Even just this morning he couldn't have imagined it as a possibility. He'd thought they were together for life. He still loved her. He told her that over and over as he held her. But the "still" said it all, even if only he heard it. He'd taken one of her pills. Combined with the alcohol it made him forget enough of his angst to be able to lapse into sensation. They could do this for hours.

◆

THE WHOLLY GREEN GIANT
9:15 PM

It's getting dangerous out here. There's guerilla warfare all around the city. Horrible stuff going on. Here we thought corporate Calgary & their government lackeys were our adversaries & instead we're being pummeled by criminal elements & by ordinary good ol' boys who usually spend their time ripping up the backcountry in their quads & ski-dos. Wildcatters. These guys who believe in an illusionary sense of personal liberty. Which we threaten. To them it's a fight between individualism & some kind of collectivism we're supposedly advocating. They'd rather have their fate in the hands of giant ruthless corporations & go on pretending they've got autonomy rather than see that government — & by that I mean real democracy — & unions & other collective stuff is the only leverage they can have. But you've all heard me on this before – probably too many times.

Right now it's like being in a cocoon in here but what if the police cordon around us doesn't hold? Folks in the camps who are being hit by the so-called Wildcatters aren't fighting back. There's no defense against a raid. What – we should build walls & a moat around ourselves? Pour boiling oil down on attackers? So far it's only harassment but you know somebody's going to get hurt soon – or killed. I've heard that a huge number of guns & automatic weapons have been seized at the border. The wildcatter freedom dudes are apparently surprised to find out they can't just carry them across. So then they're sneaking across – just like those Mexicans on their southern border whom they think should be shot for trying. Not that we don't have our own home-grown jerks & gangs & gunmen. The danger is that the tarsands are going to get forgotten in all this. A vicious culture war lets the oil companies off the hook.

Nobody was prepared for the violent backlash but you have to feel for the kids among us with their idealism & hope. They're watching the violence on their screens like it's all a video game & then reacting in horror as they realize it's all real & coming their way. Nothing like this happened to the Occupy movement or to the hundred of thousands of student protesters in Quebec this spring. Everyone has a right to protest – except maybe in a place like Syria right now – but this place is Canada. How can this stuff happen in Canada? & the police aren't doing much to stop it. I've seen the videos. The cops show up after the fact & stand around staring at the charred remains of a camp. Or this afternoon, when a homemade bomb went off in an encampment on the edge of the city. Most of the cops – being who they are – are on the side of our tormentors. The old thing about cops being latent criminals keeping themselves under control. They hate us. Us wimps out here passively protesting the way the world works. While they play tough-guy cops & drink too much & beat up their wives & spend hours target shooting & playing violent video games because their lives suck.

SATURDAY
JUNE 2 2012

Tim was at his front window again, trying to decide if he should attend the general meeting in the park, due to begin soon. As a local resident he had every right to be curious about their plans. He told himself he wouldn't be committing himself to anything, just to go listen.

He'd been at loose ends all morning, unable to remember what he usually did on a Saturday. Newspaper delivery had stopped in his neighourhood and he didn't have his regular crossword puzzles. He couldn't get his car out now to go look for a paper or run any errands. Anyway, he didn't think he wanted to know what was happening in the city right this minute. But Jason kept texting him information and developments, prodding him to join him in his obsession with it. Tim didn't have Jason's veneer of cynicism, as he thought of it, to protect him from shock.

Backlash really getting going; check it out. Bunch of yahoos tried to burn out a campsite. This is getting nasty. World war coming.

Reluctantly Tim went online, where he watched a clip about a campsite on the outskirts of town, which must have been what Jason was texting about. The camera panned a camp now heaped with the blackened sleeping bags and pulled-down tents and wadded clothing that had been used to smoother the fire. A group of sooty, disheveled, outraged Tarstoppers told their story to a reporter. Apparently a number of pick-up trucks had driven up on the grass, positioning themselves around the camp. Then at a signal, people had jumped out and run forward, dribbling some kind of accelerant from cans. They'd then jumped into the next truck left idling and tossed flames out their windows as they left. They could have blown themselves up but they'd gotten away with it.

Was this kind of thing common around the city? Tim wondered, appalled by the viciousness and danger. The news didn't say. No one knew who the attackers were, their license plates muddied up. The cameras and the interviewers and the commentators seemed more obsessive than their most rabid followers, as they circled and wove through incident and disasters. He didn't want to watch any more of this kind of thing. He didn't want to think about how many good citizens, like his neighbours on both sides of him, were probably attached to their TVs and devices and cheering the vigilantes on.

A few minutes later Jason texted again. *Court order. Clearing the school playgrounds. Starting with Windsor Park near the M house.*

Not going easily, School near you ll be next.

Tim resisted looking but then brought it up. The police were carting off limp resistant people on stretchers. A lot of other Tarstoppers had chained themselves to trees or benches or playground equipment and the police were patiently sawing them free. There were hundreds of people on the school field. The removal seemed futile. Once they'd been evicted from there, they'd only join other camps. A police spokesperson, a young woman, said they were just carrying out the law. An official from the school board, so red in the face he seemed inflamed, demanded to know who was going to pay to clean up the mess. The camera panned the abandoned tents and the rubble of lawn chairs and bulk food bags and makeshift tables and indecipherable garbage.

Ardith had also been texting him this morning. Earlier she'd worried about their safety but Tim had reassured her that her mom had escaped to Gizelle's. Now she texted *I cant believe this happening in Calg ur in middle whol world waching I can't stop but makes me so mad those grubby no counts r goin 2 cause global collapse.*

His guilty pleasure: Ardith's frankness, her lack of equivocation. It was as if he'd given her license to be brash and opinionated. What he disliked in most people, in Deke especially, he indulged in Ardith. It was projection, he knew, of all those sides of himself he couldn't muster. Whereas Armie was deeply familiar to him, Ardith sometimes seemed like one of those unattainable cheerleader types from high school who for some reason gave him the time of day. His daughter. To have a wife like Shannon and a daughter like Ardith was like a costume he kept at home, not to be used to bolster him in the eyes of others. Except of course people did know, the people at work had met Shannon any number of times over the years. If he was honest, he had to admit he got great satisfaction from the image: ordinary smallish quiet Tim (except when he had the floor somewhere, his surprising oratory) and his glamorous women.

Where was Armie? Tim had texted him to no response. At the moment his son seemed like the only person he could think of who seemed as troubled by what was not being said – that basically we're fucked regardless – as he was. The look on Armie's face as he'd listened to Deke and Jason last evening had mirrored Tim's own reaction. Armie had taken it all in straight. He'd believed them both.

Should he go to the meeting in the park at noon? Would it look like a commitment, a move off the fence? He didn't want to be seen as endorsing the call for a total shutdown of the oilsands. After all he was the Director of a charitable agency: he knew what happened when the economy wobbled.

And then there was the other reason not to go to the park: Deke would be there at the meeting and he'd gloat if Tim showed up. He told himself he should not still be planning his actions in reaction to Deke. But he imagined a whole field full of Dekes, people outside the system, students and artists and old hippies and the feckless from all walks of life, people proud of their ignorance of economics. Maybe he'd be surprised by who was there. He told himself to keep an open mind.

It was quarter to twelve and still no word from Armie. He'd been hoping to talk Armie into going with him to the meeting, the two of them standing back as spectators. He watched as the people in the park moved towards the baseball diamond, carrying their folding chairs. This was stupid, being so equivocal. Why shouldn't he go?

As he stepped out onto the porch he felt exposed, in the process of taking a giant step, which he told himself was ridiculous self-inflation. He hoped none of his neighbours were watching. Were any of them reading Deke's blog? No wonder he felt self-conscious. Most of the people in the park would have read every word. They'd know all about him. Had Deke posted pictures of him along with shots of happy campfires and sitting on the Wall?

As he joined the stragglers heading towards the baseball diamond, people smiled at him, none with any recognition, and he smiled back to show good intent. Everybody looked a little rumpled, a little shaggy, but no different than any other bunch of campers. They all wore the green and black badge; they were all ages, as diverse as any group except there was not a button-down among them. He looked too clean. He should have put on a sweatshirt, changed his shoes.

He stood on the edge of the semi-circle that had formed around a group of people at a table pushed up against the wire mesh of the backstop. The facilitators, he knew they were called. Six of them, mostly young, three men, three women. A few more piercings than usual, two male ponytails, but nothing untoward. They were as rumpled as everyone else. With all the money now arriving from worldwide donations, who could blame them for upgrading? They could say to themselves they needed to get their sleep to better play their role and thus take the first step towards entitlement and power.

A middle-aged woman stood at a microphone (how many stationary bicycles powered the battery to feed its amplification?) and began by outlining the day's events. She had the look of someone long used to organizing against the system, the patriarchy, the elite. She was someone like his mother, although his mother had more style. Then she read the manifesto Wendy and the boys had put on the Net before the hostage-taking, a ritual, no doubt, to start every meeting. Basically it said, stay the summer, stay as long as it takes. No negotiations. The woman said that the problem now was how to stay motivated and not devolve into squalor and acrimony. And how to protect themselves from rogue roughnecks.

First there were reports from some of the working groups: sanitation, structure, food, as boring as any committee reports anywhere. Although he was interested in their arrangements, Tim couldn't stay focused. He couldn't imagine that anyone else was really listening. But then when they opened up the mike, Tim could only listen for a few minutes to the first speaker, an orange-haired young man whom everyone had obviously already heard too much from. Something about spies and germs. Tim scanned the crowd for Deke. He expected him to sneak up on him and grab him like he'd been caught. Talk about your paranoia.

Someone rang a bell, time was up, a restriction probably put in place because of people like the orange-haired young man who was just getting going. He tried to argue but he was led away, gently but quite firmly by someone who looked like a bouncer. The problems of participatory democracy. Tim knew them well. The world was not made up of rational, thoughtful citizens. People had issues, agendas, obsessions, illnesses. The quiet moderates stopped talking and eventually gave up no matter which strategies you used, and the bullies and obsessives took over. Non-profits tried to be non-hierarchical, being in the caring business, but leadership and structure usually became necessary once you were any size at all. He still had to remind both himself and his staff (he corrected himself: the staff) to collaborate, not to take over and run with things.

There were at least twenty people in line to speak. Tim had to leave. He couldn't bear to watch the process. It was easy to slip back into the maze of tents and camper trailers that surrounded the baseball diamond. Was Deke watching him leave? As he walked home, Tim passed some campsites as neat as suburban lots, with lilacs in a jar and the grass clipped, while others, after less than a week, were collapsing or they were a jumble of garbage and bedding. Already the grass of the path system through the encampment was wearing thin. It would be a quagmire after a couple of more days of foot traffic and rain.

Deke was sprawled on his front steps. It was too late to avoid him. Luckily a large spruce tree shielded Tim from view as he crossed the street towards the house. Olsen's signs on his front lawn were as venomous as Tim had imagined. GO HOME GREEN SCUM. DEATH TO ENVIRONMENTALISTS. Tim was starting to feel like Shannon, just get him out of here, anywhere but here.

From halfway up the walk – the walkway offset so he wasn't walking straight towards his brother – Tim called out to Deke, "It's pretty hard to listen to some of the more delusional and obsessive stuff." It was meant to sound understanding of why Deke wasn't across the street in the audience but it probably came out like he'd caught him shirking.

"I didn't think you'd last long."

Tim remembered how impossible it was to embarrass his brother, and how easy it was to embarrass him. Reaching the steps, Tim said, "Let's talk about something else, okay? Family, the past, whatever. And in the back, not out here." He unlocked the front door. Deke, he knew, was judging him for locking up the house and for avoiding the only topic of any relevance, for hiding from the reality in front of his own house. Deke wouldn't say anything right now though, only smirk knowingly. Tim felt trapped in a vat of something viscous and inescapable.

"Do you want a beer?" he asked as they walked back through the house and of course Deke did.

"And a few munchies if you've got them."

When Tim emerged onto the back deck, Deke had both his iPad and his phone going, tweeting and texting at the same time. He nodded as Tim set down his beer and a plate of nachos but he didn't look up. Tim waited. Deke's thumbs moved fast. Every few seconds one of the devices pinged. He was wearing grey sweatpants, dirty ones, a green t-shirt onto which he'd painted the Tarstoppers emblem, and huge once-white untied sneakers. Tim didn't know anyone who wore sweat-pants outside a gym or during a run. He could hear the voices in the park. He'd drunk half his beer and eaten too many na-chos before Deke even looked up. Then Deke drained his own beer and shoveled down the rest of the nachos. And burped.

"Okay, Bro, what do you want to talk about then?"

"Maybe I should text you. We don't do well face to face."

"What would the text say?"

"I'd really appreciate it if you could keep me and Shannon out of your blog."

"You've read it?"

"No. But my friends and my co-workers are reading it, which is a little more exposure than I want."

"I'd have thought you'd take a little more interest. Some-times I even think I'm writing it for you. Trying to get through to you."

"Just not the personal stuff, okay?"

"What does Shannon think?"

"She doesn't know."

"Jesus fucking Christ. You're doing it again. Trying to control me. You've been this fucking lid on me my whole life. Big brother standing to the side and disapproving. Fuck."

Tim let a silence develop while Deke ignored him, check-ing his phone. This was his brother. They shared a lot of genes, a childhood. They knew one another deep down. It shouldn't be this difficult. After a few minutes he said, "Okay. Let's try again. Neutral subject. How's Mom? I talk to her on the phone but I haven't seen her for a while."

Deke didn't take his off his screen. "Don't think I don't hear about that."

"So how do you find her these days?"

"Busy. What else? Being retired hasn't slowed her down one bit."

"Have I ever told you Shannon's theory? She thinks Mom made us into the kind of men that she wanted in the world. She'd made the mistake of marrying a tough businessman like her own father and she vowed her two boys would never be like that. We were feminized. A whole generation is like that, brought up by women to be good fathers and unaggressive and considerate and not wrapped up in work."

"Shannon thinks."

"We're not talking about Shannon. It's the theory. She says it's why you're so good with women."

Deke snapped his attention off his screen. "Which is otherwise totally inexplicable. Right. Well, I do prefer women. They talk about the best stuff. Aside from all their other advantages. Do you notice how almost everything you say to me is an insult? How are we going to talk about anything if you put so much off limits, like Shannon? You're always going into your shell. Into a bristly ball like a hedgehog. Then shooting off your quills."

"I think you're getting your animals mixed up."

Derek's eyes were half-closed, evaluating him in that knowing, infuriating way. "Okay, I'll tell you want I think. Our dad was a bastard. Self-obsessed, bad-tempered, bullying. I've never been as happy in my life as when Mom told me he'd left.

I will be forever grateful to her that she had the guts to toss him out. Twelve years old and no longer terrified when I heard the garage door roll up at suppertime. After that everything would have been blissful if it hadn't been for you. You don't know what you were like. Always on the outside. Always by yourself. Scowling. You don't know how much you're like our old man. And you're getting more and more like him. His mannerisms. It's tough being around you sometimes."

"It's not an insult to tell someone they're identical to a bastard? I don't want to fight. I was talking theory. A bigger picture. Us as a product of a generation of new feminists. You concerned about the poor ailing planet, me feeding the hungry. It could be said that all the people in the park are the result of the ongoing feminization of society. In the sense of caring, of tending things, rather than exploiting them. Of thinking widely about the implications and consequences of what we do, rather than narrowing in and bulldozing straight ahead."

"This is Shannon's theory?"

"She was talking about our particular family but I've been thinking about it more generally. Let's keep everything on a theoretical level, right? So we can think about it. Not get into the particulars. Not have to take any action."

Someone had come through the side gate, Tim heard the latch. Must be a Tarstopper. The Tarstoppers coming in to take over. Tim imagined a long line of Deke's friends. But then he was relieved to see Lori appear around the edge of the deck, although surprised. He had to get his imagination under control.

"Hi," she said, "I can't keep away. There's something there in the park, something important." She said to Deke, "I don't know if you remember me. Tim and Shannon used to live next door to us. I'm Lori. I was hoping to run into you."

Deke didn't remember. But he was keen to talk to someone showing enthusiasm. After all, she might be teetering on the edge of commitment. An attractive woman. "Of course," he said, "Lori. Hi. Isn't it amazing? We're trying to create a template for an alternative way of life. I can't tell you what a high I'm on with this. What is it you do again? Are you able to join us?"

"I teach high school. You can imagine how the kids are talking. I need to know more."

Tim didn't want to listen to Deke again. "What about lunch? Can I make you both lunch?" He stood up. "Is anyone else hungry? I can probably rustle up something from inventory."

Deke and Lori barely glanced at him as Deke said to her, "Come on over and I'll give you a tour. We'll do a video for your class."

"Will you be back?" Tim asked him. "Tonight? Maybe I should give you a key."

Sometimes he was buffaloed by the things he did. Why had he brought up his staying here again? Showing some stubborn loyalty to his only sibling, with Lori watching. Being the nice guy, still.

Deke did that stretch-faced thing to show it was immaterial to him. Tim wondered if he kept trying with his brother in hope of getting some gratitude out of him. Deke never thanked anyone. To be fair he was quite generous himself and never looked for acknowledgement but this just left Tim feeling petulant. He went in for the key.

When he came out, Lori and Deke were already on their way out. As he handed the key to Deke over the deck railing, he could see him struggle with the need to justify in front of Lori his preference for a bed and a roof over his head while his Comrades slept rough in the park. Had Tim offered it just to show him up? Tim turned away, to spare them both.

◆

THE WHOLLY GREEN GIANT
3:32 PM

I had a blast this aft showing a friend of the Bro's around the camp. Lori. A high school teacher. She was really into it – taking pictures & recording everything. One of those satisfying people you can pour information & perspective into. She wanted to know it all. She was so enthusiastic I started to wonder if she was a spy for one of our enemies. Not really. She gave me hope but we're in for a long struggle if we have to bring around each Calgarian individually.

Lori was telling me the hoops she'd had to go through to get into this area. Nobody was home at the Bro's when security called so she had to make up a story & finally connect with her principal who lives in here. Lori has such an open face no one would doubt her but in lots of ways – & this is beyond ironic – us

Tarstoppers are only safe in here because the army & the cops are doing our security for us – keeping the badasses & vigilantes out. The cops as our protectors. Geez. But they're stretched very thin – even with the army & the RCMP called up from across the country. & it's taking massive manpower to remove the Tarstoppers from the school grounds.

6:28 PM

First fatality. It was inevitable. A woman blown up by another bomb plant. This time in a park in the city – though not inside the zone – but not too far outside. Man can you feel the fear now. Folks talking about the terrible things that might happen. It gets all mixed up between speculation on the possibilities & rumours & reports about what might have happened. A water supply poisoned. This seems to be fact. Some lone shooter picking people off. This can't be confirmed. Unlikely. Threat of arson in the middle of the night. More & bigger bombs. The really ugly stuff is down at the border in the camps there. Folks getting killed at a sickening rate. How long will folks stick around under these conditions? I want to get out to tour around the other camps – see for myself – but I probably wouldn't be able to get back in here. I'll see what's happening in the morning. I'll get some sleep tonight. It might be the last anybody's going to get.

●

Nine fifteen on a Saturday night. Tim couldn't watch any more TV, even a channel with no news of the standoff. He was not sleepy. On the other hand, he didn't want to be up when Deke came back. He heard the back door and that was his first thought. He listened intently, hoping for Armie, or even Shannon, but not daring to look. Someone in the fridge could be either his son or his brother. This was nuts, standing here in the darkened living room, the shades down against the chaos across the street. "Armie?"

He appeared in the living room, carton of juice in hand.

"You okay?" Tim asked him.

Just by the way he turned his head Tim knew he was not, even if he said, "Sure."

"Want to talk about it?"

"No, it's okay. Is Deke here?"

"Not now. But I expect him. I gave him a key."

Armie wandered back into the kitchen without looking at him. Don't pursue him. Don't. Tim sat down. All afternoon and into the evening he'd been standing around, in front of the TV, at the front window, in the kitchen where he'd snacked but never really eaten. There was a hum coming from the park, so many people in a small space. He'd been texting Shannon but she wasn't responding. She was out there living her vicarious life with Gizelle, single, selfish, raucous Gizelle. It always made him uneasy, the possibility that one day the balance might tip and Shannon would do more than just play around in her head with the idea of living on her own, being as free as Gizelle. She sure didn't need him financially. She knew it made him uneasy when she was out on the town with Gizelle but she never rushed to placate him. Tonight it was just convenient for her to be in the relative safety of downtown where there were few Tarstoppers thanks to early police action to fence off Olympic Plaza where the Occupiers had camped out last fall. He told himself not to get paranoid. It was not that she was chafing. She herself liked to put confines around her life. That fact kept him secure.

"Dad? Can I ask you something?"

"Sure." It helped, it made it easier for Armie, that it was dim here in the living room, almost dark.

Armie remained standing at the edge of the room. "Like with you and Mom. You don't think the same on a lot of stuff. Like she's more conservative than you. Like she just hates this whole Tarstopper thing and you're more sympathetic. Stuff like that. Doesn't that cause, like, problems?"

Tim would have liked a few minutes to think about the best tack to take but he didn't have that luxury. He had to talk off the top of his head, which he didn't trust. All he knew was not to relate Armie's question back to Katie, who had to be at the root of it. "We're together on the big stuff. Like the way we want to live. Not too much ostentation or phoniness. We trust each other. The ethical stuff. That's probably what's most important. I understand why she thinks the way she does. She's not wrong. It challenges me." He smiled. "What would we talk about if we agreed on everything?"

"Some people think that love means that."

"I don't think there's anyone anywhere who thinks exactly like me. Or you. I don't know about you but my mind is pretty inconsistent. The whole Tarstopper thing has left it in a jumble."

"A lot of people are very sure what they think. Some of the guys at work say some really nasty stuff. They hate the Tar-stoppers. Like loathe them. It's hard to listen to sometimes."

"There are a million positions out there. There are even some people, believe it or not, who don't have any opinion, who are barely aware there's something going on in the city."

Armie glanced over at him. Was he referring to Katie? Armie knew he and Shannon thought Katie was a little clue-less. Armie changed direction. "What if both sides are right? What good's an opinion then?"

"It's strange how people have to be on one side or the other. Then they project any doubt they have onto the other side and vilify them. It seems to be part of human nature. It's a psychological relief to do it, I guess. It's hard to stay aware and stay neutral."

"But I don't want to be neutral. What's coming at us, either way, seems gigantic. We should be doing something. Some-body should know what to do."

"Well, I personally think we're stuck. We can't modify our way of life enough to really make a difference, environmen-tally, without unbalancing it. I wish I could be more optimistic. I wish I could believe that if we just switch over to electric cars and solar and biofuel we'll be fine. I don't think any or all of it would begin to cover the world's needs. And they all have their own problems. I guess, like most people, I'm hoping for the unforeseen salvation. Something we haven't even thought of yet will rescue us in the nick of time."

It was not helping Armie much. Tim added, "On a personal level I do what I can to be as responsible as possible. But I'm not joining the Tarstoppers because they don't really have a workable plan. I hope they have an influence though. I wish I had more to give you. It's your only life, so far as we know, and you have to figure out something to do with it, even though the conditions at the moment look dead-ended. All I can say is, you're only one person out of billions, you can't save the world, just find your small bit to contribute."

He told himself to shut up and wait for Armie to assemble his thoughts. Without looking too expectant. But then the silence dragged on too long as Armie squirrel-caged inside his own head. Tim had to relieve him.

"Well, right now I should get to bed before your uncle, speaking of people who know what they think, gets back. I've had enough of him for today."

He got up and as he went by him he squeezed Armie's shoulder.

"I'm glad you are the way you are. Even if it's not the easiest way to be."

Armie smiled but didn't interrupt his ruminating.

"Do you read Deke's blog?" Tim asked before he left the room, curious.

Armie was a long way away. "What? No. I already know what he thinks. He kind of puts me off."

Tim, relieved, said, "I know exactly what you mean."

●

"Hi."

"Hi. Still at Gizelle's?"

She'd needed to hear Tim's voice. It surprised her, how she needed to grab it now like a lifeline. "Yeah. I lost track of her last night. I haven't seen her."

"You mean she didn't come home?"

"I don't think so. Either that or she was up awfully early." Shannon didn't want Tim to start marveling again at Gizelle's lifestyle. He was a little too intrigued by her sexual casualness. She said, "What about there? I left several messages and texts with Armie today but he hasn't gotten back to me."

"He's here. Came home about an hour ago. I think something's happened with Katie. Maybe he tried to talk to her about global warming, I don't know. As we've said, eventually he has to see her limitations. He was disturbed by Deke and Jason last night, I know that."

"Speaking of whom."

"I'm letting him stay. You're not here. He is my brother. He's not home yet. I don't think. I gave him a key. He and I had one of our abbreviated conversations this afternoon, which ended with him stomping off. It was a relief to see him go. With Lori. Who turned up and wanted to be shown around."

Shannon had known Derek would be right back in there. She would try and be generous and not assume it was Tim's weakness. Instead it could be his need to somehow connect to his brother, which she had to respect. She said, "I don't want Armie listening to him. He's trying to recruit him."

"Come on, Shan. He's twenty. You can't tell him who to listen to. He knows Deke's take is only part of the story." He changed the subject. "So what did you do today? Did you just end up going back into work?"

"Actually I indulged myself. I went to a spa." She hated how she had to watch her tone with Tim, not defensive, just factual. Or was it the idea of Derek ever finding out how she'd spent her day and jeering at her? Pampering herself while the future of civilization was being decided. She had needed to go somewhere sealed off, where no one could reach her. The guy from ABC News couldn't find her there. She knew this was delusional, to think he was in pursuit of her. Maybe she'd wanted a way to stop picturing him, sensing him. Or maybe her mind was bringing him up in order to avoid the real menaces.

"That's good. You needed that." He rushed on in case he'd insulted her by saying she'd needed rest and indulgence. "So you probably haven't heard that somebody got killed a little while ago. A bomb. Of course that's no comparison to what's going on at the border. It's like the wild west down there. I think the tally's now something like twenty or so Tar-stoppers have been killed there."

"I'm trying not to hear anything but it's hard to be completely sealed off. I heard. This is getting really scary. We should leave. We should get Armie out of here."

"There are no hotel rooms and we can't get the cars out, the roads are impassable around here. You can't get a flight out. Anyway I don't want to leave the house empty. Stay at

Gizelle's. You're safest there. Come and get what you need for the coming week."

"I'll come home around lunch tomorrow for my stuff. Just make sure your brother's not there. And try and keep him away from Armie."

●

THE WHOLLY GREEN GIANT
11:20 PM

Let's call him the neph. Actually anything would suit him better than his real name. My nephew. We share the basement at the Bro's house. The upstairs is all set up for the Bro & wife – what was a three bedroom bungalow is now a master bedroom plus a dressing(!)room for the queen & a den for him. All decorated & ready for the photo layout. I never venture out of the kitchen for fear I'll smudge something or somehow befoul the place. They used to live further out in a bigger house & I have to applaud the downsizing – if not their way of life with the two cars & the vacations & eating out & all the consuming.

So I'm in the basement – which is more done up than any other basement I've ever been in & looking not any different than the upstairs – with the neph. I hear him still up & I'm wondering what he's thinking after he listened to me & his dad's friend going at it last night. He's a tough kid to get too much out of. He's learned fence-sitting from his dad & I take it as my duty to pull him over. I've given up on the Bro himself. Course the kid's leery of me. I can imagine what's been said about me around here.

The sis-in-law has decamped to live someplace else – thank God – & I have a feeling more because of me than the tent city across the street. So I'm careful. It matters. I don't have kids of my own to further the over-population of this world so he's the closest I have to a son. I try not to hold it against him that he's like his dad. Not physically – the kid's as tall as me if maybe a hundred pounds lighter – but as the kind of person you've got to pry out & you never know what they're really thinking. You keep hoping it'll be something specific & forward thinking but usually it turns out to be more circling. I'm almost desperate to get this kid off his circuit but just like with the Bro if I come on too strong he'll pull right back into himself. I try to remember what I was like at 20.

As you know I never went to university. I barely graduated from high school. It was the fall-out time from the sixties 30 years ago & as teenagers we were stoned all the time, hanging around on street corners in our ragged jeans & long hair. Even then the Bro barely got his hair over his ears. He had a scholarship. I didn't think university had anything to teach me & I'm still pretty much of that opinion. Nowadays they function for corporate-funded research & the actual paying students are an afterthought passed off to graduate students to lecture on a pittance. Don't let me get going on universities. Anyway most of you have heard it before. A lot of you followed me this spring when I spent time in Montreal banging pots & wearing the red to protest tuition hikes & the way the government colludes.

Anyway back to the neph. So I knock on his door. I mean that's him to have shut his door. Private as his dad. I know he's awake. I'll be really pissed off if he pretends to be asleep. So I just open the door. But he doesn't pretend. He's on his iPad. I stretch out on the other bed & ask what he's on. He won't tell me – just kind of shrugs & shuts it down. So I ask him straight out what he was thinking last night listening to me & his dad's friend. & the kid says he believed us both. This flummoxes me for a bit. Then I ask him to consider that everyone in the system has a vested interest in keeping it going & they'll lie about how possible any real change is. They'll wildly exaggerate the dangers. I keep my voice low & under control but the kid isn't convinced. What do I know about economics, he asks me & he answers the question himself, saying probably no more than he does which is almost nothing. He says he knows economics aren't the whole of life but they're pretty central. It's kind of interesting he says. He's been reading up & figuring out what stuff like leverage is. It's like a whole other language he doesn't know. I'm a little fuzzy myself – I think it's just a fancy word for financial gambling – but the kid's going on about risk & how you have to have protection from it to have a free market & I'm going into a total panic. Next thing you know he's going to be signing up for an MBA like his sister. I won't go into what I think of the new breed of Amazon females like my niece who play the corporate game even more slickly than the guys do. I used to think women were the saviours of the world but not any more. My niece is a clone of her mother polished up even brighter. Scares the bejesus out of me.

I'm up off the bed & almost yelling – didn't he hear what I said last night about the consequences of our lovely economic system, which isn't remotely free anyway? Just ask a third world farmer or an illegal Mexican or a daycare worker how free they feel to sell their stuff & their services. But just like with the Bro I have to pull myself in. That same closed alert face. The curve of the body like towards a ball. I hate that. Come out & fight. Argue back. Okay I'll listen I promise. But I've scared him shut. He only says he heard me. He believes me. I lie down on the bed again & wait him out though it's hard. I promise not to jump on anything he says. I feel like I'm holding onto him as he dangles over a cliff – thinking. He's a polite kid – they're all too polite these days – so he feels he has to say more. Reluctantly he says he just wants to learn more. To figure out if the economic system has to work the way it does. Because he was as convinced by his dad's friend that we have no choice but to keep the system going.

This kid is way too open-minded. Way too cerebral. Reading economic theory in his basement while the world is convulsing right outside his front door? Are you kidding me? But I know there's no point arguing. He's the type that has to look at all sides & figure it all out for himself. Wasting time. Reinventing the wheel. At least he's aware of the environmental disasters all around us. I've made sure of that. I think that awareness paralyses a lot of people – not much different from denial that it's even happening, or that it's only a minor hazard. I can't let the kid drag me down. It's so easy to despair. The forces against us are so strong. We have fantastic numbers – better than we ever thought possible – & so much optimism but I don't kid myself. This is just one step – albeit – neat word – a big one. The biggest yet by far. We've shown our strength. I didn't mean to do that – put it in the past tense. I give up on the neph. He's got to do it his way. At least he's aware. Which is not much consolation.

SUNDAY
JUNE 3 2012

Armie had always avoided anything to do with numbers. Why was that? After all, his dad had a business degree. He ran a business with forty employees and thousands of volunteers and an annual operating budget of millions. His granddad had an economics degree and had worked his way up the banking hierarchy. His mom ran her own business. So why had he, Armie, shied away from anything involving numbers and a spreadsheet? Partly it was that his sister had claimed the territory early. But it was more that he'd felt he had to find something lofty and innovative to pursue. Why had he thought that? It was fine for Ardith to fast-track on business but something different was wanted from him. His dad had urged him to search widely, not settle for the usual. His dad was always telling people about Armie's early interest in paleo-anthropology.

It was like his Dad got off on just saying the word. Like this interest alone was proof of something and not just a variant of all the other kids and their fascination with dinosaurs.

His dad liked to tell the story of following his own father into business, just trying to please him, and how disappointed his mother had been by his choice. To even just read about economics somehow felt like a betrayal of his dad, who'd rejected it himself. But then it was weird how his dad had never objected to Ardith's path, even seemed to take pride in her success in business school. Anyway it couldn't hurt to learn more. It wasn't as if he was going to become an accountant or anything. The theory interested him and he knew so little. Do we have to have growth and markets and high finance like Jason said? He'd been unnerved though to discover how little consensus there was. The expert opinion seemed pretty well divided on something like whether the best way out of a debt crisis was austerity or stimulus. Economics was called the dismal science, which Armie took to mean dismally unscientific.

It was almost noon. He texted Katie. *slept in. sorry im so freaked by whats going on. ill explain. be there in hour. love u.*

It was going to take all afternoon and probably much of the night to reassure Katie again. He had to do it. He couldn't lose Katie. Images of Katie, of her body, were crowding out any coherent economic thought.

Deke's door was open, the bed empty. When Armie reached the kitchen, it was full of people. Some bearded curly-haired guy he'd never seen before was sitting at the kitchen table. He was introduced as Abe. Deke was frying eggs. His dad was leaning against the counter, arms folded. A woman came up the basement stairs carrying a stack of folded laundry. She looked like a teacher or a nurse, middle-aged, scrubbed, open-faced, a little plump. "I'll get out of your hair now," she said to his dad. "I can't thank you enough. I might be able to stand myself now." She didn't seem connected to Abe. She told him his stuff was in the dryer now.

His mom was not going to like Tarstoppers using her appliances. What was his dad thinking? Soon there'd be line-ups out front. Armie thought about taking off, eating later, but he was too hungry. He got out the cereal.

Deke said to Tim, nodding at Armie, "I hear your boy in the middle of the night and guess what he's doing. Reading up on economics. A little light reading. Other kids his age play video games."

"Oh, he plays enough of those," his dad said.

The bearded guy, who was wearing overalls, said, "Where once the future was in plastics, now it's in video games. Equally destructive. So what have you learned about economics?"

Deke told Armie, "Abe's a nuclear scientist with the Ontario government. He's been educating us about nuclear power but I can't say I'm convinced. He says the only solution to clean electricity is nuclear fusion. I guess the next big thing is thorium, which is radioactive like uranium but not useful in making bombs."

Armie said in answer to the man's question, "I'm still on the basics."

His dad, to take the spotlight off him, went back to what

they'd been talking about. "As I understand it, there's not an infinite supply of uranium in the world. What about thorium?"

"It's much more common."

Armie stopped listening. His brain was overloaded as it was. A mindless video game would be perfect right about now. He bolted down his cereal and headed for the basement again. He didn't even shower, just brushed his teeth, dressed, and started for the back door. He called to his dad that he'd be at Katie's. His dad looked relieved there'd be one less person in the kitchen.

There was a strange racket going on outside. More than just the noise of the Tarstoppers. At the end of the lane behind the house, there was a small triangular park also covered in tents and lean-tos and cars. On one side of the park there was a lane that backed onto the houses on the next street north. Standing on the lane was a line of people, all banging pots and blowing horns and blasting music. They stood there making a God-awful cacophony. Some Tarstoppers had come forward to see what they wanted but they couldn't be heard. Other Tarstoppers, hearing the uproar, were running from the bigger park around the corner and more people came out of their houses.

The noise penetrated his own house and now his dad and Deke and Abe had rushed outside and into the lane. Neighbours had come out from their backyards to find out what was going on on this already unusual Sunday morning. Some of them started walking towards the park, some went back into their yards, maybe to get their own pots and spoons and old ghettos blasters. Dan Parker from down the street waved at his dad to come. The Olsens from next door were already among the noisemakers, both of them. So funny to see the two old people out there disturbing the peace, screaming away. He couldn't read their sign from this far away but he knew it wouldn't be nice. Little kids were jumping up and down and playing their drums and letting off sirens and every other deafening toy they could find. Of course Deke and Abe immediately raced off for the park, Deke looking like an elephant as he ran, so much weight on such narrow hips.

His dad said to Armie, "It feels like we should take a side. But I can't join something with Olsen in it. And there's that Nazi, Lyle Grogan. He doesn't even live on the street. This is going to get ugly. Get out of here. Go to Katie's."

There was no one else just watching like him and his dad. Every neighbour who came out ended up joining in, some reluctantly, standing off to the side when they got there and keeping quiet, others joining the yelling and hollering. His mom would have been right in there if she were here, though it was hard to picture. She'd be screaming, her face distorted with anger, something Armie had seen only a couple of times but never forgotten.

The raggedy line of homeowners began to press forward, as if cued. An unanchored tent at the edge of the park got pushed over. In response the Tarstoppers, who'd been staring at the noisemakers in dumbfounded amazement, all sat down on the grass where they were. Some of the homeowners stepped right over the Tarstoppers on the grass at the edge of the lane. Armie turned and loped off the other way down his lane, not quite running. His dad went back into the yard.

●

Tim opened up his house to the injured. Although there was a first aid station in the park across the street, they were overwhelmed and there was little water there. Tim didn't hesitate when Deke brought in the first casualty, a young woman whose hand had been stomped on in the melee. The next person, a middle-aged man, had had his face slashed by a broken bottle. A nurse accompanied him. There were apparently quite a few nurses in the camp, even a doctor, a resident in psychiatry from Oregon who said it had been a while since he'd stitched anyone up. Tim boiled water and washed towels and ran up and down the basement stairs. They needed more painkillers, more bandaging, and Tim volunteered to find what he could.

He only approached houses where he thought the residents might be sympathetic, in the opposite direction from the triangle park, and skipping both of his immediate neighbours. He was beginning to dislike them all, the Olsens who he could imagine at home in Nazi Germany, and Mike and Mandy, the young couple who'd built the huge new house next door (putting the whole of the McKays' old bungalow in a dumpster first) and lived with such affluence (nannies and two vacation homes and four cars) that even Shannon was put off. It had become a joke: what next? as they spent a hundred thou on landscaping, as Mandy told Shannon about the horse for the seven-year-old that was boarded outside town.

Most people didn't answer their doors. Only Sally down the street, who volunteered at Tim's agency, put together a box of everything she had on hand. Jeremy, an emergency room doctor who lived on the next block, gave him a stash of mostly out-of-date narcotic samples that he said he'd deny ever came from him. He was not otherwise getting involved. He said he hated the Tarstoppers and they'd brought it on themselves: what did they think would happen? He stared Tim in the eye, unabashed.

At another of the new big houses that were replacing the old bungalows, a young, good-looking man, the father of three small boys whom Tim had often seen in the park before its invasion, said to him, "Not on your life. They can die for all I care." After Tim, stunned, had backed away, his long-haired blonde wife came running after Tim to thrust a pile of tape and gauze into his arms. At another house, a woman, an ordinary plump woman who Tim didn't know, glared at him and demanded, "Why are you helping those criminals? Give me one good reason."

When he got back to the house, Shannon was outside on the porch, standing stiffly in her sweater and jeans, her face deadened. Tim passed off the medical supplies to someone going into the house and then he beckoned Shannon to come with him. He didn't dare touch her, even her elbow in guidance. The only private place he could think of was the garage, in one of the cars. At least she followed him around the side of the house. There were strangers on the back deck. He wanted to shield her from them like they were the leftovers from a wild night he'd had. In the garage, he and Shannon got into her car, the first one in past the door, him in the driver's seat as if they were going somewhere.

She stared straight ahead. Finally Tim said, "I had to do it. There was a big skirmish in the triangle park. Our nice neighbours attacked the Tarstoppers. It wasn't the wildcatter guys this time, just our neighbours. It was pretty upsetting. Over in the big park they don't have enough water to clean everyone up."

"And I'm the bitch because I don't want a stranger in my bed bleeding on my sheets. I need to get my stuff for tomorrow."

"I'll clear the bedroom for you. The dressing room, the bathroom."

"I hate this."

"Me too. I didn't want to know that my neighbours could start kicking people who were just sitting on the grass. Then hitting them over the head with the pots and stuff they were carrying as noise-makers. That's how it started. All the people living around the triangle park were trying to force the Tarstoppers out. I know everyone's beyond frustrated and angry, but still. A lot of kids were involved. Lyle Grogan started waving a gun around and threatening people. It really got out of hand. And now very few of our neighbours want to help the wounded. I'm really shaken."

She still hadn't looked at him, as if she couldn't bear to do so. She asked him, "Aren't you furious that the Tarstoppers took over our community and made life impossible for us? What gave them the right to do that? And we're supposed to just put up with it? And they've caused us to lose nearly half the value of our investments. Sometimes I think you don't have emotions like the rest of us. Just that all empathy of yours. Where's Armie?"

"He was here. He saw the beginning. But then he took off for Katie's. Something's happening with her."

"At least he's not in there dressing wounds. I'm sorry people got hurt. I didn't want that. But they should leave. I'm not coming back until they do. I mean the whole park."

"I understand."

"No, you don't. But never mind. Go clear out our bedroom and the dressing room of people. Half my stuff's probably gone anyway."

Tim didn't bother protesting this assumption. He didn't like her right now and he had no idea if this was fair. He knew she didn't feel any better about him.

It took a while to move people around, to rip off the sheets and remake the bed, to clean up a little of the mess. There was blood smeared on the bathroom walls; all the drawers in the vanity were open and ransacked; towels and old sheets and anything anyone could find to staunch the wounds lay wadded and stained on the bathroom floor and in the tub. He went back to the garage where she sat in her car occupying herself on her phone. She went around him without meeting his eye.

Tim sat it out in the car. He couldn't stand to watch her in the house. Her face would be screwed up in anger and disgust and the others would exchange looks and keep out of her way.

She didn't come back to the garage. He imagined her walking down the street pulling her big red suitcase on its wheels, her heavy purse over her shoulder. On her walk she'd avoid Stanley Park with its thousands of campers and head across MacLeod Trail and then north to the LRT station. She didn't need her car downtown, if it was even possible to get through the streets. She could walk to work from Gizelle's. He imagined she felt exiled, trudging her suitcase across an inhospitable part of town, but maybe her anger cut off everything else. She thought he'd been weak to give in to Deke. He hadn't protected their home. She might never forgive him.

Deke opened the passenger side door of the car and slid his bulk in. "She's gone. You can come back."

"Did you keep away from her?"

Deke nodded. When he opened his mouth to say something else, Tim said, "I'm not talking about Shannon." He went to get out. "We should start moving people back across the street. I'm not setting up a permanent clinic here or anything."

Deke gave him the face of disapproval for always setting limits and trying to control things. Fuck him, Tim thought but didn't bother to say.

Back inside he tried not to see the house through Shannon's eyes. After everyone had gone, he'd clean it up, fix what was broken. A painting in the front hall hung askew, its thick oil paint chipped on its ridges from someone knocking into it so that the white gesso showed through the paint like snow drifts on the landscape. He'd pay to repair everything.

He wondered how many of the participants in the melee in the park were appalled now by what had happened. Surely most of them had never intended to hurt anyone. He was glad he hadn't been there and was not now stuck with an image of his neighbours bashing people on the head as they passively cowered on the ground. His imagination was enough.

●

THE WHOLLY GREEN GIANT
4:01 PM

Welcome to all my new readers at FlashPoint. Just a little background info before I get to the day at hand. I've been writing a blog for a number of years on environmental issues & the general need for extreme systematic change. I live in Toronto but I'm here in Calgary with the Tarstoppers. As it happens, my brother & his family live here almost in the centre of the protest. The park across from their house is a Tarstopper site. I'm about to describe what happened today at a small park around the corner from his house. I'll try to remember to give some explanation for anything that comes up that I just assume most of my readers already know but otherwise I'll just let rip. I'm sorry to have to begin with such a dispiriting incident.

What I can never get through my thick skull is how people cling to what they've got — even if you can show them it's all based on destruction. So these nice property owners — solid citizens all I'm sure — are so incensed by the presence of the peaceful protesters in their little park that they attack them. They think it's their park because their houses back onto it. At first they just make a lot of noise trying to get us to move on – they've even got little kids screaming at us to get out. They're banging pots like the student protesters in Quebec – the appropriation is beyond ironic comment – & then very quickly some of them start hitting us over the head with them. Get this – it's a woman who starts the bashing. Maybe 50. In her tight jeans like a teenager. Maybe the organizer of the whole thing. The usual happens – soon as there's violence the more humane types run away. Wouldn't you think you'd try to stop your neighbour from clobbering someone sitting undefended on the grass? There's this one guy waving a gun around & yelling at us to clear out or else. A handgun like you see on a crime show on TV. Some of us dial 911 but we're only put on a list. All the folks from the bigger park – my park just around the corner – come running when they hear the pandemonium at the little park – a block long but a thin triangle – & it's soon piled with sitters. We're really packed in – the lucky ones squished inside the tents – & the homeowners are stepping over us & screaming & swinging at us.

Our passivity seems to incite some people. One woman just keeps whacking a metal lawn chair hard as she can with this pot she's carrying. Pulverizes the thing. Imagining it's one of our heads she's thwacking. Beyond fury. I get hit by someone. Course the first impulse is to jump up & thump somebody. I'm a big guy – I could do some damage. I'm halfway up & this girl I'm sitting next to is pulling on my pant leg. She stops me with just a look – remember why we're here. I have a second where I want to kick her off & then I sink back down. The guy who hit me – a teenager – has surged away anyway, kneeing people in the head as he goes & squishing body parts with his big feet & swinging his mother's stainless steel frying pan. It's a video game to him. We're all hunched on the ground with our hands over our heads until the good citizens run out of piss. It takes a while. When we don't react – just sit there & take it – they have to give up & start straggling back home. They look almost in more shock than us. I've got blood on my hands & my ear's bleeding. There's a lot of blood. A lot of puffy mangled hands. It's like one of those old paintings called After the Battle. Nobody left standing. Only a few of us get up. We're in shock.

We're the rest of the day dealing with the wounded. Nothing major but a lot of broken bones – mostly hands – & a lot of cuts & bruises & sprains. We've got a doc who assesses & a bunch of nurses. I'm so proud of how we took it. Only one real donnybrook with one of us losing our cool & fighting back. But the hate shown by our temporary neighbours has left us all reeling. Even the Bro is with us now that he's seen his fellow citizens & what their sense of private property has done to them. There's a big assembly tonight to decide what to about the triangle park – give it up or rebuild & stay. Some jerk went around slashing tents with a knife – even ripped the skin of some of the folks inside. We've all been brought low. The thing we can't get our minds around is how little it has to do with what we're trying to accomplish here. It might have been naïve but we all thought there'd be more support from the community – even here in oil-dominated Calgary. These are intelligent, educated people, not right-wing weirdoes or roughneck Wildcatter types. Directly or indirectly they might owe their livelihood to oil but how can you disregard the evidence that it's destroying the ecosystem we're all dependent on? You want to take one of those prosperous burghers & have a debate – challenge him or her in a big forum. They can't all be as cynical as the Bro's friend from Friday night who acknowledged the truth but shrugs & says we're stuck in the game. Was that just the night before last? I've got to think that the fury today must be partly because they know we're right & it scares them to death – what it means for their futures – so they lash out at the messengers. Do we get up a committee to try & talk to them? Should I volunteer to meet with a representative? The Bro can find me one. Right now I'm bushed from lugging people around. We've got everybody sort of settled. The Bro wanted everybody out of his house after they'd been bandaged up. That's his wife's influence. To know about her – the sis-in-law – go back through my reports here. Can't stand the sis-in-law – which is mutual. It's cloudy & cool & there's the threat of a thunderstorm. I thought you needed to have heat for lightning. I really feel for the banged-up folks now having to suffer a wet night in a bashed-in tent.

●

Are u okay? Shannon texted Armie. *Heard about the fight in the park. Yr dad opened a clinic in house for injured.*

im okay. at Katies. does he need help?

Cleaning up now. im staying at Gizelles. u can come here too if u want.

Maybe Ill go home now.

U and K ok?

Yeah.

Worrying about Armie. All the mothers she knew worried about their sons. She remembered Marilyn, her mother-in-law, worrying about Tim and Derek when she'd first met her. At the time Tim was unhappy in business and Derek was refusing university. Shannon wanted so much more for Armie, most of all for him to become sure of himself, although not at all in the way of his uncle. Armie seemed to be drifting and all his thinking seemed only to take him further out of range. She had tried to tell him that life didn't make analytical sense, that it didn't add up, that he'd never figure it out. It was best to just go along with the craziness. But he was young and he still thought people, adults, and their institutions had to be rational.

She was sitting in a downtown coffee place leafing through a magazine, trying to settle her mind enough to go to the office and get something done. Stampede and all her events were only a month away and there was so much to do, even with the Tarstoppers in town. The price of oil was way up, but the stock markets were down hundreds of points. How would the oil companies and their support players react if this trend accelerated? Cancel everything peripheral, like Stampede events? Her company would be bankrupted.

She was watching for Matt so she could either duck or she could catch his eye, she wasn't sure which, which she knew was crazy. Normally on a Sunday afternoon there'd not be nearly this many people downtown.

"There you are," said Gizelle, plunking her big red bag down on the small round table, taking it over. The purse glittered with chains and rivets and locks and buckles, not Shannon's style at all. "I never see you, even though you're living with me."

She left the table again to order a coffee. Gizelle, Shannon had come to realize, viewed herself from the outside even when alone. Her life was a video she was watching along with her imagined audience. Here I am having coffee with my close friend Shannon. Shannon could tell by the way she stood at the counter now in her skinny jeans and tight white top, swinging her hair, how aware she was of everyone in the room and to what degree they were taking her in. Shannon herself tried to confine that kind of exhausting self-awareness to her work, where she had to constantly feel for impression and reaction, but she was fascinated by how Gizelle seemed to thrive on it.

"What was going on with that guy from the bar Friday night?" Gizelle asked her, teasing, sitting back down with her latte.

"What do you mean? Did you talk to him after I left? What happened?"

"Oh he wanted to know all about you. Very attractive in an older grizzled way."

"What did you tell him?"

"Hey, what's this? Why so uptight?" She grinned at her. "Is there a little attraction going on here?"

"What did you tell him? Did you tell him my name?"

"Yeah. Why not? Just your first name. Probably not your last. I don't think, anyway. I told him how wonderful you are. Why are you looking at me like that?"

"I didn't like him. I don't want him looking for me."

"You can't fool me. You're attracted, I can tell. I don't know how you can't be just a little bit intrigued by it. You don't have to sleep with him but it might be fun to play along for a while."

Gizelle laughed at the face Shannon made. It had become one of Gizelle's purposes in life, Shannon thought, to loosen her up. Gizelle seemed to need to pull her offside to feel better about her own easy surrender to impulse and emotion. "You emphasized that I'm married, I hope."

"I saw you practically thrusting your ring in his face. Actually I ran into him to him last night again. I think he was looking for us. Very disappointed we weren't together."

"I don't want to hear about it. Did you tell him where I was? Does he know where your condo is?"

"Hey, I wouldn't do that." Gizelle was a little offended that she would think she would, as if her limits on disclosure were obvious. "We just talked generally. He said he was interested in what you had to say. He says he wasn't hitting on you. He's looking for background, people's reactions and stuff."

"Don't ever talk to him again. I mean it. I don't care how prim that sounds. This isn't funny."

"Oh, Shan. Okay. I think you're being weird about this, but okay."

After Gizelle had left, Shannon felt much more vulnerable.

He wouldn't have any trouble finding her now that he knew her first name. Combine that with an event planning company and she'd pop up easily for anyone looking.

This was paranoid. The man wasn't after her. She'd blown one moment up out of proportion. This feeling of hers that she was about to be broached was because of the Tarstoppers invasion, because of Deke and his friends in her house. It had nothing to do with the American journalist. Maybe she was just trying to keep her mind off the mess in her house. She hadn't even looked around. She'd kept her head down, stuffed her suitcase, and left. When she finally could return home, she would don her rubber gloves and scour everything with bleach. Erase it from memory. She'd turn over her mattress and buy a new cover for it. And she wouldn't wonder now what she would have done if she'd been home and injured people had started showing up at her door.

Her preoccupation with the American was a diversion her mind had come up with from the takeover of her house. He'd go away now. But first she'd just look up ABC News on her iPad. His name was not anywhere she could see. Nothing came up on Google that was him, but both Matt and Matthew Brown were very common names. While her name and life might be easily searched and information found, he would not be anywhere near as easy to trace. He was probably not who he seemed. She'd heard that there were thousands of plainclothes American security people in town, most of them pretending to be somebody else. They'd infiltrated both the Tarstoppers and the Wildcatters and they were chatting up the locals. Now that she thought about it, she didn't have the card that Matt, if that was his real name, had placed on the counter in front of her Friday night. It had disappeared before she could take it.

Nothing was as it seemed. She knew that but didn't want to live with it day to day. Whereas Tim loved to hunt out discrepancies and snort in satisfaction at exposés, she was unsettled by the evidence. She thought of it as his mother's legacy: Marilyn's zeal to deflate and uncover. Twenty-five years ago when Shannon had first met her, Marilyn liked to declare, "That's a myth," about any preconceived idea or convention. It had been part of her times, the Seventies, when people thought they could clean up the world through exposure, part of the feminist Zeitgeist. It seemed very naïve now to think that simply bringing injustice to light could change much. Shannon thought her mania for change and digging into things had sure misled her sons.

Marilyn was probably right that the forces at work in the world had little to do with its surface appearance. Shannon didn't want to know the way corporations and governments operated outside their bland and earnest public statements. Obviously you couldn't believe everything you heard but you had to proceed with life while mostly ignoring the undercurrents. She did a good job for her corporate clients and they paid her well. She employed a lot of people one way and another. Why was she justifying herself? It was like Derek was somewhere around, chortling at her discomfort.

She just wanted back to normal, like practically everyone in the city who wasn't a Tarstopper or a Wildcatter. Take it somewhere else. Take Matt, whom she was still picturing far too often, down to the border where the real fighting was going on. Her interest in him would go away. Ignore it like the itch of a sting or a song repeating in her head or the image of her house overtaken. It was best to ignore what you couldn't control. That was sanity.

●

Every time he came home Armie had to readjust to the presence of the camps in his neighbourhood, to a whole other makeshift community co-existing with his own. There were many more Tarstoppers than residents now, all of them packed in the parks so tightly. It was one of those things that if told about it in advance, or if someone was to invent a story, he'd never believe it possible. He'd been thinking about how stubborn minds could be, clinging to the known against all logic, unable to believe what their senses told them. But then something shifted and the new reality replaced the old. This was the kind of thing he thought about but could never voice. He came across as such a dunce a lot of the time. No matter who he was with, some kind of clamp came down on his mind as soon as he tried to get his thoughts into a vocal form. Sometimes someone would take an interest in him, usually because of something he'd written, like a professor or lecturer, but they'd give up on him when he couldn't come out with anything coherent.

It was a lie that he and Katie were of one mind. It was an

illusion he'd agreed to for the other benefits. Sex. He used to think no girl would ever give him free access to her body. But more and more he felt lonely when he was with her. They'd finally seemed back to normal today but part of him was hanging around watching, left out and bored. He wouldn't take any of her drugs, which upset her. He was done with the pills. Why did everything have to be so heightened? He didn't know what most of her pills were for. Katie did a lot of acid, which he'd only tried a couple of times. It had been mind-blowing, so that he felt like he understood the sixties for the first time, but he didn't need to keep doing it. He'd probably never forget the intense and vivid world he'd entered but he didn't want to live in it. He liked to think too much, which was not a concern of Katie's. He'd worried for a while that he'd become addicted to her sex bombs, as she called them, but this afternoon he'd managed okay without them, to his relief, although he thought a lot of the diminishment in sensation was because of his emotional distance from her.

As he went in the back gate he could see the triangle park at the end of the lane, now mostly put back together. One tent close to the street was covered in strips of duct tape, bandaids on the slashes. His very own neighbours had done this. He didn't have any real friends around here since his parents had only moved here after he'd left for university, but he could imagine one guy he only knew to say hi to, a real jerk, out there happily beating people up. But the adults? Again, if someone had foreseen it and told him about it, he would never have believed it.

The house seemed okay inside. The dishwasher was running, the kitchen had been cleaned up. It was just after five. He always headed straight downstairs when he got home, needing a little interval between things, even between the trip home on the LRT and talking to his dad, even to say hi. His bed had clean sheets on it, which meant someone, a Tarstopper, had been on it. The dryer was going. He didn't care about somebody's body in here so much as people looking at his stuff. His books, his drawings, the stupid little collages Katie had gotten him making. He didn't have a password on his bedroom computer.

His dad was lying on the sofa in the living room, the blinds down against the chaos across the street. "It really got out of hand," his dad told him. "A lot of people got hurt."

Armie sat down on one of the two modern wooden chairs in the room. If he stayed standing he felt a little like a balloon, his head bobbing up near the ceiling. "Mom texted me. I guess you had a hospital going here for a while."

"Your mom was pretty upset. She came to get her things. She's going to stay at Gizelle's for a while."

Armie nodded that he knew this but couldn't think of anything to say.

"The part that got me," his dad said, "is what ordinary people are capable of. You read things in history that are incomprehensible. Armenia. Rwanda. Huge slaughters by ordinary people. Obviously it can be anyone, any group of people wound up and let loose, but I don't want to believe it. Okay, maybe the Wildcatter types. But then you think of them as sort of damaged somehow, outlaws and full of hate for some reason. But ordinary people? Educated upstanding people? I understand they're scared. The city's taken over and their investments are in freefall. But to do this? Afterwards I went up and down the street trying to find medications and bandaging. Hardly anyone wanted to help. Some people even yelled at me for helping the Tarstoppers."

He had to say something. "You sound like Mom."

"I've always thought her gloomy view of human nature was a little extreme. I'm not so sure anymore. Lyle Grogan had a gun. Some you're not too surprised by."

"Did he shoot anyone?"

"He waved it around and threatened to but I have to believe it wasn't loaded. Are you hungry? Should I start supper?"

"Not yet. I'm okay. Where's Deke?"

"Across the street. He and I actually worked pretty well together today. He's got more stamina than I do though. I'm bushed. How's Katie?"

He shrugged. In order not to talk about Katie, Armie jumped into another topic he didn't really want to talk about. "You heard Deke say I'm reading up on economics a little? Like the theory. Not business. You know – after what Jason was talking about, how we're stuck with the system we've got. That we have to keep growing or die. I don't know much but even I can see that capitalism is dead-ended. All the money ends up concentrated in a few corporations and individuals and then you run out of consumers to keep the whole thing going. Not to mention the environmental side-effects. It's hard to believe there's so little out there as an alternative."

He had his dad's attention. He could feel the effort it took for him not to sit up and quiz him, to start suggesting directions for him to go with his new interest. "After my day today I've lost faith that there's any rational system that can be imposed on people."

He couldn't go on with this conversation. He didn't really understand why his dad wasn't someone who made him relaxed enough to be able to express himself. There was really nobody. His mom sometimes, but she had to be slowed down enough to be really listening. Every once and a while with a stranger he could get going — but how pathetic was that, needing anonymity? He was keen to get back to his reading. He was looking into Marx. Communism was such a bad word that it was tough to come at it with an open mind but he was intrigued by the theory. It was not anything like he'd imagined. He left his dad on the sofa, just lying there.

●

THE WHOLLY GREEN GIANT
9:10 PM

I've become friendly with a nice nurse from Ottawa. We're all starting to feel like a big family of friends here. It's what being attacked will do for a group — a real bonding experience. Some of the idealists among us — mostly kids — are traumatized by what happened this afternoon. This is a neighbourhood like the one they grew up in. How could people have turned savage? We all thought it was just the outlaw types we had to guard ourselves against – the Neo-Nazis & the bikers & the rightwing fanatics – & the cops of course. Patti – that's the nurse – & I've been talking about what happens to people when they're stressed & scared. She's a psychiatric nurse in her regular life. In the end people protect themselves & what they value – like their property & their retirements & what they think they're entitled to. She says she doesn't have any property but she'd sure fight for her pension. She says you can't reach people with logic or reason. She wasn't at all surprised by today. She doubts we're going to be strong enough to survive what's brought down on us. Which you've got to think the organizers – facilitators – know & it's why they're practically like cheerleaders trying to pep us up now. It's not going to help us that we know we're in the right. The earth is being so desecrated it won't be able to sustain life as we know it. Governments have to stop colluding with corporations whose only motive is profit & become responsible for the welfare of their citizens. But people are afraid of change – they have their vested interests. But what's next? All we can do is stick to our course. We're not leaving until there's a moratorium on the tarsands no matter what anyone does to us. What happens after that we're not responsible for. My personal opinion is that after the panic that will set in with the tarsands shut down, the country & the province & the economy will adapt.

Our job now is to protect ourselves. There's a drive on to provide everyone with some kind of helmet. There's a new committee to patrol the park on the lookout for bombs or arson or anything suspicious. We don't trust the cops not to be letting the vigilantes & so-called Wildcatters into this part of the city to do their dirty work for them. Another bomb blast in a park today – luckily no one was hurt. The real one-sided war goes on at the border, the Wildcatters actually slaughtering the passive Tarstoppers – not just hitting them over the head with frying pans. It's hard to take in. They say the American army's been called in to send everybody packing. That'll be a real war. The Wildcatters are probably getting tired of killing off Tarstoppers who don't fight back. They're all itching to have real death battles. They'd love to have a superclash with the federal government. Americans take things to such extremes – why is that?

As for the triangle park every Tarstopper resident has to make their own decision about whether to stay there. We don't have the room in this park to take them in so they'll have to go further afield. At the assembly when it's input time I wait in line for the mike for almost an hour & then pitch the idea of using my contact in the neighbourhood – the Bro – to talk to our assailants of today. Nobody seems to think this will do much good – & I'm absolutely not to negotiate any withdrawal – but the vote on it goes my way though not by much. My nurse friend says I just want to argue with someone & maybe I have to do it to see that it doesn't go anywhere. We could never compromise enough & as for convincing one individual after another of the legitimacy of our position that's an illusion of grandeur. Don't you love her hard-won wisdom? But I'm still going to try. I'll probably never totally believe that you can't reach people with the facts.

●

Tim knew it was stupid to want praise or even a little acknowledgement when he'd only done what any reasonable person would have done when people were hurt. But it seemed one more instance in a long history of waiting for something to come back from his brother. Could you go through your whole life lonely for a brother you were never close to from the beginning? His first memories of him involved protecting himself and his toys and his haunts from him. Tim had looked after his things, while Deke used and broke and discarded almost everything that came his way. He was downstairs now, using Tim's house as a campsite, challenging his son in conversation, and now he could hear him rummaging in his fridge.

Tim went out to the kitchen. He was pretty sure Deke was not giving him a thought, even enough to say goodnight before he went downstairs. Shannon would say he didn't have to let him stay here and if he felt he had to, for whatever reason, then he should ignore him. As if almost fifty years of interaction and frustration could so easily be suppressed. Shannon didn't have much to do with her own sister, an airhead, Tim thought, who lived in Winnipeg and was consumed by appearances. Their attachment had been easily severed, which she thought of as an example for Tim. He didn't understand why he was so much more compromised than she.

Deke was making himself a sandwich of cheddar cheese, jam, and pickles. Like in childhood. "So what have they decided to do about the triangle park?" Tim asked him. "Abandon it or stay on?"

Deke talked with his mouth full of the cheese pieces he'd

stuffed in to tide him over until his sandwich was ready. "Left it up to the people camping there. There's not a lot of extra room in our park for them." He licked the jam knife. "So do you think your lovely neighbours are going to go on a killing spree if the protesters stay put?"

"I don't know anyone who lives along there. But I feel less and less able to predict what anyone will do, no matter how well I know them."

"I've volunteered to try and dialogue with them. Can you introduce me? I might get a better reception than if I just knock on doors."

"I don't think any of them are going to want to talk to you, no matter how you approach them. Your charm and your oratory have their limits."

Deke was shaking his head. "I keep thinking that if people just hear the facts, they'll have to join us. I think it's got to be ignorance and they just have to be enlightened. I know that's not true but I keep hoping."

"They're not a monolith. They're all coming from different places."

"I'll bet they're very similar. Any visible minorities among them? Even any non-professionals?"

Tim had to shake his head. Not as far as he knew. It was not the kind of dense cosmopolitan diverse area Deke thought a person should live in, not like his in Toronto. "They're scared. Don't you understand that? They see everything they value being torn apart, their investments plummeting."

"Oh let's all worry about the well-off and their investments.

As long as they're alright. Who was the bitch who was screaming the loudest?"

"Probably Kelly Rigaud. She likely organized it. I don't know her but she's something of a legend. The type who opposes everything. She put the couple who live behind us through hell blocking their new house from a city by-law approval. You two are probably pretty similar, on your opposite sides of the fence."

Deke ignored this last comment. "Could you set up a meeting with her and a few others along that street?"

This situation felt so familiar, Deke trying to get him to do his bidding. Be his campaign manager that time he ran for student council in high school. Explain to their parents why he wasn't going to university or why the garage door was broken. Send him money when he was stranded in Africa. Cosign a loan a few years ago. Deke always wanted something. And wanted and wanted, for all how he prided himself on living on next to nothing. Leaving Tim feeling anemic for never wanting anything as badly as even Deke's minor desires.

"They don't want to talk to you. They want you gone. They're united in that, no matter how they otherwise differ."

"So that's a no?" Deke was incredulous. Which again was very familiar. How could any right-thinking person turn him down?

"You and Kelly would make explosive combatants," Tim said. "I might be able to sell tickets to the match. But I don't think you've ever in your life had to talk to someone as reactionary as she is. You'd be in for a shock."

Deke wasn't paying any attention. "Which house is she in?"

"The big greenish one in the middle. I'm pretty sure. Wear protection."

"You're coming with me."

"No, I'm not."

The theory was it got easier the longer you resisted a stimulus. It seemed to Tim like he'd been at this most of his life, struggling not to give in to his brother. He'd only made modest gains in being able to withstand him, or the people he encountered who were like him, inflamed and demanding, and there'd been no decrease in the amount of turmoil produced when he was around them. People with insistent domineering personalities had vexed and ensnared him throughout adulthood. At work, Connor was that type, trying to bowl over anyone in his way. Resisting them had always left Tim feeling diminished, dismayed by the passivity of his fallback position.

And Deke was probably a stand-in in his psyche for their impassioned parents, whom Tim had never been able to challenge, not that this awareness had any effect on his responsiveness to the type. Their mother had causes she'd dragged them into, protests, marches, abortion rights, Take Back the Night. No wonder he'd spent so much of his childhood in his room. His mother might be hunting him down to participate in her rally or wanting him to organize something at school, Deke already on board and gloating.

From in his room Tim as a child would hear his father excoriating Deke at top voice while his mother yelled at his dad to leave him alone. Bully! she'd be screaming – and Tim would wonder again why Deke had started it, why he needed to provoke their father, why he couldn't fly low and stay out of trouble. Like wanting to take on Kelly, still unaware of how hopeless that was.

Deke, also stuck in old patterns, thought he just had to look very aggrieved to bring Tim around. When this didn't work, he said, "Fine then. I should have known better than to ask. Tell me, Timothy, are you committed to anything? Do you care enough about the fate of the earth to inconvenience yourself even a little?"

"Oh, come off it. I do those things that have a chance of success." He stopped himself from going on. But he wanted badly to say, you want to talk to Kelly so you can grandstand and show off your expertise and bully someone. You're so arrogant you think you can sway the whole world. He knew he was no match for Deke in a verbal fight. He'd end up not sleeping and feeling sick with regret while Deke would be so energized by it he'd clomp around the house half the night. "Good night," was all he said.

"You're doing it to your kid, you know," Deke said before Tim could get out of the room. Deke didn't have many inhibitions, an approach to life that he'd gladly defend. "It's really getting to me to watch. He's down there studying economic theory because he fully realizes the crisis we're in and that's the only solution he can come up with. Never mind getting out there on the front lines and actually making himself count. You've taught him well."

"Good night, Deke." And this time he kept going.

MONDAY
JUNE 4 2012

Act as if this will all end soon and go away. Shannon thought of all the people in history who had gone on acting as if calamity was not approaching. The Jews in Germany and Poland, the Tutsis in Rwanda, the educated glasses-wearing middle class in Pol Pot's Cambodia. She understood how such wishful thinking could happen. Those preparing to flee must have seemed alarmist and paranoid. Mass hate and violence couldn't happen in somewhere as civilized as Germany in the twentieth century. Or Calgary in the twenty-first. Why was she thinking like this? Tim would say she was always too primed for disaster. But she couldn't stop her foreboding. Conditions seemed ominous.

She told herself to concentrate. She was way behind. She never did make it to the office yesterday, uneasy about being alone in the building on a Sunday afternoon. She'd worked on her computer in her bedroom at Gizelle's, answering e-mails, contacting suppliers and clients to reassure them, but it was never the same as actually being in the office.

She was doing quite well now, but her assistant was in and out and Shannon knew she was constantly checking her phone and her Facebook. It was as if just the access would conjure some terrible news into being. Madison was in her twenties, a former dancer, with dyed red hair and an ad hoc wardrobe that once involved wearing a net tutu to work. Her cell phone had always been an issue. Shannon had had to block Madison's personal access on her work computer and had on occasion had to confiscate her phone if there was something urgent for her to attend to. Shannon was doing fine concentrating but then she was aware of a commotion in the air outside her sanctuary. She thought she was imagining it until Madison knocked.

"I know you don't want to be interrupted," Madison said, poking her head around the door, "but I've got to tell you this. Wendy and the boys have let the Morrisons go. They've all just walked out. Course the police were waiting. There were a lot of them in the crowd pretending to be Tarstoppers. Undercover. I know I'm not supposed to be watching but I had to see it. I'll get back to work now, I promise. But I thought you'd want to know."

"Thank you Madison."

All she could think was that maybe now the Tarstoppers would disperse. They'd made their point. Maybe this whole thing would be over soon. Even though she knew it wasn't likely to be true, this thought allowed her to get back to work, her door closed. But then her cell phone rang. It was in her purse. She never used it to talk to clients or suppliers. Her friends didn't call her at work. But she was too much a mother, even with both of her kids grown up, to ignore a personal call. She took out her phone. Caller unknown, no number displayed. Matt would have no way of finding her cell phone number. And it was still possible it could be one of the kids, some emergency, and so she answered.

"Shannon. Matt Brown. We met the other night."

"How did you get my number? Don't do this. Don't come after me. I'm distressed enough by what's going on in the city without you phoning me. Leave me alone." She was aware of how her voice had risen. She hung up.

She sat looking at the phone, waiting for it to ring again. When it didn't, she picked it up and dialed Tim at work. "Hi." She knew she sounded stressed but that was easily explained.

"What's going on? You okay?"

"I just heard about the hostage-takers letting the Morrisons go. Maybe it's all going to end."

"As I understand it, they did it because they don't need to keep them now. The mass of people in place is enough on its own. I wouldn't count on it being over. Sorry."

"What's going on with Armie and Katie? Did you talk to him over the weekend?"

"You know our Armie. He keeps things to himself. But something's going on. It may well be ending."

"Let's hope so. Although I don't underestimate her ability

to pull him back in. I've got to go. I'll talk to you later."

"Are you sure you're okay?"

"I'm okay."

That was stupid to have reacted to Matt that way. She'd sounded hysterical. Don't come after me. It was totally unlike her. She was smooth, she was professional. Her response had probably piqued his interest.

She needed something to wipe Matt out of her mind but not what came next, Sevaris calling to cancel their event. Not even nicely, regretfully. Abruptly, with no apologies. Now she was afraid to answer her office phone in case the next call was another cancelation.

●

THE WHOLLY GREEN GIANT
1:23 PM

As I'm sure you all know by now, Wendy & the boys are out. They stepped out the front door of the Morrisons' house a couple of hours ago as if they were just going out for a coffee. A thousand devices started filming — everyone in the inner circle pressed up against the house & in range. Wendy & the boys are immediately grabbed by the plainclothes cops in the crowd — we always knew they were there but wow there's a lot of them. It's weird how they materialize out of the mass of people & you know at once who they are. They really fitted in — men & women both did an amazing job of getting the look right which was more a matter of a kind of benign casual passivity than the right hair or clothes – but then their faces tighten up & their posture stiffens & you wonder how we ever missed them. There's nothing the cops can do to shield Saint Wendy & the boys from view – no van with blacked-out windows to shove them into. Nothing was able to get through. Huge cheers & hollering go up for the trio. Wendy's surprisingly petite & quite plain. She doesn't even wave – she's one cool chick – but the boys – bearded & scruffy James & Paul – look confused & embarrassed & they nod at the crowd & squint. Do they even know much of what's been happening around them? What their act has come to? Has any outside info been able to reach them?

When the Morrisons step out they're scooped up by the cops as well. The Morrisons look no worse for their ordeal. Tanya still has that Barbie glaze on her skin & hair & clothes. The kid – that pampered little prince – seems a little dazed.

Now I have to admit I wasn't there when all this happened. I wish I had been there. Instead I was in my park doing some of the shit jobs. Somebody's got to.

So these undercover cops have to lead Wendy & the boys through the gigantic crowd of hooting & cheering & clapping people. All these other undercovers emerge to line a path for them. Cop cars are trying to come towards them – & an ambulance – but nobody's moving out of their way. I've put this version together after viewing & downloading all the videos I can. Somebody's got a huge job ahead of them to get some coherence in the mass of video being downloaded from a thousand devices. The mainstream press has always been a part of the Wall but their content's probably no different than anybody else's. Bastard

Morrison & family have to walk the corridor as well. You almost feel for them. They probably think of themselves as leading citizens – the envy of all – richly deserving of all the wealth & rewards that have come their way & here they are being stared at with contempt & dislike by the throng. You can tell Tanya just doesn't get it. Her forehead would be squeezed with confusion & puzzlement if the Botox would allow it. Bastard's got his chin jutted out & he's staring straight ahead. He's got his arm holding up Tanya who's stumbling & the little boy's got a tight grip on his mother's hand as she pulls him along. Eventually – after what seems like hours of slow parade – all the flashing cruisers & paddy wagons & ambulances & the whole hoopla meet up with the hostage-takers & the hostages & the billion cops & it all gets sorted out.

Now I'm out here milling around & getting the feel. Everybody's pumped & buzzing. It seems Wendy said something like, "Keep it up, it's all of you now," to the crowd as she emerged from the house. I haven't found anyone yet who caught it live & I can't find a download of it anywhere.

The cops have the house wrapped in yellow tape like a birthday present now – everybody pushed back. Folks say it makes no difference & everyone's staying up but it's kind of ominous to have the cops now at the centre of our protest. I'm scared the whole thing'll come apart without something or someone to keep us focused – especially now that we're so threatened by those animals who call themselves Wildcatters. What was it – like ten people killed overnight? It's like being in bloody Afghanistan or somewhere & being blown up by roadside devices. I don't trust the powers-that-be not to start hassling our people & roughing them up & maybe even encouraging the Wildcatters to put the squeeze on us. I have to admit I'm a little nervous. But we're not leaving until the tarsands are shut down – no negotiations.

4:22 PM

We don't have a Wall now for people to spend time on. There's no point to it now that there aren't any hostages. People are milling around here now not knowing what to do with themselves. No one's thinking of leaving but as it gets more uncomfortable – & apparently June is the rainy month around here – & it drags out – how are we going to keep people motivated?

There's talk that the cops won't be able to hold Wendy & the boys 'cause there was no threat involved – no weapons – & the Morrisons were free to go at any time. If the Morrisons felt threatened by the wall of people outside their door that wasn't Wendy & the boys' fault. Technically there were no hostages, we're told, so our heavenly trio could be out on bail in no time. Which could really stir up both sides. Then Saint Wendy & her Apostles could come back & lead us – even though I don't believe in leaders. We'll have to wait & see what comes out of all the meetings tonight now that Wendy & the boys are out. Much as I hate to admit it we do need some kind of executive body now. We have a goal & we have to coordinate. It's not like we can just go on living in our peaceable camps forever. Now that Wendy & the boys are out something's got to happen soon – in the next 24-48 hours – to bring us Tarstoppers together again or all the forces against us – & some in our own midst – are going to destroy us.

All day Tim had kept his head down, feeling like a fish in a bowl even when he closed his door for a while. Connor was out at meetings most of the day but he wasn't really the problem. Tim didn't care what Connor thought. It was the not knowing when he talked to his assistant or to the Head of Operations or anyone else in the building if they'd read the blog, what they knew about him. He'd get over this, he knew. Like anyone, he'd survived a lot of embarrassments in life. It would take time but he'd get himself tucked in again, not feel like his innards had been spread out over a table for viewing.

Should he read it to know what was being said? How could you go ahead with life, oblivious to what was being said about you? Like a celebrity learning not to read their own press. If he read the blog, he knew he'd only wish he hadn't read it.

His phone rang. His dad, the display said. Tim picked up because it was a distraction, a way to recalibrate his mind.

"Are they clearing out now?" Garth asked, not even saying hello as was his way. "I heard about the hostages being released."

"Hi, Dad. I don't think that was the point of releasing them. They weren't necessary anymore, now that so many people have been attracted to the city. Nothing's changed."

"And your brother's still in the middle of it. Do you know how much money I've lost in the last week? Does he ever think of that? He's out of my will. I made sure of that."

"Talk to him. I'll give you his cell phone number. You

can call him."

"I don't want to talk to him. He doesn't want to talk to me. He hasn't called in years now. It's hard for me to remember I even have two sons."

Garth's feelings were hurt. This fact came as a surprise to Tim every time. Garth wanted the opportunity to straighten Deke out and Deke continually, infuriatingly, denied it to him. Tim said, "It's supposed to rain this week, lots of thunderstorms. Maybe that'll discourage the campers. There are all kinds of shortages, food, water, sanitation. This thing has a natural life span. Not to mention all the vigilantes and rednecks and white supremacists around and itching for all-out war."

"It's a real war at the border. I've been watching. The Americans aren't putting up with it. Not like our wussy government. They're fighting back. They brought in the National Guard and the army and they're forcing all those Tarfuckers to go home. Smashing up their camps. Forcing them back on the road. Forcing them onto buses. But they know better than to take on those Wildcatters. Just get rid of the Tarfuckers and the whole thing will go away. Makes you wish you were an American."

"I'm busy, Dad. Call me at home in the evening when I have more time to talk."

But by evening, with Toronto two hours ahead in time, Garth would have drunk so much wine at dinner that he'd have done all his ranting to his girlfriend Eva, his huge anger like long belches, and he wouldn't think of Tim again. Poor Eva.

Tim kept waiting to hear she'd had enough and left him. Then who would Garth yell at about the government and the Natives and Quebec and all his fellow Canadians? And worst of all his two sons, one a fucking Tarstopper for Christ's sake and the other some kind of passive peacenik in a nonprofit. What did he do to deserve that? Tim knew exactly how his dad thought.

He turned back to work to avoid any more thoughts about his family.

●

Coming home from work, crossing MacLeod Trail, it took Armie a few seconds to realize the change. The barricades were gone around his part of the city, the checkpoints and the army personnel. He had to guess that now that the Morrisons had been released the Wall of people surrounding the house was down. With no Wall, this part of the city would no longer be a magnet. The fact that he'd once had to show ID just to enter his own neighbourhood would come to seem like a curiosity in his memory. He half-expected all the Tarstoppers to be gone, like a change of screen on a device he was studying, but no, Stanley Park was still full. The blockades had at least been some protection for the camps around here from the Wildcatter guys but now it'd be wide open.

What were people going to do with themselves now that they wouldn't have the Wall to go to? What would he do with himself if he didn't have Katie? He kept pushing his mind out into the possibility of breaking up, trying to imagine it. Even to be thinking it seemed hugely disloyal. He'd spent all of yesterday reassuring Katie, wondering what he was doing. Sex like four times in one day. Her parents downstairs. Which seemed weirder and weirder.

How could you go along accepting things as normal and then one day have it all shift sideways on you? And then the weirdness spread and you were no longer at home with anything you once thought or felt. You couldn't even remember what you once said to yourself. About Katie, about global warming, about the economy. What was he doing with his life? Working a mindless job with a group of people he mostly didn't like. Spending most of his free time locked up in a room with Katie. Not thinking too much about the big issues of his day.

It was how things worked, he was beginning to see. You went along and then suddenly life lurched. From his study of ancient human beings, he knew it had always been like that. Going along with the same tools and no change for hundreds of thousands of years, even millions of years, and then in a short time something new swept them all up. Like how Cro-Magnon popped up fifty thousand years ago in this huge leap forward. He felt like a Cro-Magnon, in Europe for the first time, barely able to remember the life left behind in Africa. Running into Neanderthals who were so backwards they were a different species. Would this whole Tarstopper thing change the world that way? Or would it eventually get forgotten as some other crisis, a plague or a war or an approaching asteroid, preoccupied us?

●

Shannon felt caged, just walking west along Eleventh Avenue towards Gizelle's condo in the late afternoon sunshine. It was the first breakthrough in a gloomy overcast day. She'd just come from a yoga class, which usually gave her a temporary stretch of calm afterwards, but not today. No one else had cancelled. At least not today. But she could see that if this went on, the rest would. There was nothing she could do.

She couldn't look around, only stare west through her sunglasses. Multiple cages, Matt circling her, all the forces in the city circling them both. All her apprehension seemed to have condensed down into a fear of this man. She'd turned off her phone, but it was like a defused bomb she was carrying around. As the one-way outbound traffic crept along, keeping pace with her, she felt very cut off, which seemed like a primal state for her. She realized she was rushing and slowed down.

At the Co-op grocery store she went in to find something to take to Gizelle's for dinner. It was odd enough these days how many people wandered the grocery aisles talking on their phones and checking their messages, but now it seemed like everyone in the store only had half an eye on their shopping, baskets at their feet while they stared at their screens, carts at a standstill. It was like moving around in a zombie movie as she collected her in-store squash soup and some bread and milk for the morning. She went through the self-check-out and was back on the street in under five minutes.

No Matt outside Gizelle's building, no Matt in the lobby. She was in a cage of self-consciousness, like the elevator that took her to the eleventh floor, mirrors on every wall. No Matt in the hallway, or inside the condo. Only then could she take out her phone and call Tim, without looking for messages. She knew she was being paranoid, she knew she'd blown him hugely out of proportion, but the knowing didn't seem part of the same brain as her fear.

"Hi. I'm at Gizelle's. What's going on there?"

"Why haven't you been answering?"

"I just wanted some quiet while I walked from yoga. Is Armie home?"

"Yeah. In the basement. Tell me. Something's wrong. I can hear it in your voice."

"Sevaris cancelled today."

"I guess it was bound to happen. I wish I could reassure you that this will soon be over and they'll come back. But there are a lot more people in the park now without the Wall to go to, now that the hostages have been released. And they've taken down the barricades around our part of the city. Without the Wall and the hostages, I guess the authorities don't think our area's the centre of this movement anymore. It feels more chaotic than ever."

The Wall dispersed, the barricades down: she imagined armies of people clashing, hand-to-hand combat in the streets like they said was happening in towns along the border. "You're really vulnerable now. All our protection's gone.

Without the barricades, Wildcatters can come in and blast everyone out of the park and take over. This is really scary. Keep an eye on Armie."

"Are you going to be okay?"

"No. Of course not. It feels like Armageddon or something. I'm going to watch a movie with headphones, take a long bath and go to bed early. So don't worry if I'm out of reach. I'll talk to you tomorrow."

He wanted more from her, like always, but he was lucky, she thought, to be getting this much reassurance.

TUESDAY
JUNE 5 2012

THE WHOLLY GREEN GIANT
11:09 AM

They've taken down the blockade around this part of the city. Without the Wall around the Morrisons I guess there's no need to close this area off. There goes any protection we might have had from the maniacs out to destroy us. So when we should be planning for our long-term habitation in the city instead we're talking about self-defense. That's what the assembly focused on last night rather than mapping out our glorious future. Setting up some kind of alarm system. Somehow digging a bunker for if we get raided by a bunch of Wildcatters. It's like preparing for war. We're so pathetically vulnerable – as we found out in the triangle park – & those guys only had noise-makers. These other dudes have automatic weapons & bombs.

At least the Wildcatters are never going to get organized – given who they are. Course they're not all coming from the same place – just like us. At one extreme you've got the white suprema- cists who think we're funded by China or by the New World Order to take down the white free world. They think they're fighting for Western civilization. It's infuriating that some people would see us as the other extreme – trying to tank civilization – when we've got indisputable science on our side. Those armed hellcats are just ignorant loudmouth gun-crazed morons. But they're scaring the crap out of us. Another death – in a camp on the edge of the city. Not to speak of the carnage at the border & the cops & army going after the peaceful Tarstoppers rather than those murder- ous thugs attacking them. Just from watching last night at our own meeting I could see how difficult it's going to be to get folks focused now that we're in such danger. Folks are terrified.

On another front – have you heard the absolute hogwash coming from Baxter Morrison & the lovely Tanya? Bastard pre- tends like he's seen the light. Oil companies & pipeline compa- nies have to pay attention, he says gravely. What he means is he's seen our numbers & power & he's a little scared – not because he's had any change of heart on the actual issues. We used to be so dismissible – just a small bunch of radical loonies obsessed about minor damage caused by the development of the lifeblood of the nation. Have you seen him on the news or on the Net? I know the type well. Like my old man. Affable on the surface & in public but a pitbull underneath. He's out to win. But we really scared the guy. All the execs & government guys are quaking. Even if we haven't convinced them of the environmental dangers we should take what we get. They're paying attention. Although it's hard to watch Bastard mouth the words out of fear – with so little conviction. At least he's not quite as puffed up with himself as before.

& did you see the lovely Tanya going on to a sympathetic reporter about how awful it had been? She moans about all those horrible people surrounding her house & imprisoning her & her family. She doesn't get any of it. She asks, all perplexed: how do those people think the world would run without oil? You know she'll go back to her fat life now & need to recover at their 10,000 sq ft place in Palm Springs & make herself feel better with shopping & golf & visits to the spa. She never questions her right to it. She really thinks she's superior – more civilized – than grubby rabble like us. She thinks we're just jealous of her. It's amazing to watch her blindness & stupidity. Our own Marie Antoinette.

But at least we've scared Bastard Morrison. Almost as much as the Wildcatters have scared us.

●

Lunch with Jason. They did lunch on a regular basis, but given what was going on in the city Tim would just as soon have put it off. On the other hand, who else was he going to talk to about what was going on? Definitely not Shannon.

They were eating around the corner from Tim's work, out on picnic benches near an old bus that served hamburgers. They both still wore their coats.

"Have you heard the latest?" Jason asked him, having

waited, bursting with it, until they were settled at a table. "The real war is down at the border. Like a civil war right there at the border. Nobody knows how many have died but the guess is, close to a hundred. It's wild. The Wildcatters are now shooting at the cops and the army because they're removing the Tarstoppers and taking away all their fun. It makes no sense. Those guys are so full of rage they just want to kill, they don't even care who."

"Thank God it's down there and not here. I still don't really understand the Wildcatters."

"I watched an interview with this one guy wandering around southern Saskatchewan waiting to get picked up. They asked him what he thought he was doing and this guy, your average ball-capped rough-edged loser type, said he worked in the oilfields in North Dakota. The new ones where they're fracking. It's a real boom area, with thousands of guys moving there from all over the States. He said he'd been out of work for years down in Texas and now he's making a bundle and nobody's taking that away from him. The bleeping Tarstoppers and their Commie ideas had to be wiped out once and for all."

It was like Jason was telling him what had happened on an episode of a television show he'd missed. Tim hated the excitement in his voice. His own voice deliberately flattened, he said, "Who'd have ever thought that needing a passport to enter Canada would save us from an invasion?"

Jason raised an eyebrow at his cool wryness, surprised maybe that even this extreme real life story couldn't get Tim going. He sat back a little. "So what's going on at your house?

Deke still living with you? Shannon still at Gizelle's?"

Tim nodded about Shannon. "She lost a client; they cancelled Stampede. She's pretty upset. I don't see much of Deke, though he comes back every night. God knows what he tells himself about his comfort when so many others are out there shivering. But you read his blog. You know much more about him than I do."

"You really should be reading it as well. You don't know how personal he gets."

"I can guess. I told him to stop but I don't suppose that had much effect."

Jason shook his head. "I've learned stuff about you I never knew."

"Oh, great. Deke's version. Take it with a grain. Connor at work is lapping up every detail. Everyone at work is reading it. Taking it as the truth. It's tough. There's no protection against it."

Jason gave him a quick nod of empathetic agreement and moved on. "So what's going on at your park?"

"It's overflowing now, without the Wall to go to. Usually I guess at any one time half of them were there on the Wall. They've got to be losing steam. Rain and hardship is one thing, the danger of being blown up or shot is another."

"Without the barricades around your part of the city, they are in real danger. I'd stay indoors if I were you. Never mind the border, there are thousands of Wildcatters already here, Canadian and American and from all over the world. I've heard that the price of a handgun in the city on the black market has gone up by thousands of dollars. I may come over tonight just to get the feel of your neighbourhood. Easy to get in now."

"Could we talk about something else? I hit overload on this stuff way before you do. I'm actually quite terrified of where this is going. It's not in your front yard."

Jason smiled. "Shannon's influence."

"You don't have to be as ready to see the dark side as Shannon to be afraid of this. I'm doing fine on my own. I'm starting to think she's been right all along. About the potential in all of us."

"These are the extremes. From both ends of the spectrum."

Tim shrugged. But he couldn't shrug any more without imagining Deke mocking it. "That's what I'm not so sure of anymore. I'm not sure that the majority of people in the city wouldn't agree to whatever violence it took to clear this all away, even if they're not going to pull any triggers themselves."

"Hey, this is really getting to you."

"You could say that."

●

Shannon was alone in the office at six in the evening. She wanted to barricade herself in and wait this out, however long it took. At least there hadn't been any more cancellations. Each day now without one was a victory. She'd have to leave soon to find something to eat. She had eaten nothing all day. She didn't want to go to Gizelle's, either to be alone in the condo or to talk about the Tarstoppers. She wanted to go home but not with Derek there, not with her neighbourhood full of strangers. She wished she could get a hotel room and bring Armie with her. She was on waiting lists all over town.

She couldn't concentrate. It was too quiet. Out her window, cars and buses moved slowly west on Eleventh Avenue like on any day at the end of rush hour. She glanced out.

He was across the street. Matt. Standing on the sidewalk staring up at her office window. She ducked back instinctively, as frightened as if he were a sniper.

Was her brain conjuring up what she feared? She couldn't look again. She had to believe he really was watching for her. Calm down and think. She could go out the back of the building and avoid him. She started to gather her things together but then realized that he could be on his way up, easily bypassing the security code on the front door. She was rushing now, even as she tried to tell herself that she was over-reacting, that she could get rid of this guy, that he was no threat to her. He was hardly going to lock her in here, wrestle her to the floor and rape her. Why would he want to do that? She was a fifty-one year old woman. Well-kept maybe, but uptight, not seductive, not a come-on. Just keep going.

She took the stairs, her heart pounding in panic and made it to the back door unaccosted. She burst out into the alley among the dumpsters and the short-cutting cars. She was wearing heels. She liked to wear heels, her vanity, but she couldn't run in them. Where was she going? A restaurant, somewhere public. Edouardo's around the corner on Twelfth.

It was open. She half expected the whole city to have shut down. There was almost no one in there. She sat at a table with her back to the door so she wouldn't be constantly watching for who came in. She knew that would only increase her fear. She ordered a glass of wine. Her muscles were so tensed waiting for his hand on her shoulder that she almost felt it, again and again. When the wine arrived she gulped it down.

She texted Tim. *I'm at Edouardo's. Any way you can join me? I need you to.*

She ordered another glass of wine. The waiter, a man in low-slung jeans and a long white apron, asked her if she'd heard the latest.

"I'm trying to avoid it. I only want the news in bearable snippets at the end of the day, if that."

He smiled at her but told her anyway. "Two more deaths. Wildcatters shot up a Tarstopper camp. A lot of people injured."

Alarm buzzed through her body. "Where was this?"

"On the edge of town. No one even saw the shooters. Just all of a sudden the Tarstoppers started keeling over."

She interrupted him to repeat that she didn't want the news. Let him think her a bitch. She ordered a salad to stop him from lingering, to stop his excited voice.

She knew Matt was in the room, although she hadn't heard the door because of the waiter. Matt slid into the seat across from her, so real she knew she couldn't be hallucinating. Older than she remembered, in this stronger light, and not as good-looking. But still magnetic. She did not want to be involved with this man. Even if she'd been single she wouldn't have wanted it. There was no appeal to the idea of feeling like this, heightened, sexualized all of the time. She didn't want it.

She said coldly, "I'm meeting my husband here. He's on his way."

He smiled. "I'd like to meet him."

"And get his views? Shouldn't you be out covering events? I'd have thought it would be 'round the clock right now."

He just kept smiling. He was good at not reacting to provocation, trained to it no doubt. But he had serious stuff on his mind. He locked her eyes. She didn't know how he did it, but she couldn't look away. "I really liked talking to you the other night. Someone whose livelihood depends on the oil industry and yet has some objectivity."

"Well, you're wrong. I'm as angry as anyone."

"I looked into you. I have to confess I've become a little obsessed by you."

"Don't say that. I don't want you investigating me, talking to my friends. I don't want you here. I'd like you to leave."

He smiled and shrugged. "Too late. I know everything about you. Your mother's maiden name, the whole bit."

What would he be able to access? She felt like a mother hen trying to locate her chicks to herd them into safety. What private information of hers was out there? She wasn't the kind to put her personal life on display. Her Facebook page was all work-related. "I don't believe you. I'm careful with my walls."

"You have no idea what's available." The waiter had returned. Matt ordered a glass of Malbec. "I know you feel it," he said after the waiter had left. "We've got a connection."

"No, we don't."

"I'll make you a deal. We'll have a nice impersonal conversation until your husband gets here. Then I promise I'll go. What's the harm? I really want to hear what you have to say."

Shannon paused, thought. "Explain the Wildcatters to me then, if you're just going to sit there."

"I want to hear what you have to say."

She shook her head and took a big mouthful of wine.

"Okay. The Wildcatters, otherwise known as Freedom Fighters. Well, it's huge. There's more anger out there than anyone can imagine. And they're everywhere. The military is riddled with secret militias. Did you know that? There are covert organizations all over the country. The Tea-partiers are just a mild form. Homegrown terrorism is a much much bigger threat than Muslims. At the moment we're just glad they're marching north and not blowing up national monuments and subway stations in the States. They can't do much damage in those hick border towns except kill Tarstoppers, which is one problem cancelling out another."

"That's a horrible way to talk." She didn't mean to engage. She didn't trust herself, what she'd say.

"I thought you hated the Tarstoppers."

"I don't want anyone killed. I want it all to go away. I'm a Canadian: I have to say I relate more to the Tarstoppers, if I was forced to choose. I don't get the American violence thing." Stop talking. Don't engage with him. Just shut up.

"Don't think you don't have your share of the Wildcatters

up here. Don't go all superior." He was laughing at her.

"Whoever they are, how'd they become so extreme? What's your theory?" Maybe the only solution was to keep him talking, wait him out until Tim arrived.

"Powerlessness. They don't recognize the world now. They feel they've been left behind and they've got to blame someone."

"But environmentalists?"

"Liberals. Anyone who wants more change. There's been too much change. They want to go backwards."

The waiter brought her salad. When the waiter asked Matt if he wanted to eat, he said, "It's six fifteen. No one eats this early."

After the waiter left again, Matt nodded at Shannon's plate. "Not waiting for your husband?"

Don't react, she told herself, don't become defensive. "So do you think the Tarstoppers will start to leave now that it's getting violent?"

"There'll be a hardcore element that stays. Like your brother-in-law."

She heard someone come in but it was not Tim. The waiter led a young couple towards the back of the restaurant. Her shoulders hurt, waiting for Tim. When had she ever texted him that she needed him to come? "I don't want to know how much you know about me and my family. It's creepy. Is that what this is about? You're investigating my brother-in-law?"

Her body was buzzing. Like the tingling before vomiting. It had to be the stress; and she was not breathing properly.

Every sensation was magnified, painfully: the acrid smoky wine in her mouth, the slick texture of the glass in her hand, the male smell from across the table, the clarity of her sight and how sensually vivid his skin, his hazel eyes, his mostly grey hair all were. She wouldn't be able to eat her salad. The mix of tastes – greens and walnuts and raspberries and some kind of lemon vinaigrette – could so over-stimulate her she'd have to run for the bathroom or for the street. She'd need to find a dark closet where she could desensitize for hours and hours.

"It's part of why I'm interested in you," he acknowledged, watching her discomfort. "You seem to embody the whole conflict."

"Are you really with ABC News?"

"Don't get paranoid on me. I'm here because of your level-headedness. I was struck by that."

Where was Tim? Ask another question. "So how do you think this is all going to end?" She kept her voice as cool and level as she could. She imagined him a difficult client. She was good at flowing over the top of strife. She was a professional. Use it.

He knew what she was doing. He even smiled in understanding. He kept his eyes on her as he said, "It's unpredictable. Once roused, who knows what anyone will do. And it's not possible to suppress it now. They'll act it out. They want to fight someone. They crave violence. The old thing about how cleansing it is. If you ask me, that urge to periodically clean everything out and start over from some kind of new pure beginning has been the undoing of civilization all along."

He reached over and put his hand over hers on the table, then as quickly withdrew it. "I just had an urge to calm you down. Sorry."

She had to leave the table. There was nowhere to go but the washroom. But in there the smell of a flowered air freshener brought the wine back up into her mouth. Why hadn't she run out the restaurant front door instead? But he could just have followed her so maybe she was better off in here. There was no point in calling the police, the city in crisis the way it was, and she didn't want to ask the waiter to intervene. She probably couldn't outwait Matt in here. Her only hope now was Tim.

She texted him again. *Help. Are you coming?*

She held the phone out in front of her waiting for him to text back. *What's going on? On train. Approaching downtown. Be there soon.*

She just had to wait. Think about Tim. Reliable Tim. His voice. His voice that could unite and empower a room full of people. That Tim. Her mind wouldn't stay with him. She grasped after him as the panic careened back like water thrown at her. She told herself to breathe, that she was in no danger right now.

He crashed into the washroom. Matt. He said, "Just checking that you're alright. You seem so upset. I'm sorry if I've caused it."

She pushed by him, their bodies touching, and she was thankful he didn't grab her. If he had she'd have started screaming. Screaming and screaming until Tim finally showed up.

Tim! He was here. Tim, Tim, Tim. In the vestibule, red-faced from running, out of breath, looking around frantically for her. She ran for him, for the relief and delight in his face on seeing her. But then he noticed the man coming out of the bathroom behind her. She was running from this man but he couldn't figure it out. She grabbed his arm.

Looking back she saw Matt approaching them, his hand extended. "Matt Brown," he said to Tim. "I was just borrowing your wife for a while. We'd been talking and she suddenly didn't feel well."

Tim stared at his hand.

"Actually," Matt went on, "I was hoping you'd join us. I'm a journalist."

Shannon couldn't speak, only shake her head at Tim. She knew he'd understand.

Tim said to Matt, "I think you'd better go. I can see you've upset her."

Matt smiled and conceded. "Maybe another time." He walked over to her table and swallowed down his wine. He left a bill on the table. He was in no hurry.

Everyone in the restaurant watched him. Two women at a table at the front were openly listening, mouths slack. As he walked by Shannon at the door, he said, "It really was just a conversation. Everything I'd learned about you suggested you were not the nervous type."

She had to sit down somewhere before she fell. She stumbled across the room to her chair against the brick wall, to the small white-clothed table, which seemed like a kind of home or refuge. After a pause Tim followed her. He took Matt's wine glass and the ten-dollar American bill and put them on another table. Then he sat down. He watched her, mystified and concerned, waiting. She couldn't meet his eye. She couldn't drag herself into forward motion and yet everything in her was so vividly present. She would remember the way the light slanted in the window, the texture of the linen napkin, the small pinkish glass lights hanging over each table. She'd never be able to come back to this restaurant again. She pushed her salad away but there was nowhere for it to go, nowhere far enough. She finally met Tim's eye and he took the plate and put it with the wine glass and the money on the other table.

"When you're ready," he said. He signaled the waiter. He'd have a scotch. Neat.

"Where's Armie?" Shannon asked, suddenly remembering him. "Have you seen him?"

"Texted, that's all. He's okay."

She dropped her eyes again. She thought of the funeral phrase, in the midst of life we are in death. In the midst of life we are in derangement. In a city taken over by protesters who were being picked off by armed maniacs, she had responded to a man trying to get something out of her. Some large part of her not controlled by her mind, by her choice and preference, had reacted to that man. Other people got caught in dramas and farces, not her. Gizelle's life was one emotional saga after another. Shannon was not like that. This city was not like that.

When she still couldn't say anything, Tim said, "Okay. Start from the beginning. How do you know him? Do you have a relationship? You have to talk about it."

Okay, step by step. She and Tim were good at this, a team, talking things through. "I met him Saturday night. At a bar. With Gizelle."

"And what happened there?"

"He's in town with ABC News. Or so he says. He talked me up. I left. That's all."

"But you talked to him?"

"Not for long. I didn't even tell him my name."

"Go on. What came next?"

"He grilled Gizelle about me. She told me. And he called me at work one day but I hung up on him."

"And then?"

"He showed up outside my office tonight. On the street. I left by the back door and came here. He followed me."

"You should have said that in your first text. I almost didn't come. I couldn't get my car out. If it hadn't been so unusual for you to need me. So how did he end up in the bathroom with you?"

"He followed me in. I was trying to get away from him."

Tim took a sip of the scotch the waiter had just brought. She could feel the scotch in her own throat, the warmth and comfort and taste of it. She desperately needed to dull down. She wanted to take a cold bath. To drug herself with tranquil- izers or sleeping pills.

"And you didn't give him any encouragement?"

"No." She wouldn't tell him about her physical response, all that she couldn't control. She was sure this was right, not to tell him. He would only be hurt by it. As much as he disliked how she kept things to herself, he wouldn't want to hear this. Marriages, relationships, went day to day on their balances. She didn't have any faith that tipping the balance could result in any good. Maybe there was some small chance that after a long long readjustment they could be closer than they were before but she was not taking it.

"He's with ABC News?"

"They deny any knowledge of him. I tried that. I think he's CIA in anti-terrorism or something. He's been tracking me. He knows everything about me. It's scary to think about. He knows Derek's my brother-in-law."

"You think he's after Deke? That doesn't make any sense. As far as I can tell, Deke is all talk. He's no ringleader. And how would talking to you get him closer to Deke anyway? Does he know you're staying at Gizelle's?"

"I don't know."

"This is really weird. It's like something out of a movie."

"It scares me, what he's really after."

"What do you want to do? Come home? Go back to Gizelle's?"

"You'll come with me?"

"Of course." He twisted his face at her, surprised she was even asking. "I can understand what you're going through. All the normal limits on behaviour seem removed and your mind goes leaping. Like should we search you in case he's planted a tracking device on you? It seems paranoid but it's hard to keep your mind in check when such incomprehensibly extreme things are going on."

"Okay, let's go. To Gizelle's. We don't know that he knows I'm at Gizelle's. And she has security. Although if he's any kind of agent that'll present no problem. I know he knows where I live. I don't want him showing up. With Armie there. Derek."

Out on the street she was surprised by how bright it was, like the whole world should have dimmed in preparation for what was coming. Matt could be watching them from any-where. Luckily it was only three blocks. She took Tim's arm, more for steadiness than comfort.

"Is Gizelle home?" he asked her.

"I don't know." She got out her phone and pressed. "No," she said after Gizelle's message clicked in. She texted her. *Need to know when you'll be home.*

Gizelle checked her messages every few minutes. There was no wait. *What's up? Home a few hours.*

Shannon texted back. *That guy harassing me. Going to condo now. Don't let anybody in when you come.*

Upstairs on the eleventh floor Shannon let them into the condo with her key. Tim went through looking for anything suspicious, but the condo was such a mess, Gizelle always run-ning late, that it was impossible to know if anything was differ-ent. He seemed to half-expect Matt to jump out of a closet, dagger in hand.

"I'm okay now," she told him. "You can go home now. I'll be okay."

"You don't want me to stay?"

"No, I want you there. For Armie. I don't want him alone with Derek. I don't want Derek bringing his friends to the house. You should go now. I'll be all right."

"I hate to leave you like this." He wanted to hold her, she could tell, to comfort her, to reclaim her, but it was their pattern that he never touched her without her permission. They had their signals. It had been worked out all those years ago when they'd first met. Nice respectful kind-of-ordinary guy meets pretty but stand-offish, not-to-say-prickly girl. She knew she was not like a lot of other women. She couldn't imagine wanting to be dominated. Or even to have someone think it was their business to know where she was going, what she was thinking, who she was talking to on the phone, like some husbands and boyfriends.

"Call me," he said. "Even if you're not sure."

She couldn't hug him. She should have but she couldn't. He knew that she withdrew when distressed or upset, that she didn't seek solace. As she held the door open for him he put his hand on her hand but that was as far as he went. He didn't push at her with his eyes, for which she was grateful.

After he was gone, she couldn't think what to do with herself. A hot bath might help but she'd feel too defenseless. She didn't want any more to drink. She rooted through Gizelle's medicine cabinet and came up with out-of-date Ativan. She took three and then stood and waited with her eyes closed.

◆

Armie, sitting in the park near Katie's house, in an empty serene green space like a park was supposed to be, was getting ready to break up with Katie. He'd made up his mind. He had all these images in his head of things breaking, dissolving, falling apart. Slow things. Eggs cracking, sand being washed away, a humpback breaking the surface of the water, a house listing on its porch. At least he was not imagining explosions, carnage, not like one friend of his who told him he sometimes imagined mowing down rows and rows of people with a machine gun. Katie had been the first person to tell him he was not alone with his images. Life for her was also accompanied by a visual track, although she did everything she could to intensify it while his seemed mostly background. He was in his teens before he realized the constant imagery was even there. Now he pictured a ripe green fruit – a gooseberry? – splitting open. The imagery wasn't too hard to figure out, like the stories in dreams that mirrored the day.

It was a June night but cold, not too far above frost. He needed to break out but how do you do that without affecting the other person? Like slipping out of bed without waking them up. He loved Katie. He would always love Katie. But not enough to wait out the long process of trying to bring her along with him, with no assurance she'd ever want to engage with the world. He would explain it to her, but he was pretty sure the moment he revealed any dissatisfaction with the way things were she was gong to panic and stop listening. She'd start to wail, that horrible keening noise like when her dog Max died. She gave herself up to her emotion. Which he used to envy but now found a little self-indulgent.

She texted him. *Where r u?*

He'd been wandering around since he'd left work, trying to get up the courage. He'd hopped off the LRT downtown, mid-way, procrastinating, feeling ill. He'd thought the city should feel foreign now with the thousands and thousands of protesters and Wildcatters and security and media that were supposed to be around but it was only in his own section of the city he was aware of them, and then overwhelmingly so.

He got up from the park bench. He wished it could be neat and quick but it would take hours of explaining and holding her and listening to her cry. It was going to be a long, long time before he ever got in deep like this again. It really was over when he had thoughts like that. He'd thought they'd be together for life.

●

THE WHOLLY GREEN GIANT
9:37 PM

I'm at the Bro's, nobody here, but then that dickhead friend of his shows up. Can't remember the name I gave him. Last person I want to see. He's the kind of guy always has to feel in the centre of things – in the know – but never puts himself at the forefront or in any danger. He doesn't like me any more than I like him but he wants the insider info. He can tell his buddies he got it from a real Tarstopper. We have a little jostle to start with – him wanting in & me trying to keep him out. He says the Bro's expecting him but I say he's not here. The guy's coming in anyway to wait – like he's got more of a claim on the house & the Bro than me. Everything's a competition for this kind of guy. So we're in the kitchen at an impasse. I don't want any more of the guy's cynicism & I'm not feeding him any of the details he wants. For those new to this site the Bro's friend works for a pipeline company – I kid you not – & is well aware of the environmental facts but says we don't have any choice but to keep playing the game. Otherwise total financial collapse. The old lie. The old blackmail. The guy's in suit pants & a button down. The guy wants to argue with me again. We've already had one go-around, which went nowhere. It's like he's desperate to convince me we have no choice but to keep the oil flowing so he can silence his own doubts.

I have to say to him that I just can't get my head around intelligent people buying into the corporate scam & then I'm kicking myself for getting into it. But motor-mouth that I am I can't stop. I say they've scammed the whole world into thinking there's no alternative – that what's good for General Motors – or Apple or Google or even that good ol' standby Exxon – is good for the USA. & what's good for the USA is good for the planet. It's crap. Corporations make money for their owners or their shareholders. End of story. They don't care about their employees or what happens to the environment. They have zero interest in the tangential consequences of their drive to make a profit unless it's forced on them & who's going to do that? The jerk friend doesn't deny this – which blows me away every time – but says we're stuck with it. I want to jump up & down in a tantrum like a kid. We've been here before. I stop listening. This guy depresses me even more than the Wildcatters – who at least believe in something even if it's debauched & crazy. This jerk thinks the Wildcatters are the real villains in all this & us Tarstoppers are to blame for stirring them up! Can you believe it? & then corporate malfeasance – the whole point – gets forgotten.

I start looking for something to eat even while he's yakking. Into this situation comes the Bro. He's not happy to see either one of us. Eventually we get it out of him that the sis-in-law is being stalked by some American who might be the CIA or the like. We know the city is crawling with them. We know that to security forces we're all terrorists – Tarstoppers or Wildcatters. Anybody who wants to stop the flow of American commerce or the government's support of it is a terrorist. Both the friend & I want the details but the Bro is in a weird space – all self-involved & quiet. I hate when he gets like that. It's real passive aggressive control. As a kid it used to infuriate me. He'd know something & not tell. Or we'd be somewhere like on vacation & he'd not want to do stuff with me. Or with the old man & he'd watch me get it & he'd go hide in his room rather than stand up for me.

Now I acknowledge that the sis-in-law is a looker – if you like that sharp-faced buffed & polished blonde type. She's much more sleek than who you'd expect the Bro to have attracted – if you think like that. You should have seen our old man when the Bro first brought her around. The Bro went up like twenty notch-es in his estimation & the old man goes all suave & flirty around her. The old man's single at the time. It was kind of disgusting. He'd have taken her away if he could have – the old alpha male. To her credit the sis-in-law didn't play along, which soured the old man on her. To this day he has nothing good to say about his daughter-in-law. One cold bitch, in his view.

So this American operator's harassing the sis-in-law. The friend & I are speculating on what he's after. Neither of us thinks he's hitting on the sis-in-law because she's all that interesting or because she's hot. Let's be reasonable. She's over fifty. Of all the women in the city it's her who's attracted him? – when he should be out there infiltrating the Wildcatters? Come on. The Bro seems to think it could be the case though. I'd hate to have a beautiful wife. I used to wonder how he didn't go loco with the guys staring at her. The Bro seems to think the guy's legit – like he really works for ABC News like he says he does. The Bro says to me not to go thinking the guy's after me. But it turns out the guy did bring me up. He knows who I am & that I'm her brother-in-law. He's probably reading this right now. The friend & I are on the same page – which is not entirely welcome – that this stalker guy is after something. The friend's a complete cynic who thinks everybody's after something. The Bro's fiddling with his phone but he's not going to text the sis-in-law while we're around. He really shuts down then. He goes to his room – his bedroom – like we're back in high school. Doesn't even say goodnight.

The friend & I really get into trying to figure it out. We're both dumbfounded that neither the Bro nor his wife got a picture of this guy on their phone. It's the first thing I'd have done. Despite what the Bro says I know this guy is after me. The CIA & the Mounties know this blog-turned-column – now that I'm with FlashPoint – gets hundreds of thousands of hits. They know who every one of the Tarstoppers is & they track every computer that has sites & blogs like mine. Sorry to frighten you. They're spending billions & billions. & the public is so terrified of Islamic terrorism & things that go bump in the night that they don't blink an eye at the money spent. Their money. Or the loss of their own privacy. You want to just give up on the human race. The friend treats this like an espionage thriller he's watching. All of life seems like something he's just watching. You get hooked in & you go along like a sheep without any awareness that you can question it – you can fight to influence it, even change it. To him it's all just a given.

I was brought up to question. My mom made me see it was my responsibility to get involved & try to change things for the better. Not everybody had that. I was lucky. But you'd think it'd dawn on you that you don't have to just go along once things don't make sense – once you disagree. The Bro thinks he's doing his bit – he's the Director of a local charity – but to me charities are just a sop to corporate & government failures. He won't even talk about it with me any more. He's on these committees to end homelessness & all that kind of thing but I think of him as a lackey trying to clean up a little of the mess that the system's left behind. I can't get him engaged in changing the system itself.

But I'm spooked by the CIA operative. We have far more enemies than we know. I don't kid myself that there aren't huge files on me. Are they planning to take me out? Silence me? Have the Wildcatters been whipped up to kill Tarstoppers & do the CIA's dirty work for them? I don't put anything past the system. If you don't hear from me again it's because I've been targeted.

WEDNESDAY
JUNE 6 2012

Tim was surprised that he'd slept. Six hours ago he'd have said he was awake for the night. Now it was almost seven. He reached for his phone and the texts he might have missed while he slept. Big swerves could have happened in the lives of his family overnight. At least Ardith was out of this, living her disciplined school life in Vancouver, unaffected. Ardith had always been mostly self-sufficient, even as a child. Without obvious vulnerability she'd been less loveable than Armie but also a parental joy in her reliability. Ardith had just gone ahead, school, basketball, the debating team, the business she started in grade twelve.

He was holding onto the thought of Ardith and resisting the replays of the night before in the restaurant, that Matt guy coming out of the bathroom after Shannon. Swaggering out, smirking. No texts from her yet this morning. Didn't she appreciate how anxious he'd be? Okay, don't wait around for her to contact him, take action. He called her. "Is everything okay?" he asked her when she answered, slipping back into his old sense of being the supplicant with her, which he hated, which he kept thinking he'd finally moved beyond.

She seemed a long way away, her voice distant. Any solidarity from the night before seemed gone. He had to ask her for any news, like she didn't know he was on edge.

"He was outside last night when Gizelle got home. She says he wanted to apologize to me for frightening me. You can imagine how that intrigued Gizelle. I wouldn't talk about it. At least she didn't bring him up just to create some drama for herself to enjoy. It's really unnerving to think of him waiting outside the condo hoping to talk Gizelle into letting him up. In a way it was worse than having him show up at the restaurant. What does he want from me?"

"I don't know. He scared me too. I don't trust Gizelle not to lead him right to you."

"Where's Armie?"

"He slept over at Katie's. Something going on there. Maybe they're breaking up. We can hope."

"Sometimes I picture him swaddled in Katie's pink bedroom, trying to fight free of the netting and then giving up and letting it wrap him even tighter."

"Do you want me to come and escort you to work? I don't like the thought of you out there on the streets with that guy hovering around."

"No. I'll be okay. I can handle him."

He could never get enough out of her. And he seemed incapable of demanding more. His mother had once told him that a pattern had been set in him when Deke was born. Tim had given her up to the demanding new baby without a struggle. There were just his big-eyed looks of loss and betrayal as he went about his quiet pursuits. He'd never demanded, never insisted or fought back. He'd become stuck in the pattern, according to his mother, who was given to this kind of analysis. Meanwhile someone like this Matt could just shoulder his way in and try and take his wife over.

He didn't check for messages again until he was in his parking space at work. Jason. Jason loved being in the middle of this mess. He'd probably come over last night in the hopes of being close to events as they happened, to history forming just outside the window. When Tim had told him about the melee in the triangle park, Jason seemed almost envious of his involvement, without hearing how perturbed Tim had been by his violent neighbours.

Been searching for yr guy. Not ABC. Probably after yr bro. Know D gets 100 thou hits on Net? Gone to his head. U should look at blog. Know u don't want to but should. About u and S 2day. U cant keep head in sand 4ever. Getting bad.

It wasn't until lunch that Tim went online to search for Deke's blog, after a morning of resisting even the idea. He didn't want to know. If he read it, he knew he'd wish after that he hadn't. But it seemed inevitable, a hurdle, something he had to get past.

When he found it, he only brought up the latest entry, posted the night before. It had to be the one Jason had alluded to. He read the first few lines and had such a pile of reactions he had to stop reading to try and sort them out and calm down. First of all the "we." Deke made it sound like he was one of the inner circle, in the know, but as far as Tim could tell, Deke was more like a reporter wandering around. That aggrandizement of himself was so familiar and so irritating that Tim might as well have been a teenager again as he sat in his office.

Although it was his brother's voice in the words on the screen, it was improved in ways he couldn't explain. More easy-going and likeable, although it was true that in person Deke could be smooth and loquacious. It was one of the few things they had in common, a deep mellifluous voice. It had taken Tim years to realize the way people responded to his own voice. As a hesitant and self-conscious teenager he'd thought the talent was all Deke's and envied it. Deke never doubted his own appeal. How did he end up so full of himself after the drubbing he'd received from their dad his whole childhood? That was the mystery.

Deke really thought he was the rational, observing, assessing person he heard in his own head, the one he entered on his blog. He didn't know what a small part of him it was, however huge in his head. Noisy, dominant, slobby, argumentative, exasperating Deke had no idea what he was really like. Could Tim post a comment saying that the Deke in the blog was nothing like the real Deke? Was the real Deke the one he was in action, in interaction, or the self he knew in his own head?

Who was Tim: the person Deke thought he knew or the self he himself knew? Was he now going to find out things about himself he didn't want to know but couldn't dispute?

He started reading again and suddenly he was in his own house. How personal was this going to get? How dare Deke invite his readers into Tim's house! And slag his friend like that? Jason didn't seem to be holding a grudge but then he might be enjoying the notoriety, even unnamed. Tim could see that Deke was using Jason as a paper dragon, making his points, but there was no reason for him to bring him and Shannon into it, to expose their private lives. At least Shannon would never read this intrusive ranting. She didn't have that kind of curiosity. She was all too ready to find offence and disquiet if she went looking in places she had doubts about.

It got even more personal. Deke's version, loud and intrusive. About how annoying Tim had always been. There might even be some truth in it – Tim liked to think he knew most of his own shortcomings, especially through Deke's eyes – but it was the public airing of his faults and those of his family and friends that seemed indefensible. The story about their dad and the ass he'd made of himself over Shannon, coming on to her. Why tell that? Garth had indeed gone primal and mindless around her, embarrassing everyone. Garth couldn't be reading the blog or Tim would have gotten a call about it. He and Deke had never talked about their dad's barbarism and now Tim was reading about how Deke had seen it along with thousands of strangers. Weren't there privacy laws, libel restrictions, on this kind of thing? Shannon, were she to know about it, would feel as violated as by the CIA guy stalking her and digging into her life. You couldn't use people like this. Was Deke feeling badly now that he knew about her stalker? Did he worry that he'd exposed her? Endangered her? Not a chance. It was all about him and his pride in being high up on some security list.

Then Deke got into the old argument against aid organizations. He thought if you shut them down it would force the government into providing more to the poor and sick. Tim should be out on the front lines demanding change instead of looking after the damage. The old charge. But he was not going to get back into worrying his duty to the world and to his mother, who like Deke thought he should be doing more. He was not giving up his hard-won balance, his peace of mind, to re-examine their demands of him. He was enough of an adult now for that.

He shut down the site. He would never look at it again. He was so full of emotion and reaction it was like water up to eye-level. Heavy turbulent water that stuck him in place and would take hours, days, to begin to recede. What he'd learned over the years was how to stay afloat, eyes open, brain working, while the emotion, either rage or despair, possessed the rest of him. He used to drown in it. It would close right over his head and leave him depressed, the ability to vent his emotion having been squashed out of him early.

He'd known he shouldn't have read it. What had he been expecting? And who knew what personal stories Deke had told earlier about their upbringing, about Tim's personality, about Shannon? He wouldn't look. He knew Deke didn't have limits. Motor-mouth was right. Without a rearview mirror or any brakes.

He would not be able to talk to Shannon about what he'd learned. It felt like more and more was kept private between them. There was more to what was going on with the Matt guy than she'd said, too. He knew when she was being more furtive with him than usual. It seemed a danger sometimes that, as strong as the bond between them was, they'd withhold so much that they could end up too far apart for everyday life.

He had to distract himself somehow until his mood started to ebb, as he knew it would, a life lesson. He texted Shannon. *Still no sign? You okay?*

She texted back: *Eating lunch with a client. No sign. Tense.*

He could imagine. He'd try to transfer his anger at his brother over onto the American jerk harassing his wife. It didn't work, which said something about Deke's power.

He could act; he wasn't powerless. He had some control. He texted Deke: *Just read your blog from last night. Beyond even my tolerance. Did you even think about Shannon and this guy after her? You are no longer welcome in my house. Please be gone by the time I get home. All your stuff. Don't come back.*

●

When Armie arrived home around four, having left work a little early, he found Deke at the kitchen table, writing his blog. Armie really wanted to be alone for a while but Deke was not going to let him go so easily. Catering to other people's needs: at what point, Armie wondered, would he become the kind of man who just went his own way? He couldn't even think of himself as a man yet. Deke put up a hand and it was like a stop sign.

"I hear there's trouble with the girlfriend. As someone who's had more than their share, I'm like an open advice book. So what happened?"

"Did Dad tell you there was a problem?"

"Hey, we're family. Family's where you talk about stuff going on."

When Armie had been in university in Toronto, Deke had wanted all the hot details, the excesses Armie'd seen, the girls gone wild. Second best, he'd wanted to hear about romantic involvements. Deke had been incredulous that Armie was staying true to Katie over their year apart. You're young, Deke had kept telling him: now's the time to cut loose. The best way to deal with Deke, to avoid his scrutiny, Armie knew from experience, was to get him talking. "How do you break up with someone without hurting them?"

"It never gets any easier, trust me. By the time you're my age and still single there's a long string of women left behind. But we have to do it. You have to evolve. In the end it's not your problem if they don't understand. I'd say you've been with this chick way too long."

Armie nodded like this was great wisdom that had been a great help. Why was he so responsive to other people's feelings? It was like a disease. He'd been at it all night with Katie, coming at it from a long way away, circling, approaching and retreating, trying not to be a jerk. She wouldn't let him leave. She'd half-threatened to kill herself, not seriously, but an indication of the pain she would be unable to survive. What could he do but stay with her through the night? He was not going to tell Deke anything about himself and Katie. Move on.

Deke filled the gap in the conversation. "You heard about the Tarstopper just gunned down out of nowhere? Yesterday. This is a whole new ball game. Strike that. I hate sports analogies. Even when we try to stay separate from the warrior culture it's hard. It's so much part of our conditioning it's inside us. We're going to have to rethink. And the Wildcatters are the least of it. We estimate there are at least fifty thousand cops and security in the city right now. In the city and all the way south to the border. Canadian and American. CIA, RCMP, military, ordinary cops from other jurisdictions, Homeland Security, you name it. Your own mom is being stalked by a CIA guy who's really after me."

"What? What do you mean, stalked? Is she okay?"

"Relax. He's not really after her. He hit on her because that's one of the tools of the trade. He knows she's my sister-in-law. She's a little freaked but she's in no danger. Do you see though what a war this movement is facing? Strike that too: military analogies are as inculcated as sports ones. Worse, even. You have to come out on our side. It's more important than ever. What are you thinking? Where are you in thinking this stuff all through – which I guess I understand you have to do?"

Armie would much rather talk about economics and the

environment, if he had to choose, than relationships. What he really wanted to do was study. At least after he'd had a nap. He needed to learn more. And not from someone as biased and uneducated as his Uncle Deke. "What I don't get about the Tarstoppers is how limited the movement is. Like small-minded. I read somewhere about hedonistic sustainability. Like ecological awareness that's not all about making do with less. Not about privation. Like inventing creative solutions. The Tarstoppers seem kind of dead-ended. Like they're just against things."

"I have a thousand responses to that. Like that big think-ing and mega projects and the whole macho Ayn Rand idea of massive objects thrusting into the sky are inherently destruc-tive. They're dwarfing, not human-scaled for anyone's com-fort. Innovation can be just as exciting on the human scale. We've been brain-washed into thinking bigger is better and small is mingy."

"Isn't there something in us though that likes grandeur and awe and all that stuff? We've been building things like Stone-henge and the pyramids forever."

He didn't really want to listen to Deke's answer; he was just making conversation. As Deke went on, Armie wondered why he did that, asked a question rather than just going his own way. Here he was, looking at his uncle like he was dutifully, politely paying attention and actually learning something, while his mind wandered. He knew Deke's position; he'd heard it all before. He'd heard it from his grandmother, who always seemed so sure she knew the best way forward. The year he'd spent in Toronto involved quite a few dinners at his grand-mother's, Deke usually there, other people, like Marilyn really believed something would come out of all the talk and argument around the table. She used to challenge him when he was too quiet, like he was her representative of his generation and he had to speak up for her guests. He had very mixed feelings about his grandmother, admiration for her drive and involvement, unease with her bullying. She was the opposite of his own, nonintrusive mother.

He broke in. "I didn't get a lot of sleep last night. As you say, relationship problems. I'm really in need of some down time."

He waited for Deke to let him go, wishing he could just turn and leave without it. He got a glass and the milk out of the fridge.

Deke was checking his messages. "What the fuck's this? I'm being kicked out? Your fucking old man's just told me to get out. He's finally read my blog and he's in a high snit."

What could Armie say to that?

"Do you read it?" Deke demanded. "Do you take offence? I can't believe he's taken it so personally."

Armie shook his head. "Sorry, no." Sorry, sorry, sorry. He shouldn't apologize. "What are you going to do?"

"Move into a tent, I guess. But that's not the point. You'd think the least he could do for the cause is let me stay here. He's always been too thin-skinned. I've had to be careful around him my whole life. I was born with this lid over me, the big bro already there and keeping me down. Fuck him. I'll write what I want to write. This thing is bigger than us. It's just like him to make it petty and personal."

"Hey. This is my dad you're talking about."

Deke was startled for a second. "One part of growing up is seeing your parents for who they are. As very, very human. I don't think you've got there yet."

Agree with him or he'd insult you. Armie was starting to lean heavily towards his dad. "What kind of stuff did you write about him?"

Deke rubbed his head all over with both hands, a characteristic gesture of frustration with the details of life, his curly ragged hair even wilder afterwards. "I can't even remember. He thinks I put your mom in danger writing about the guy stalking her but it's me they're after, not her. Maybe I used him as an example of the kind of well-meaning guy who fails to get involved. And I make no bones about how much I dislike that friend of his."

"Jason."

"What? Yeah, I guess. I'm making points. It's not personal. Your dad takes everything way too personally. We're trying to change the world here."

"Look, it's got nothing to do with me. I'm not even going to say sorry. Maybe it's better for you to be in the park with the other Tarstoppers. Right now I've got to get some sleep. I'll see you later."

From downstairs on his bed, he could hear Deke banging around in the other bedroom, then in the bathroom. Armie felt like a zombie, so tired his mind was dying. The worst part had been this morning when he'd slipped out of Katie's bed, leaving her asleep, but then he'd had to confront her parents in the kitchen. What were they even doing up at six? It had taken him a long time to get used to the idea of sleeping with Katie in her parents' house, to realize they would indulge Katie in whatever she wanted. Katie was like a rare plant her parents had nurtured and brought to bloom and they looked to her for what nutrients she might need. If it was sex and intimacy with Armie then so be it. If she sometimes seemed high and disoriented, that was Katie's business. Maybe it was because her parents were older and they'd waited for her for so long. Armie's own parents found Katie's parents a little peculiar, almost laughable in their fixation on Katie.

So what could he have done this morning? Run out on them and never have seen her parents again after practically living in their house off and on for three years? Said so long, it's been nice? In the kitchen, they'd looked at him with such concern and apprehension he'd wanted to hide or back out. He mostly thought it was Katie's mom, Sheila, who was the protective one and Jim just went along. Sheila did volunteer work; she read a lot of fiction and went to book clubs; she played bridge. And she was there for Katie.

Jim had said, "Katie told us you're probably breaking up."

All Armie could do was nod.

"We don't blame you. Really. You kids are only twenty. You're nowhere near ready to get married or anything. We understand that you can't just stay in this pattern for years and years. It's just hard for us when Katie suffers. You want somehow to be able to spare her, you know? When she suffers, we suffer even more."

And with that Sheila had begun to cry on a big intake of air. When Jim had gone to put his arms around her, Armie had had to leave. He'd sort of waved and Jim had nodded over Sheila's shoulder. He'd escaped the hugs. He was getting awfully tired of being constantly hugged.

It had almost come to seem normal, how they hovered, how they drove him and Katie wherever they wanted to go, how they cooked just for their tastes.. Her parents were united in their dedication to loving and encouraging Katie, like the support team of an elite athlete or a politician. To leave them was like leaving home and as soon as you were out the door you realized just how queer the whole arrangement and dynamic was. What had he been thinking all this time?

He was too tired to think. He had the feeling he'd sleep now for a couple of hours and wake up in a new place, his head totally rearranged.

●

THE WHOLLY GREEN GIANT
5:31 PM

The Bro's thrown me out because of what I've written here. Can you believe it? He finally read it. Wouldn't you think he'd have had enough interest to have been reading it all along? I'm just as glad to be out of there though. He & his wife are such representatives of the well-meaning solid citizens who make their token efforts like recycling & are aware of what's facing us but would fly off to Europe tomorrow without a qualm. Fly over the Arctic on their way & dump all that carbon dioxide into the air over the most sensitive part of the planet. They fly there all the time. The sis-in-law loves Europe. The sis-in-law who is an event planner for the oil industry – I kid you not. Corporate functions. Getting their name out there as good guys who contribute to the community – like they're meanwhile not paying nearly their fair share of taxes & royalties – not to mention raping the earth & causing the end times with their contribution to global warming. But I'm not supposed to criticize the sis-in-law. With her expensive German car and her high heels and designer-label wardrobe.

●

Shannon had been out of the office most of the day, one meeting after another with clients. It felt better to be on the move, not pinned in place. She'd walked to her meetings downtown, down back alleys and through buildings, aware at all times of who might be watching. Only one of her clients seemed to be wavering on her Stampede commitment. A number seemed to think that the Stampede itself would go ahead but Shannon knew her city: nothing would stop it, which was a point of pride.

Aside from a brief text exchange at lunch she hadn't been in touch with Tim all day. Now, back at the office late in the afternoon, she accessed all his messages, text and phone. *Where are you? Are you okay? I need you to stay in touch. Things happening.*

"What's happening?" she demanded when he picked up.

"Don't panic. All good things. But you can't just be un-available with all that's going on. First of all, has that guy been bothering you? Anything more? Any more cancellations?"

"No, everyone's holding tight. I've been on the go all day. Tell me what's going on. What good things?"

"Armie's broken up with Katie. Just a short text when I texted him. That's all he said: broke up with Katie, don't want to talk about it."

"Halleluiah. What else?"

"I've thrown Deke out. I read his blog at lunch. I wasn't going to tell you about it but I have to. Jason alerted me to it. I'd really been resisting reading it. It was quite a shock. Way too personal. Our childhood, my failings: it's all out there for anyone to read. I know Connor's reading it and everyone here at work is reading it, thanks to him. Luckily I had a meeting downtown this afternoon and I could escape. And God only knows what Deke wrote before this. I didn't go back in it to see."

"Why did you read it at all?"

"You of all people should understand that. Sometimes you just have to know the worst. In the end evading it takes up more energy than knowing."

"It's for sure I'm not going anywhere near it. I can imag-ine what he's got to say about me. Why would I want to know? So did you talk to Derek or just text him?"

"An e-mail."

"It doesn't mean he'll go. Be prepared. Just like Armie

breaking up with Katie doesn't mean that's over. I don't trust either of them, Derek or Katie, not to find a way back in."

"Can you really just not want to know what Deke's written? People you know are reading it. I know Lori is, Jason, of course. Probably Madison, she could have found it. Maybe everyone in your office. Aren't you curious about the information they're taking in about you?"

"Misinformation. No. Would I go on Madison's Facebook, if I could, to see what she has to say about me? No. Do I want to know what Ardith says to her boyfriend about me? Again, no."

"Connor's been smirking at me since this began."

"Another reason to get rid of him. Maybe if you've stood up to your brother and thrown him out, now you can do something about Connor."

She'd been encouraging Tim to get rid of Connor for months now. Single, good-looking, full of himself, Connor had treated her, at fundraising events when she ran into him, as a fellow superior being as he'd made sly jokes about the hapless do-gooders. She'd wanted to knee him.

"One thing at a time," Tim said. "I was hoping there might be some chance of you coming home tonight, with Deke gone, to talk to Armie, but it doesn't sound like you have much faith Deke won't be there."

"Maybe on the weekend. If he stays away. We'll see. I'll call Armie later."

"That Matt guy's probably reading the blog. Have you thought of that? You don't know what he's gleaning about you. He could be outside waiting for you again. I could come and pick you up."

"I'll be okay. I don't care what he knows about me. You're getting a little paranoid."

"Oh, no doubt."

"I'll talk to you later."

After work, as she walked west on Eleventh Avenue towards Gizelle's again, she faced straight ahead. Dense towering thunderheads advanced in the sky. She could smell the ozone in the air. That's what she needed, a crashing deafening storm, the opening up of the heavens to clear the air. And she wouldn't even be at home to rush around trying to protect her garden.

She knew Matt would be waiting for her. She hadn't even looked around for him on the street, she was so sure he'd be at the condo when he wasn't outside the office building. He stood with his back to her, on his phone. Why had the shape of this man, the rough texture of his hair, the breadth of his shoulders, the compactness of his body, penetrated all her defenses, causing her body to jack like this, her brain to stall? She felt she knew him in a more fundamental way than she did Tim. Which had to be totally illusory. She'd almost snuck by him but then he grabbed her arm.

"No, you don't," he said. "Nice try."

It was as though they were long beyond civilities. Hazel eyes right into hers. He wasn't even that good-looking. Rougher, coarser, than Tim. Older. She was not the kind of woman who responded to other men this way. She would never have believed she could feel this electric around another man. Some ancient part of her brain had to have been turned on by the stress of the situation for her to crave this man. She pulled away.

"Have a drink with me. Dinner. You have to eat. What could it hurt?"

"No. Why would I?" She started to walk towards the door.

"Your husband seemed like a nice guy but he's a little pale for you, I thought. Don't you ever feel trapped in your safe and careful life?"

She turned. "You don't know anything about me. It's all cliché, anything you've found out. Or in the case of my brother-in-law, it's from a very unreliable witness. You don't need me. Everything you need to know about him is on his blog."

"What makes you think I'm after your brother-in-law?"

"I'm going up. Please don't find a way into the building and follow me. I'll call security. I mean it."

She kept walking, into the lobby. She pressed the security code. After she'd been buzzed in, she heard the satisfying clunk of the door behind her. She didn't look back. She wouldn't tell Tim.

●

The first big rumble of thunder jolted Tim awake. He must have dozed off on the sofa. It was almost ten. The light was on in the kitchen and he hoped it wasn't Deke. He didn't know what he'd do if Deke had just returned, ignoring Tim's order. But it was Armie in the kitchen, in his pajama bottoms and a grey t-shirt, his laptop open in front of him while he ate from a bowl of cereal. How many bowls of cereal could someone eat in a day? He'd slept through supper. What was going on with Armie?

Outside the bay window the back yard was flashed out of the darkness by a vertical slice of lightning that illuminated a sudden wind whipping the trees. "We're going to get it," Tim said to him in passing as he rushed out onto the deck to protect Shannon's begonias and dahlias with the wooden boxes he'd years ago devised against hail damage. Thunder exploded to the north and the first heavy splats of rain hit his hair and his shirt. Armie came out to help.

Back in the kitchen at the table after they'd dried off, Tim nodded at the iPad and said to Armie, "So, are you still studying economics?"

Armie laughed. "No. Just surfing." He closed it down. "Are you feeling guilty about exiling Uncle Deke out into a storm?"

"How'd you know about that?"

"He was here when I got home from work. He read your e-mail while I was with him."

"He'll find a tent. He should be sharing the experience with his fellow travellers, don't you think? He can't write about it properly if he doesn't."

"He was pretty mad. He said you were thin-skinned for taking his blog so personally."

"Anyone he tromps on as he goes after what he wants is just being overly sensitive if they complain or object. I've had endless experience with Deke. You're still not reading it?"

Armie shook his head. "I hear more than enough of his views as it is."

"It's about a lot more than the environment. He really gets into his relationship with me, and with your mom."

"Has she read it?"

"Luckily, no. And she won't. Thank God. You know your mom, she doesn't go looking for trouble. But she'd be furious."

"Does he talk about me?"

Tim shrugged. "I only read the posting from last night. He didn't mention you but that's not to say you're not in there earlier. My advice is not to go looking."

Armie was thinking through the implication of this knowledge that his personal life might be out there for anyone to read. As seen through his uncle's eyes. "Like do people at the Agency read it? Are you like notorious?"

"I'm sure everyone at work is avidly reading it. Everyone I know probably. It's something I'm going to have to live with."

The rain smashed down like it had been hurled towards the ground. The beginning of a storm was when hail in the mix could start shattering glass, shredding leaves, exploding on the pavement. At the beginning or at the end of a storm. The rain hit so hard it sounded like hail but in the next flash of lightning Tim could see no white balls bouncing off the lawn or the deck. Usually storms moved quickly. This one seemed to be settling in right overhead. Long splits of light ripped the sky with the explosive noise of it almost simultaneous.

Tim turned to follow Armie's sudden peering into the yard. In the next flare of light he saw the cluster of people who had caught Armie's attention. With black plastic bags and blue tarps over their heads, they looked like ghosts bent towards the back door, with a giant monster in the lead. Tim met Armie's eye. There was no choice here.

Tim opened the back door to the wind and the sheets of driving cold rain. Deke lifted his head and said, "Just the small kids and the sickest." Tim stood back as they pushed down the basement stairs, most of them lifting their head coverings to smile at him or nod. As they headed down the stairs they were like mounds, dripping, miserable, maybe ten people in all and a couple of children. Two babies in their mother's arms as they threw back their plastic coverings. Was one of them the young woman whose tent faced his house? He'd never seen her up close.

Tim said to Deke, who was still at the top of the stairs, "There are two blow-up mattresses in the main cupboard. More blankets in the closet in the laundry room. I'll see what I can find up here. Wait here a sec." He found towels and hairdryers and thrust them into Derek's arms. He himself was not going downstairs. "Better make sure no one's gone into Armie's room. And everybody out first thing in the morning."

Deke gave him the exasperated look that said, always with the limits, always protecting yourself. Tim stared back. But Deke had people to look after and he couldn't spend any more time on the shortcomings of his brother.

Back at the table, Armie said, "You had to do it. Let's hope Deke cleans it up in the morning."

"His cause is more important than petty details like that. And surprise, surprise, he's got himself in out of the rain. I guess that's pretty cynical of me. Sorry. I'm at a low point."

"What's with this guy stalking Mom? Deke told me about it."

"Did he tell you it's the CIA and they're really after him?"

Armie smiled. "No?"

"We don't know who he is. He says he's here with an American news network and just wanted to talk to her. Who knows? Maybe he's legit. He's scared her though. He's pretty persistent."

"Have you seen him?"

"Last night. I picked her up at a restaurant. He'd even chased after her into a bathroom."

"What did you do?"

"I didn't have to do anything. He left. Very cocky." Oh, what the hell, Tim thought, let's get everything out. "What's happened with Katie?"

Caught off guard, Armie shrugged, flailed around for a response. He seemed so distressed to have her brought back to the forefront of his mind that Tim had to let him off. "No, it's okay. You don't have to say."

"No, it's okay. I guess we're breaking up. Very slowly. It's me. I told her I need a little time on my own to sort stuff out but we both know it's ending. I really hate hurting her."

"Sounds like you're doing it as gently as you can. We outgrow people. Or go in different directions. It happens."

"And yet you and Mom have been married for like twenty-five years."

"Amazing, isn't it? It's a lot of luck. I think Katie's on a very narrow path. You're more wide-ranging. It was bound to happen. Nobody's fault. But not easy."

"She shouldn't have to change. She is who she's always been. It makes me seem fickle."

"You're twenty. You're still forming. You've been exposed to a lot of influences. You're a thinker. Katie seems to be all feeling."

"I'm going to feel guilty for a long time. Maybe forever."

"Maybe. But it'll fade. It'll be a scar. They accumulate through life. Me and Deke. Speaking of whom, I'm going to bed before he comes up. Anytime I'm around him, all kinds of scars start itching and acting up like crazy. Use the upstairs bathroom if you want. There's a new toothbrush in the drawer."

It obviously hadn't occurred to Armie how many people he would be sharing the basement with tonight. Tim put his hand on his arm in consolation and said goodnight.

●

Armie had been talking to Katie for hours now, listening to her cry and encouraging her connections to help her incorporate this break-up. She was no better than she ever was at finding words for any of her feelings. He had to think like her, play her game of connections and repeats, trying to make this break-up fit. For her, all of life fit together in a mosaic of images and time. She had her special days – June eleventh every year, November third – six or seven of them a year when magic was supposed to happen. She had her lucky numbers, letters, signs. She could turn an ordinary day around in her mind and dramatize it with three sightings of her totem bird, a flicker. She'd text him in a frenzy of significance: three, three, three! She'd wait for the appearance of a certain shade of very dark red or the random hearing as she surfed the Net of an obscure Tunisian singer who communicated directly to her. She ate an avocado every day and they figured everywhere in her art. There was a long list of talismanic objects and states. This break-up had to be augured. June eleventh was less than a week away. There had to be an epiphany coming or some kind of transformation after the darkness. It was the least he could do to suggest possible meanings while she picked over the clues and divined the images.

He'd always resisted her efforts to impose meaning on his own life in this way, insisting on the randomness of good days and bad. Lately he'd told her less and less, withholding incidents and memories because of how she'd start knitting them into a pattern for him. To counteract Katie's conviction of meaning in everything, he'd been reading about the science of the brain, about its firings and trillions of interactions, how it was designed to make connections and find patterns. It's in your brain, he wanted to tell her, to insist. It's your brain linking things up, it's not in the occurrences and events and objects themselves. It no longer fascinated him how she made her art from these themes and repetitions and images.

But as much as he had once been intrigued by her self-referential universe, it had been the sex, not the shared left-handedness or the flicker that had flown above them the first time they'd talked back in high school, that had kept him rapt by her. Every bit of sensation in her body was as encouraged by her as the repetition of signs and symbols. Freed by her pills, her chemical enhancers, she'd indulge any fantasy, pursue any desire no matter how gross or peculiar. She'd scared him sometimes. And then it would turn up in her art, not blatantly, but in among the other themes and repetitions. Only he would know what some of it referenced. Tongue-like snakes in holes. Snakes were another of her totems. And breasts, her fascination with breasts, cutting pictures of them out of magazines, downloading images from specialist porn sites in search of the perfect ones. He could imagine that one day she'd come out as a lesbian. For a while anyway. Someone in art school would come on to her and she'd end up with a brush cut and Doc Martens, for a while, he thought, though he wasn't proud of his pettiness.

He'd stayed because of the sex, which he'd admitted to her. They were both loath to give it up. "What if I never have that with anyone else?" she'd wailed and Armie, too, worried that he'd never get to that place of freedom and trust again.

"Don't talk it out, remember?" he said to her on the phone now. "Get back to your work. Use the images." This was pretty much all he'd been saying to her, in different ways.

As he listened to her ramblings again, he was aware of the dozen or so people in the basement with him, the toilet flushing so many times, the shower going non-stop, voices, a baby crying for a while, a lot of coughing. How could he be this physically close to so many strangers and yet be talking to Katie in such an intimate way? For a while the thunder had masked their conversation but it had rolled away now. He thought about the distance between him and Katie. They no longer shared a way of seeing the world, if they ever had. Walls upon walls.

Deke had looked in on him a while ago and Armie had been just glad to be busy on the phone. Growing up, he'd always wanted a brother but he could see that a brother could be even further removed from you than a sister.

His mind had drifted, as it had more and more with Katie except during sex. He wanted to stop listening and get back to what he'd been reading.

"Katie, enough for tonight," he said. "Don't talk it all out, remember? Save it for your art. Let it incubate."

He thought of how predictable she was, how he knew what to say to her to divert her. It was like giving up the knowledge you had of a city when you no longer lived there, like his of Toronto, as the sense of a place faded and was forgotten. He'd probably never know anyone again as well as he knew Katie.

He wanted out. Like an escape to the surface. Out of his job, out of his relationship, out of living at home like a kid, just out.

What had Deke written about him? If he read it, would he see himself clearly and would an obvious course of action occur to him? But he knew what Deke would say about him. He was too much like his dad; he was too much on the fence, thinking too much. Which was no help. He wouldn't read it. For tonight, anyway, he had enough strength to resist his curiosity.

THURSDAY
JUNE 7 2012

THE WHOLLY GREEN GIANT
1:21 AM

To add to our woes there's this massive thunderstorm tonight. What a mess. The mud & the temp dropping to down around freezing. Folks are low anyway. For the sick – which means almost everybody – & those with little kids & not a very waterproof tent it was desperate. So I round up the worst off & bring them over to the Bro's basement. He'll probably want a medal now for letting them in – like it's this big sacrifice, what any normal person would do for another. We're a sorry group of humanity though – folks coughing & kids crying & everyone dirty & wet. They're all demoralized. & meanwhile the Bro is harassing me about including him & the sis-in-law in here. Can you believe it? With all that's going on?

No hope of getting his car out this morning, with a couple of tents set up in the alley. Tim thought he might drown in people, as his house filled up, basement first, as his neighbourhood overflowed. None of the Tarstoppers in the basement were up yet, as they no doubt relished the warmth and cleanliness. He'd heard the shower downstairs run for what seemed like hours last night. Armie would have long since left for work.

He started walking east to catch the bus. Now he knew how most of their clients got around. Not easily. Sitting on the bus, he felt like he was in high school again, caught up in one of his brother's schemes that left him exposed and frustrated. Powerless. Like the time Deke had showed a goopy letter around school that Tim had written to Melissa Drainy, never intending to send it.

There was nothing he could do about the stories of him that Deke had now planted in people's minds. It wouldn't help to know what other stories he'd told, although he could guess. Was it really any different than the portraits people created from all kinds of sources, from expressions he didn't know he wore, from gossip and overheard remarks and assumptions? Didn't everyone live in a cloud of outside opinion about them that they mostly knew nothing about? A lot of people were oblivious as to how they came across. Connor, Deke. His dad, everyone to some degree. Those who read Deke's blog would add it to their impression of him. It was all beyond his control. He just didn't want to be too self-conscious today, looking into people's eyes. He'd be tamping his imagination down all day.

●

THE WHOLLY GREEN GIANT
11:17 AM

So where are we now? I've been here a week although it feels like half my life. Conditions are deteriorating with all the rain but we're hanging in. We've mostly adjusted to not having the Wall to go to every day. There are lots more folks around now that there aren't barricades around this part of the city. We're having trouble feeding everybody & finding places for them to sleep but mostly we're managing. At our camp there's a big assembly tonight to talk about the next step & the long term. Everybody's committed. We're okay here.

But we're just one small park. The scale of the thing is now way beyond anything that's ever happened. Even I have to admit this whole thing is getting a little unwieldy. Whoever thought there'd be this many of us? The different camps aren't communicating very well. You can go online & find all the efforts to get us organized. It's only been a week & a half since Wendy & the boys sprang into action. Which is unbelievable. It's blown up so fast – which is both a good thing for our purposes & a bad thing in that it's really tough to get organized with this many people & demonstrate to the world the kind of alternatives we're proposing. There are camps that are not reporting so we have no idea what's going on & some that are more for anarchy – burn down the city. Some of the newer ones outside the centre are coming from some very strange places. There's a coven of witches out there. It's a wild read on the Net with all the weird ideas. One group thinks aliens are returning to lead us. Every loony out there seems to be coming to Calgary to get their wacko views out to the world. Like environmentalists are just another fringe group & this is one big fringe convention. It's more than a little galling. So we've got all these bands of people who are almost like different species. This could become a big problem. They sure aren't going to be listening to us. They've got their own agendas to get out – which will just mess up our clear message. We all get called Tarstoppers but Occupiers & anarchists & anti-globalists have quite different agendas than us. The Occupier-types are more about inequality – the whole one per cent having all the money thing. While we agree it's an issue we think it's nothing compared to environmental destruction. We're with the anarchists in wanting to bring the whole capitalist system to its knees but we want more regulation not less.

& then there's the Natives. They're using the occasion to come together from all over the continent to push for more than just protecting the environment. They're our natural allies on the sacredness of the land but they've got lots of other issues they want to push. Treaty rights & land claims, poverty. If this many Natives had gathered on their own it'd be an earth-shaking event but now they're just one of many.

And even among ourselves there's a big split between those who want to accommodate industry and make them environ-mentally responsible and those of us like me who want a whole backtrack into a pre-industrial world. These days the Nature

Conservancy is working with Dow Chemical to establish forests around their plants. How misguided it that? You want to bang your head.

So that's what all the talk is right now. How do we bring everyone together under a common cause? When you think about it it's a big question for the whole society. We think of the culture as being full of mindless consuming sheep, all conforming to the corporate agenda, but thanks to the Net there's more & more fringe stuff out there. & a lot of it is no help to us.

It also means the Wildcatters are no more a homogenous force than we are. Far from it. You've got Tea Partiers & neo-Nazis & libertarians & evangelicals & paranoid schizophrenics & your average criminal out there against us. & thousands of ordinary know-nothing rednecks. The only thing they'd agree on is their hatred for lefties & governments.

The whole thing can make your head spin with its complexities & inconsistencies.

In my darkest moments I don't know which thing I fear is going to defeat us in the end – our own success or the murderous thugs out to get us.

I was going to delete that last downer but I'll let it stand.

●

She was safe at work as nowhere else. At noon, Shannon realized she'd been so immersed in what she was doing for the past hour that she hadn't once thought about the Tarstoppers or about Matt. Progress. Madison seemed not to be constantly checking for news but was instead actually working. Shannon knew the crisis wasn't over but she could feel the loosening in herself. It would end. It was inevitable. She just had to keep her head down and wait it out.

She called Tim, who'd left a number of messages. She'd texted him first thing that she was fine but that was as much as she felt she owed him. And she was fine.

She could cope with clients' jitters, she could soothe them, it was what she did. And she could deal with Matt. When she'd reached the condo last night, Gizelle thankfully not home, she'd gone to her room and sat in a mediation pose until the two parts of herself, the watcher and the wayward body, got back into better balance. She wouldn't give in to this hormonal obsession, this lust, whatever she should call it. Infatuation was much too pale a word for it. It was just the weird way her very deep anxiety was manifesting.

On the phone she immediately knew from Tim's voice, as he said hi and asked how she was, that something had happened that he was afraid to tell her. She wanted to hang up. Instead she said, "Tell me what's going on. I can hear it in your voice. I don't want to play around."

"How do you do that? I've only said a couple of words."

"Tim. It's about Derek, isn't it? You weren't able to keep him out. He's as at home in my house as he ever was."

"Not so fast. He did pack up and go, he did, but then there was that big thunderstorm last night. He brought over some people. Some small children, a few people who were sick. What could I do?"

So that was why he was sounding apologetic. "They stayed all night? What does the basement look like now? And I'll bet Derek had to stay as well, to take care of everyone."

"He was supposed to be cleaning up this morning. Everyone will be gone. Deke will go. I'll throw him out again if I have to. I was hoping you might consider coming home but I guess that's less likely now."

"As I said before, maybe on the weekend. We'll see what happens. How's Armie doing? He texted me that he wasn't ready to talk about the break-up yet."

"We talked a little bit last night. He feels really guilty. You know Armie. I think he's still talking to her as much as ever but he seems pretty sure it's over."

"Let's hope. For lots of things. The end of Derek. The end of this whole horrible time."

"No word from the guy?"

"I'm hoping for the end of him as well."

●

On his way home from work, Armie stopped at the end of his alley. What was going on? Where had all these people come from? The alley was full of people and tents. Were Tarstoppers from all over the city congregating here near the old centre of action, seeking safety in numbers? Weren't they even more vulnerable densely packed like this? How were they going to feed all these people, accommodate their bodily functions? The shower had run for hours last night, long after it would have run out of hot water. He'd heard that everyone was sick in the park. It never dried out and it reeked. How long could they go on?

Deke hadn't done too bad a job of cleaning up the basement. The towels and blankets were all heaped on the laundry room floor and Armie put a load in the washer. Last night, between the coughing and the toilet flushing and arguing in his mind with Katie, he again had not gotten much sleep. Now he planned to sleep until midnight; then he'd get up for something to eat. With luck he would have missed any confrontation between his dad and Deke, if Deke came back, and any more talk with his dad, who seemed more jacked up than anyone, between the guy stalking his wife and his brother exposing him on his blog, never mind the Tarstoppers taking over. Armie just wanted oblivion.

FRIDAY
JUNE 8 2012

Now what? Sitting at his desk Friday morning, Tim could hear the commotion outside his office. Was no one doing anything but tuning in to updates on the Tarstopper situation? It was getting out of hand. He was like Shannon: he didn't want to know, but it looked like he had no choice now as Connor, who lived on the leading edge of what was new, swung his big head into Tim's office. Hands on the doorjambs like he'd arrested himself in midflight, he said, "All hell's broken loose. A bunch of Wildcatters started shooting at a park full of Tarstoppers. At least fifteen dead. It's a massacre."

"Where was this?" That was his first thought. After looking after all those Tarstoppers last Sunday, they'd become real people to him, no longer a little tainted with otherness. "Not in my park."

"Oh, yeah. No. Windsor Park. South of you. I'll keep you posted." And he was gone.

Tim phoned Shannon on her work line. "Have you heard?"

"I don't want to talk about it Madison couldn't stop herself from telling me. Are we sure Armie's at work?"

"Very sure. I've texted him but no answer yet. I can just imagine all the wild opinions he'll get from the guys at work. He doesn't check his messages until noon."

"I bet every single person in the city knows about this. Work has stopped all over town. Everyone's on a device. We should hear from him soon."

"You know, I think I'm starting to agree with you that it's dangerous to stir people up. I know you think I can be naïve. Too trusting. But first the triangle park and now this."

"I don't want to be right about how people can go amok. I drive by Windsor Park any time I go to Chinook Centre to shop. I can't put the two together. People are being killed – shot, bludgeoned, mowed down – while a few blocks away shoppers walk the mall and sift through clothing racks? The attacks and deaths are my worst imaginings taking form in real life. It's like war. There are people around who will kill other people because of an idea. Because of their fear of them."

"Maybe that Matt guy, whatever he is, press or security, will be too busy with this development to come after you again."

"That seems a pretty self-involved way to think, when people are losing their lives. After the hostages were released, I'd actually started to think the whole thing was winding down, that it would just dissipate. I wanted so badly to believe that to be the case. I used to think my fear of advancing decay and imminent catastrophe was a private neurosis, something for family and friends to tease me about, me always expecting things to fall apart. But this situation is my personal fear blown out into the world. Sometimes I think I'm hallucinating it."

"You're not imagining this. Let me know if you hear from Armie. I'll do the same."

To keep his mind off the carnage in the park, Tim pictured Armie at work. It had been an education for Armie to get to know some of his co-workers. After his one year at university, he'd wanted to work at honest labour, as he'd called it, while he thought about what to do with his life. Shannon had been more distressed than Tim by Armie's decision not to go back to school, but over the past year Tim too had begun to worry that Armie would get stuck in low-end jobs. At least he was starting to think ahead, becoming interested in economics and tearing himself away from Katie's extreme inwardness. At work Armie would be horrified by the hate in his co-workers. Tim felt for him but also thought maybe it might jolt him out of the trance he seemed to live in.

A text from Jason. *Beyond belief.*

Tim texted back: *How do you explain Wildcatters? Who would do this?*

Fear and ignorance. *Deke okay?*

He hadn't thought of his brother. There'd be no reason for him to be in Windsor Park but he hadn't given him a thought. Which said something about him. He should probably show some concern and check around.

He looked at his screen. He had only written one sentence of his report for the Board meeting. He wouldn't look to see if anything more had happened in the city, although he was sure the staff was constantly checking. Someone, probably Connor, would alert him if there was more. This could be the first of many attacks. It was like the whole city had somehow got lost in a nightmare of Shannon's.

◆

THE WHOLLY GREEN GIANT
11:49 AM

I'm in deep shock. I've just come from a tour of the site. It's only blocks from here. It could have been us. Fuck. I know I've promised to be profanity-free here but fuck. What kind of animals would do this? Makes the beatings in the triangle park insignificant. We're starting to think humanity not worth saving from itself.

Official count thirteen dead & twenty-seven injured & three of them on life support. The park was so full of people that the bullets were ricocheting all over everywhere. Afterwards folks stumbling around in shock like we've all gotten too used to seeing on TV & the Net after a shooting rampage somewhere. Usually that's some lone deranged guy but this was like ten of them. Or twenty. Accounts vary. You're not counting your assailants when you've diving for cover.

Soon as we got the first tweet we were on our way. Sirens already screaming from all directions. But it was all over before we got there hoofing as fast as we could. We got in before the cops taped off the whole area. They caught two of the lunatics. This guy who's dying anyway clamps the cuffs he has from staying put at a protest onto his attacker's ankle. Imagine having the presence of mind to do that. Clamps him to a tent pole buried deep in the ground. That's part of what's so horrific about this – it was up close & personal & not long distance with scopes & assault rifles. A bunch of ordinary monsters with nice little handguns wandering among us & shooting people between the eyes. They know no one's firing back. I never do figure how the other guy got caught. Maybe the idiot shot himself in the foot – wouldn't surprise me. I get a glimpse of the two of them as they're stuffed into cop cars. One looked like you'd expect – bald & tough. But the other one looked like he could almost be one of us. Smaller & almost bookish. Wearing glasses. What were they thinking? The media'll be analyzing them forever. They can't all be mentally ill.

Why do they hate us so much? Makes me think how after 9/11 Americans kept asking that. With no awareness of how their fat friendly lifestyle is backed by their representatives interfering & manipulating & bullying countries all over the world. So what are we doing that's got these guys so riled they'd kill us all if they could? We have to threaten their way of life. Us pinkos. You sure don't hear that term very much anymore. Socialist peaceniks. Globalists. Which is really weird because we're dead set against so-called globalization & having the world ruled by corporations. You'd think that'd give us common cause. But they want to go back sixty years or so & have the US dominate again. Like ending multiculturalism or any of the other things they hate will take them back to that imaginary perfect time of freedom. Even I – the great believer in communication – know these guys are impossible to talk to. They're so ignorant & so full of conspiracy paranoia they're really like some lower form of life. Like medieval peasants.

So we're milling around in shock & then a miracle happens. Who comes walking among us but Wendy & her two Apostles. She should be in white flowing robes but instead she's in black jeans & hoodie. Again I'm aware of how small she is – almost like a kid. James & Paul are twice her size but still not big men. Maybe I should offer to be their bodyguard. They're out on bail. There are big environmental organizations & some very wealthy people backing us – mostly Americans, to give credit. Somebody would have paid for top lawyers for Wendy & her boys. Maybe the powers-that-be want her out on the street anyway – where some sharpshooter will eliminate her. But then they'd have to hope that eventually her martyrdom would get forgotten & she wouldn't become like Jesus to our movement. It's not like she's charismatic. I've never seen an image of her smiling – never mind laughing. The stuff she used to write on the Net even I found hard to read it was so dry. She never shows any personality. & yet she's our leader whether she wants it or not – she says not. There's this hush when she appears. She goes around to the in-jured – those not badly enough hurt to have been taken to hos-pital. We almost expect miraculous healing from the laying on of hands. You can see the cops watching her as they're interviewing people & you know they think she should still be in jail.

& then – I still can't believe it – she picks me out. She knows who I am. I know I'm hard to miss in my big green shirt but who-ever thought Wendy was reading this blog? She puts her hand on my arm – she comes up not much past my waist in height – & tells me how central I am to the Tarstopper movement. Our spokesperson. The human side of the story. Keep it up, she says. History will remember me. I'm staring down at this plain unsmiling oriental woman hoping for something earth-shaking & I have to confess it doesn't come. I don't mean I wasn't thrilled to my toes to have her single me out, but she's not going to change the world with her mesmerism, just by her brave actions. She doesn't even smile at me as she moves away. You have to give it to her – she's being true to herself. She's living her beliefs. She hates the celebrity culture & doesn't want to be part of it. The rumour is that she'll disappear now. She was only an instigator. She doesn't believe in hierarchy & leadership. This is a mass movement. She's written that she wouldn't trust anyone not to be twisted by the leadership role – even herself. She believes in the wisdom of the collective. Which is what all those Wildcatters hate – any threat to their precious individual freedom – never mind that it's left them alienated & psychotic & their culture so neurotic & materialistic it's practically dysfunctional. Wendy & the boys don't stay long. I hear that they're going home to Vancouver until their court date. Back to anonymity.

When I go to leave the park I'm questioned by a cop. You know – why was I here at the shooting? I explain. You can tell this guy is full of contempt for all of us. I don't have any ID on me, which irks him. He says, how's he to know I'm not one of the shooters? I ask how having my ID would help him with that. He says how does he know I am who I say I am – Derek Maddox? I don't know why I gave him my real name. Maybe I was a little full of myself after being tapped on the shoulder by Wendy. Maybe I wanted this guy to know I'm not nobody. Not proud of that.

He finds me on his computer – picture & all. I just look at him. He hates me as much as any Wildcatter does. I bet he wishes they'd kill us all. He gets excited by whatever comes up. He's got a live one. I wish I could see what they've got on me. He has to show me off to a few of the other cops but in the end he has to let me go. He'd give me a kick in the groin if he could get away with it.

All this hate is getting to me. We're trying to tell the world we're on a dangerous course – it's demonstrable – it's beyond doubt – & what do we get for it? It's not like we're pushing some weird religion or some hysterical over-reaction. Global warming is a scientific fact. The other stuff – like how bad our lifestyle is for us – is secondary. The main thing we're trying to get across is that we're poisoning the earth on which we are totally dependent. How can anyone argue with that? We've got to find ways to avoid despair. That's the big challenge now. We don't have to convince anyone of the validity of our cause we just have to stay here until the tarsands are shut down. But how do we keep up morale when we've being randomly picked off & slaughtered?

◆

Usually Armie didn't eat with the others in the lunch room at work. They called him the kid and put up with his eccentricities.

They liked to say that all kids were glued to their devices these days and have lost the ability to interact. But today it was instinctive to be among other people and not out on a bench on the lawn by himself where any passing nutcase could take a pot shot at him, like the city had been given a clearance for lawlessness now. He couldn't make what had happened seem real. Sometimes events pierced right through to him and other times some kind of internal block went up. On the Net the pictures of the carnage looked like a repeat of somewhere else, Norway or Oklahoma, not a real event that happened a few blocks away from his house in Calgary. One of the arrested Wildcatters was a German, from Germany, who'd only arrived in the city two days ago.

People had been murdered, slaughtered, not far from his house today. His mom would say it was nothing new. His mom, the History major, was always putting modern-day worries and calamities into historical perspective. Either she'd been really shaken by all she'd learned back then or it had been a corroboration of something already in her. It was a family joke that everything bad that happened was no surprise to her.

He heard the clamour of raised voices before he reached the lunch room. They talked over everything that happened in the world at lunch, watching the news the night before and listening to the radio in their cars in the morning so they'd be able to contribute to the discussion. They worked for a paycheck but also to be able to sit around tables at lunch and evaluate history as it formed. Usually Armie found their opinions simplistic and emotional. Certain topics reliably set them off: Quebec and its demands, the NDP, government spending on things like art or the new red peace bridge over the Bow River here in town. They'd be as outraged as if someone was hurting them personally. But today Armie had a need for real bodies around him, his usual Internet sources of opinion and perspective too disembodied and removed.

Even the top guys were here for lunch today. There was one big joined-together table and everyone was huddled around it. There were three women altogether, maybe twelve men. He was by far the youngest. Somebody said to him as he came into the room, "Don't you live close to there?"

All eyes looked to him. Armie could only nod.

They couldn't linger on him. There was too much to say. Brian, the loudest and most opinionated of them, who had been interrupted by Armie's arrival, raised his voice to reclaim the airspace. "I'll say it again: they were asking for it. Wave a red flag and sit there and you're going to get gored. Stupid cunts. Then we have to pay for the clean-up and the trials and the whole fucking mess. Millions and millions by the end. We should just refuse."

Curt, one of the managers, could silence Brian just by speaking up, for which Armie was grateful. "Only four of the people killed were local. This has nothing to do with us. We're just a site. Brian's right: we'll end up paying for it. It's the price of having the oilsands in our backyard, I guess. It sure makes you aware of the big forces at work in the world that usually seem remote."

This was too measured for most of them but they couldn't

call him on it because of his position. Armie'd been surprised by his co-workers' deference to bosses and their resentment of them, like kids and teachers, kids and parents. They still sucked up to them, like kids.

Brian had been silenced for the moment, which left room for Luke, more opinionated but less noisy, to speak up. "They should have put an end to it at the start. Back with the Occupiers last fall. Don't give people license. Clear them out however you have to. We're so afraid of using force in case images of violence cause outcries. See what it leads to if you don't stamp out protesters from the get-go? It was all preventable. How have the namby-pambies gotten such control over us? That's the big issue here. We sit back and let every airhead kid and hippie do what they want. Shit in the park. Block our streets. It's pathetic. I didn't think we'd be like that here. I thought we still had some frontier spirit. We don't listen when bleeding hearts want to shut down the Stampede because of the poor little animals so why are we sitting around letting a bunch of fairies take over who want to shut down the oilsands? Since we weren't strong in the beginning, all hell is going to break loose now." He was shaking his head like it was all foreseeable and everyone but him had been too dumb to see it. He'd probably been saying the same thing since the beginning and now he'd been satisfyingly validated. All these guys thought they alone saw the situation clearly.

Carly, the very overweight office manager, said, "A little kid was killed. What kind of parents put their kid in that kind of danger? What are they teaching a kid, to take it out of school to camp in a park far from home because of some stupid belief they have? The parents deserved to be shot."

Tom, one of the quiet ones, surprised them by saying, "I think the shooters deserve a medal. I wish they'd kill them all. Maybe now those Tarfuckers will get the hell out of here. They're all wimps: they'll run. You'll see."

Armie waited until someone else began to speak and then he got up and left. He wouldn't want Tom to think he was walking out on what he'd said, which he knew was way too polite of him but he worked with Tom and had no quarrel with him otherwise.

He found an unseen corner and went back online. He could easily find educated comment on the Net. But Brian and Tom could also find substantiation online for any of their wilder prejudices. If everyone sourced only the views they already agreed with, there'd be more and more polarization. They'd find proof that giant evil forces were trying to control the world, either international corporations despoiling the earth or socialist billionaires plotting to enslave everyone in a collective. It was all out there, evidence everywhere you looked.

When he first had gone to work here, he'd wanted just hard unthinking labour. He'd had the vague idea it would be an honest use of his time after wrestling with the doubt and confusion of what he was doing there in university that year. After work he could read and learn on his own without any particular goal in mind and not be dependent on his parents while he flapped around trying to find a direction. His parents had said the brewery was a waste of his abilities but he'd been stubborn. He'd gotten the job himself. Skinny as he was, he was very strong. But now he had to admit how bored he was by it. He had to find a job that didn't leave him mentally exhausted but was interesting enough so he wasn't totally bored. Or something that was so minimal, like a security guard or something, so that he could go on reading and investigating stuff while he was at work.

He walked back to the lunch room. There was something about the way he pushed in that made some of them look up. Over the top of whoever was speaking he said, "I think most of you are ignorant assholes."

Now he'd done it. No going back from this. He couldn't believe he'd done it. Who was that guy? He'd left again before anyone could react.

●

THE WHOLLY GREEN GIANT
4:03 PM
At least there haven't been any more massacres. We had this fear that it was just the start of mass extermination all over the city. A real civil war. Can you call it a civil war when one half doesn't fight back? When the other half is composed of people who don't live here or even have citizenship here? Maybe it'll end up an American civil war fought on foreign soil. That'd be the American way – leave the mess somewhere else. Don't mean to be anti-American. It gets to be automatic but I know our

movement would be nowhere without Americans. They have the numbers & the clout. But that's true of their uglier side as well.

We're going to vote tonight on how to keep going. Everybody's afraid. We've put up barricades on the streets around us so no one can drive by & pick us off. Some of our nice neighbours came out & moved the barricades but they're so scared of being mistaken for a Tarstopper & shot that they stopped doing it soon enough. The cops aren't going to respond to their complaints about illegal barricades on their street – not with what else they've got to deal with. We're trying to protect ourselves best we can but it's the old story. Might is right. If you're willing to kill me & I'm not willing to retaliate then you've won this round. But we don't go away for long. Already people are leaving. Especially those folks with kids. You can't blame them. We're not asking people to be martyrs or to sacrifice their kids. I know we're not going to be able to keep this thing going now. We're too demoralized. & shaking to our toes that we've unleashed something evil when we were trying to do good. I really feel for the young people among us. Their disillusionment. Their horrified awareness now of the extremes of hate. Their parents are phoning & texting & pleading with them to come home. It's the ruination of their idealism. It'll be a long time before we get them out again. I try to talk to the ones I can & bolster them a bit but they're stunned. They're not thinking. They're packing up. We're going to be down to the hardcore left here. Our power was in our numbers. I've heard that the government – don't know which level – is giving out bus tickets to anyone willing to leave the city. How far we've fallen. Think of our joy less than two weeks ago when we were on the road to Calgary to change the world. The revolution was at hand. We never envisioned mass murder. We knew the cops couldn't rough us up too much because of all the cell phone cameras trained on them and the public's distaste for police brutality. We never imagined thousands of armed gangsters & good old boys & rabid militias taking after us. We know this is only one step in a long process – I'm not going to say long war or campaign & use military terminology. Even if we'd been successful – see how I'm already using the past tense – in shutting down the tarsands even if only temporarily – we always knew we didn't have the power to shut it down permanently – it would still only be one step. That's what's so hard for us. Change & awareness is painfully slow in coming & the situation is beyond urgent. Dire. What we need – I hate to say – is a hurricane to wipe out Miami or a tidal surge to flood New York. Then we'd get people's attention. Mark my words it's going to happen & soon. Maybe the best thing is to get out of here without being so demoralized we lose too much momentum. We'll do it again. & again. We have to.

●

Finally a text back from Armie. *Quit job. Cant take in about shootings. Life sucks.*

Tim had known something was wrong when he hadn't heard back from him at lunch. He'd been texting him all afternoon. It was very unlike Armie not to have responded, especially when so much was going on. Even though he knew

Armie was a long way from Windsor Park, he'd needed to link with him, to know he was alright. Which clearly he wasn't but at least he hadn't been shot. Small mercies.

He phoned Shannon back on her work number. When she answered, he said, "Armie's quit his job. I don't know what's going on. Just a short text."

"Why would he quit his job today? Not that I don't think it was about time."

"I don't know. I'm guessing because of the reaction of his co-workers to Windsor Park. Come home tonight. Armie and I need you to come home. I'll pick you up. I promise Deke won't be there."

"Did he come back last night?"

"No. I was braced for it but he never showed up."

"I'll think about it."

"No. We need you to come home. Okay? Say five-thirty. Out back of your building. Okay? Nothing more is going to happen near us. The whole area will be full of police."

"Okay. I guess it's better to be there than not. Five-thirty, out back."

Tim just had to last until four-thirty. Twenty more minutes. He'd leave early, take a taxi home and get his car. Then he'd blast his way out of the alley no matter what. Meanwhile he could return some calls.

Instead, here came Connor, just barging his way in. Tim had hoped to escape before this happened.

"It's wild," Connor said. "Have you been following the talk about who was really behind the shootings this morning?"

Tim shook his head. He could say, no I've been working, as you should be, but instead he said, "Too wild for me."

"It's looking," Connor said conspiratorially, "like it was deliberate. I mean, the people were targeted. It turns out every one of the victims – except the kid, who seems to have been an unintended casualty – was a somebody of note back in their hometowns in the fight against the oilsands and the pipelines. The other things – the earlier bombings and harassments and that lone guy picked off – seem to have been the Wildcatters adlibbing, but Windsor Park is looking like something else."

"And who does the online world think might be responsible?" Tim didn't really want to know but Connor was so eager to tell him Tim thought it better to get it out. Maybe then Connor would leave. At least this hunt for underground forces had overtaken his interest in Deke's blog.

"A lot of it's the usual, like it's the American government behind it, or the oil companies. One theory is it's a group of ultra-right-wing rich guys in the States who hired pros to mimic the Wildcatters. Those guys think they're above the law. And they'd think anything is justified to keep America out of the hands of lefties and greenies. But then some of the ideas get really wild. Like the Mafia. It's just coming to light now how they've infiltrated industries in Quebec and Ontario to launder their money. The theory is they've invested in the stuff around the building of the pipelines, like the Keystone one down through the States or the one to the west coast. One of the guys shot in Windsor Park was a leader in the American effort to get the Keystone pipeline killed by Obama."

"I hate to be too logical here but isn't it possible that everyone camping in Windsor Park was prominent in the movement, not just those who were shot? It was one of the first parks taken over. They were all hardcore environmentalists. So anyone who was hit in that park would have been somebody prominent in the movement. And how would you explain that one of the shooters they caught was from Germany, just arrived? Or was he a contract killer invited in just for the day by the mafia or the CIA or some American right-wing extremist multi-billionaire? Do you see how ridiculous this gets?"

Connor was giving him the pitying look Tim expected for being such a doubter and so naïve. "What you don't get is that nothing's as random as it seems. You don't want to believe it, but who can deny that organizations and governments really do interfere wherever their interests feel threatened? They fund subversives and order assassinations. We know they do. It comes to light afterwards how much they manipulate and direct things."

For all of his arrogance and ego, Connor was basically a clear thinker. So if Connor was exciting himself with conspiracy theories, imagine how many other people in the city and around the world were letting their minds go with unlikely conjecture. Most of all, his brother. Deke would be eagerly scrolling his iPad, avid to see himself and his movement as the target of powerful international forces.

"I'm not into speculation," he told Connor. "I'm not going into the murk of conspiracy paranoia. We'll probably never know who was responsible. They could have joined up last night in a bar, unknown to each other before that."

"I haven't even got into the really wacko stuff. Apparently the whole Tarstopper thing was the beginning of a plan to unite North America. A lot of fringe groups have been predicting this for years. Powerful rich socialists in both countries have been planning it all along."

"Enough. I don't want to know. I'm out of here. I've had enough for this week."

Connor put his hands up in mock surrender and sauntered off, unaffected by Tim's sternness.

No speculation, Tim reminded himself. Not on the shootings and not on Matt Brown and his wife, not on what Connor had read about him on Deke's blog. He'd get out of here now. He'd sit in the alley behind Shannon's building and wait for her.

●

Tim's car was pulled up at the back door to her office building. As she got in, Shannon felt herself to be in someone's crosshairs, but she told herself it was just aftereffect to be so afraid. Tim looked tired and anxious. They'd get her things from Gizelle's and then pick up dinner to take home.

"Still no sign of that guy?" Tim asked her. "No calls?"

She shook her head. It would do him no favours to tell him about Matt being at the condo last night, about the call today that she'd hung up on. "He seems a pretty small harassment now. I probably over-reacted."

They stopped for food at a take-out place. As Tim got out

of the car to pick it up, she felt a wave of gratitude towards him. No one cared about her well-being more than Tim. She had to remember that. Although she had no desire to talk, she understood that he needed to, that most people would. When he was back in the car, she said, "I haven't been paying attention this afternoon. Tell me, briefly, what you've heard." She would try not to take in much of what he was saying.

"I think the final tally is fifteen dead, one on life support. Three Wildcatters in custody, although nothing's yet known about them. There've been no more shootings in the city but they're now talking about dozens of people dying at the border every day. Wildcatters are collecting into militias there. The National Guard can't cope and the American military's been called out. You don't really want to hear this. One horrible, but positive thing is that the Tarstoppers are leaving. There are long line-ups of people waiting for the government-arranged buses to take them back to eastern Canada or Oregon or Vancouver or wherever they're from."

"Even I didn't want them forced out this way."

"All this stuff you can't believe is happening. All these people acting on impulses and attitudes you can't comprehend. The Wildcatters are the real threat now. The Tarstoppers seem innocent, just peaceful little protesters."

She kept her head averted, looking out the window onto newly re-opened, tree-lined Elbow Drive, the river and a park to her left. Usually there were joggers, dog-walkers, groups of kids, bicyclers, as there should be on this first nice evening in a while. Instead it was just cars, mostly headed south out of downtown, all windows up, getting through the playground zone as quickly as possible. The Tarstoppers had not spread this far north. She wished it were storming. Torrential rain and pulverizing hail and a destabilizing wind would mean that by morning every single Tarstopper would be gone, every Wildcatter in the city on the run for home.

The Tarstoppers were gone from the triangle park at the end of the alley. The whole park had been cleaned up. Tim said, "I had to come home to get the car before I picked you up because I couldn't get it out this morning. Believe it or not, this morning there were tents set up in the alley. Now they're gone. They've probably just moved over to the big park now that space is becoming available, with so many people leaving. Don't get your hopes up that everyone's gone. But they are clearing out, a lot of them. No one's going to stick around to be slaughtered. It'll take a while, but it's going to be the end."

It was almost like normal, parking in the garage out back. Her backyard seemed unaffected, fenced off as it was from the mud and destruction. The honeysuckle bloomed pink and the bridal veil spiraea frothed white. At least she still had this beauty as consolation. Her garden in the front of the house felt lost to her for now, its unfurling unseen by her, its blossoms peaking and fading without her. It had probably been tramped and broken, at least its edges, but she wouldn't look. Once everyone was gone, she could cut everything back and, this early in the season, the perennials and shrubs would recover. She could replant if she had to.

She wouldn't look downstairs at the mess Derek had

probably left behind. She'd get Tim and Armie going on the basement tomorrow. But no matter how much scouring she did, she knew she'd feel Derek in the house for weeks to come, his judgmental eye on how she lived, his fingerprints high on doorjambs, a faint mildewed whiff of him everywhere. It was like the house had been flooded by water that had now receded.

Armie was in the kitchen as they came in. She ran to him and he folded his long arms over the top of her head in greeting. No one was as free physically with her as Armie, as shy and diffident Armie, which thrilled her, however it had happened, whatever she'd done to encourage it. As soon as he'd been taller than her, around age fourteen, instead of backing off from her like a teenager, he'd started leaning on her, slinging one arm around her, laying his head on top of hers. His eyes rarely shifted from hers the way they did sometimes from Tim's.

"Welcome home." Armie said to her, pulling back. "You'll be better off here, with Dad and me to protect you from that guy and from the maniacs loose on the streets."

Armie was such a sweetie. She said, "I think the guy has given up. Whatever he was after. But thanks. We better eat this while it's still warm. Korean, your favourite."

She and Tim wouldn't ask him yet about his job and why he'd quit. He'd tell them when he was ready. Or maybe it was so obviously the wrong place for him that they'd never need to discuss it. She was more concerned with what would happen next.

It sort of felt like normal, the three of them eating in the kitchen, except she was listening for the opening of a door, for either Derek or Matt to just saunter in and disrupt everything. Armie was doing a better job at normal than Tim, who looked at her too often, gauging her, ready to leap up for what she might need. Much as she hated macho, this was too far the other way, almost obsequious. Tim knew it; he didn't like it either, but he would get it under control.

Eventually she'd fit back in here. It would be her house again, her marriage, her life. She knew that from experience. But she'd never been yanked this far out of place before; her home life had never felt as alien. The first time she'd gone to Europe, the year before she'd met Tim, she'd had a similar sense, returning home, of her real life continuing somewhere else without her. She'd felt she belonged in Europe; she was not really a North American. Europeans cared about beauty; they knew about layers and depth. Even now, every time she returned from France or Italy she felt it again, the loss of her real home, the real place of beauty, although never quite as devastatingly as that first time. It passed. This sense of being separated from a vital part of herself would pass, just like jetlag.

After dinner, she and Tim were both aware of Armie downstairs in his room, but from experience they knew that he'd talk about Katie and about leaving his job once he had his emotion and confusion subdued enough. Meanwhile there was much to do. The first mail in a week had gotten through that morning and she and Tim sorted through it. The blinds were still down in the living room, making the house gloomy.

She'd not even looked out front. The chaos would be worse than ever out there, everyone in a panic, people packing up to leave, no longer caring about the mess they left behind.

She wasn't doing too badly, acting normally, when her phone rang. A strange area code. She was not about to start dodging everything questionable, which she knew would only increase her fear, and so she answered it.

"Shannon," Matt said. "You're home, I hear. You must be feeling safer."

His voice was a shock in her body. Tim looked over at her in alarm. She said, "Don't call me again," and hung up.

Tim grabbed her phone and called the display number back. He listened, his face twisted, then hung up. "I don't even know what language they were speaking. Nothing I've ever heard. How did he do that?"

The phone rang again, same number. Tim answered, listened again and then said, "I don't understand. I'm sorry."

Shannon said, "I'm going to have a bath. I'm going to lock the bathroom door. Nothing personal. My phone is yours. I thought it was over."

"You get the sense this guy just does what he wants. He uses other people's numbers, identities, whatever. There's no defense against him."

"Whatever he's after, he'll give up eventually. We just have to keep stonewalling him. I'm not going to let him have this power over me. I'm starting to come out of this."

Tim couldn't stop himself, she could see it. "He does have something over you, though. He's more than an annoyance or a mystery."

"Don't go there, Tim. Anything I might feel, I'm not going to act on. I'm not responsible for reactions I have. It will go away. It's tied up in my fear of what's going on. It has nothing to do with you, with us. Don't let your mind run away on this."

"Wouldn't you say that to react to someone is an indication that all's not right with what you have? Or you wouldn't. React."

"How's it different than Gloria?"

"It's not at all the same. I was just flattered that she had a crush on me."

"That's a reaction. We're not perfect together, which is safe to say about anyone's marriage. Don't go all insecure on me. I'm here. I choose you. A thousand times over. I'm going to take that bath." She hugged him because he looked so unsure and quickly left him.

In the bathroom she changed her mind. She didn't want to be naked in the tub, so much flesh visible, the water soft and sensual around her. Instead she took a quick hard shower and got into her nightgown. She was not going to question herself. She'd watch mindless TV in bed, the door shut, until she fell asleep. She'd taken a pill. She'd barely slept the last few nights.

●

THE WHOLLY GREEN GIANT
9:57 PM

We're having a big memorial tomorrow afternoon for the holy

martyrs of Windsor Park. Fourteen of them in all. Let them never be forgotten. We've found photographs of all fourteen & we'll have them blown up & we'll research their biographies. It breaks your heart – such good, well-meaning people practicing their democratic right to peaceful protest. Three Americans from the west coast & one guy from the Netherlands & the rest from all over Canada. Oddly not one native Calgarian among them – which is too bad in a way because it makes the dead seem like interlopers. It's always better to have a local hero – not that I'm wishing anyone dead. They were all ages – six to seventy-one. Only the one child, thank God. Jonah. Weird how kids all have biblical names these days like Noah & Jacob. Everyone's focused on the kid. There's lots of outrage about putting kids in such danger. Like we knew these murderous maniacs were going to start mowing us down. Little Jonah Petersen is now our patron saint. Read Wendy's eulogy if you haven't yet. We're starting to see that we've done what we can here & the next step is to play on it. Really pump Jonah – brand all the martyrs. Never let them be forgotten. Gear up for Wendy & the boys' trials & make a real display of them.

We're in such a state of chaos now that we've put off the big assembly till tomorrow evening. With so many of us leaving we'll have to reorganize everything – all the committees – but we'll want to see who we have left. Everyone's huddled down who's not packing up or trying to find a way home. I talk to a few folks but everyone's numb – not in the mood to talk.

People keep asking me if I'm staying. I promise I'll be here bearing witness until the last Tarstopper leaves. There're a lot of us determined to stay on – to not let anyone forget.

Did we really think we could get the tarsands shut down? I realize I'm talking in the past tense. I'm being realistic here. There was a chance. If our numbers had kept growing. If we'd been able to bring the whole city to a standstill for a good long time. Eventually they'd have had to make a lot of concessions. Maybe not shut the tarsands down completely but really really lessen their impact. Put climate change at the top of everyone's agenda. & of course if those murderous thugs hadn't come rampaging around. We never predicted them. It never happened at any of the Occupier camps last fall. We thought killing environmentalists & left-leaners of all kinds was a European thing – like in Norway. Oh sure we know about the neo-Nazi types in the States & here at home. If you want to have your hair curled I could give you some sites – although I won't because I don't want to give them any more publicity. But scary scary racist right-beyond-right hate-beyond-hate stuff. Who knew they had these kinds of numbers?

At least we'll be able to hold our memorial to the Windsor Park holy martyrs in peace. There might be a few wackos left around but there'll be a big police presence, like it or not. Wouldn't do to have any more mass murders happen on their beat. Makes them look bad. So if you live in Calgary or vicinity & support our cause or even just feel badly for the victims come out & join us tomorrow afternoon. Two o'clock. Windsor Park school playgrounds. The police won't let us into the community park where the murders actually took place – crime scene don't you know – but the school grounds are right across the street. Fifth

Street southwest. South of 50 Ave & east of Elbow Drive. Pay tribute to the holy martyrs of Windsor Park. Mourn their loss. We do not want them to have died in vain. I'll be the big guy in the bright green shirt. Come say hi. Wear your green & black. Remember tomorrow at two o'clock at Windsor Park.

SATURDAY
JUNE 9 2012

In the morning, Tim raised the living room blind, half-expecting everyone to be gone like from the triangle park, for the park to look green and untouched as if the whole unlikely occupying protest was either over or a dream of his. But no. Although reduced and more spread out, it was still there. The big bus that had once blocked a lot of his view was gone, as was the young woman with her toddler and her tent.

Shannon was already out back in her garden. Later they'd go to the market together. It almost felt normal, like any Saturday, if you didn't know they were in the aftermath of carnage.

●

Eleven o'clock in the morning. Armie had slept five hours past his usual time to get up and go to work. Oh, yeah, he remembered, he'd quit work, it was going on without him now. No, it was Saturday. He thought maybe he was losing his mind. For all he knew, he'd slept through the end of the world.

He'd broken up with Katie although he was still talking her through it, hours again last night on the phone. He'd listened to her cry, listened as she tried to piece together their breakup's meaning through signs and sightings and images, listened to her effort to find words for her emotions. He could only keep repeating that she should be finding visuals, not words, and fix it all in her art.

He heard noises upstairs, his parents no doubt. But then, when he got up for the bathroom, he was surprised to see Deke coming down the basement stairs, which meant that his parents weren't home.

Seeing him, Deke said, "Hey, Dude, what's this I hear about you quitting your job? The brewery sounded kinda cool. Micro-breweries instead of the giant corporations is the whole point." He was not the least bit embarrassed to be found wandering the house when he'd been thrown out.

"I would have thought you'd see high-priced specialty beers as kind of elitist. I'd have thought you'd be more supportive of having a cooperative where we make our own." This sounded a little snide in his own ears, a sarcasm that emerged when he didn't watch it. "Did my dad tell you?"

"I have my sources. Your dad and mom seem to have gone somewhere. I waited till I saw them leave. I wanted to talk to you."

"What's going on? How's everyone doing with the massacre and all? People must be scared."

"We're holding a big memorial this afternoon for those killed in Windsor Park. Have you heard? That's what I wanted to talk to you about. Are you coming?"

When Armie looked away, Deke grabbed his arm. "You have no excuse not to. You can at least do that much."

Armie shrugged and sort of nodded.

"Don't do the shrugging thing. That shrug of yours is very like your old man's, you know. Better be careful with that. You can spend your whole life on the fence just thinking about things. There isn't time for that. I know I turn you off if I get too loud but how am I going to get the urgency for action across? You need to come. You can make at least that much commitment."

"I'll see." Although he'd been doing better at looking Deke in the eye, he couldn't manage it for long. He was too busy trying to keep his mouth shut and not offer up explanations. Like that he didn't like crowds. Like that he didn't even know yet what he thought about the demand to shut down the oil-sands. Like that basically he thought that what Wendy and the boys had done was really stupid, bound to make things worse. Bound to rile up the opposition.

"You'll see? For fuck's sake. People died trying to ensure that the planet doesn't die around you and you can't even show up to honour them?"

He kept his head down.

"Do you not understand the danger we're in? Have I not

gotten through to you at all?"

"I don't have to explain myself." He knew Deke was glaring at him, hands on hips, but he couldn't look up. Saying what he had was as far as he could go, but at least he'd said it. He sure knew better than to try and explain himself.

Deke slammed his hand against the wall near Armie's head. Armie thought he'd hit him if he could get away with it, if he wasn't so against violence. Armie waited until Deke gave a huge sigh and turned away. But then as Armie tried to go around him into the bathroom, Deke knocked him sideways a little as he headed back towards the stairs.

●

THE WHOLLY GREEN GIANT
5:04 PM

It was beautiful this afternoon. It was redeeming. Thousands of people filled the grounds. Tarstoppers of course – easily recognizable in their proudly worn bedraggledness – & a lot of ordinary Calgarians who came to honour the passing of so many innocent protesters. Of course we had the horrible reminder in the park across the street, still all wrapped up in yellow plastic ribbon. It kept us focused.

It took a while to get going. The cops had the whole area fenced off & everyone had to go through security. I don't think anyone expected the numbers. They opened up a few more entrances but it still took over an hour before we could start – with still long line-ups of people waiting to get in. What's this world come to when you have to have a weapons check for a memorial to peaceful protesters? We'd erected a stage of sorts & we had amplifiers. Several people spoke & we heard the stories of the victims – our holy martyrs. They broke our hearts with their hope & then their sacrifice. After that we sang. The most amazing ad hoc band formed on stage – it's mind-boggling how many of us are connected to music in some way. It was beautiful. Everyone had a candle & the flames lit up everyone's faces. Unfortunately we underestimated the numbers & had too few portable toilets so it was kind of a shambles towards the end after all the long line-ups. I think everyone who's been camping has had it with makeshift arrangements for bodily functions & some of the local citizens who came just out of respect got a little outraged too. But before that it was beautiful. Such solidarity & common feeling. A whole sea of green. So many people wore the green & black as a show of solidarity.

We didn't talk about the future & what would happen next with what's left of the protest. Folks can stay on in Calgary in the parks or they can go home. No one will blame anyone for leaving now. We know this was – past tense again – only one step in the long process of change. Much as the situation is beyond urgent, people need to see proof in their own lives before they'll become involved. That's the horrible fact we keep coming up against. But it's coming soon in the form of extreme weather & heat. In high cancer rates. In food shortages from drought. Extinctions. On & on. It would be so much better if we acted now but that's not how humanity works – frustrating & tragic as that is. But it's coming soon. Say most of the US east coast under water. That would get people's attention.

There were all kinds of rumours that Wendy & the boys were coming but they stayed true to their vow not to take the spotlight. Yours truly was pleased to talk to so many people who read this modest contribution to this whole process online. I was like a celebrity & I had to keep remembering that's not what we're about – like Wendy demonstrates. I was surprised by how many asked about the Bro & the neph – like it was a story I was telling in installments. They asked whether that American guy was still after the sis-in-law or maybe he would come after me directly now. Everybody agrees it's me he's really trying to get at. They warned me to be careful. Thanks to everyone who's tweeted & responded to my blog telling me to be careful & worrying about my safety. I'm not quite at the stage where I'll get a bullet-proof vest but I sure do see how self-protection becomes a big deal. Like for all the folks who've left & are on their way home. I get it. I'm sorry it's come to this but I get it.

●

Tim was having a drink with Jason and Cole at five on this Saturday afternoon, since Shannon was busy during the evening, at a dance performance with Alysha. Life went on, Shannon in particular avid to re-establish routine. Tim would have preferred to stay home but he had to resist his tendency to spend too much time at home like a kid. Instead he was going to sit in a dark pub and listen to his friends. He thought of all the years of organizing camping trips with Jason and Cole, various kids along, of going to hockey games, meeting for a beer after work, aside from what the women arranged. Why these guys? It seemed very arbitrary, like the friendships could fall into disuse without effort.

Both of them were already there, at a British place they frequented, equidistant from them all. Jason and Cole were discussing something, close to arguing, Jason usually the dominant one, but Cole brought out by his rage at the Tarstoppers. Tim didn't feel up to it. He started to come up with an excuse as to why he couldn't stay long but they'd caught sight of him and they both smiled and waved. He was such a sucker for inclusion, people happy to see him.

"How about we don't talk about the Tarstoppers?" he said, sitting down. "Can we stay off it? Is it possible?"

Jason said, "I was just filling Cole in on some of the conversations I've had with your brother."

Cole asked Tim, "How can you stand to have someone like that around? Don't you just want to plow him?"

So much for not talking about Tarstoppers. "Lots of times. But not because of his beliefs. He's always been one of the more annoying people on the planet."

"I'd be hoping one of the Wildcatters would pick him off." Cole said this so grimly Tim had a sense of it as just the least of the things he could say. Quiet, affable, round-faced Cole.

"Hey, he's my brother. That's got to count. They're all family to someone. I get the feeling you hate them so much you'd see them all exterminated." He was careful to keep his tone light. Why was he always monitoring his tone when others could say outrageous things without self-censorship?

But Cole was trying to hold himself back. He knew neither Tim nor Jason would tolerate too much anger. "All I'll say is I'm grateful to the Wildcatters for scaring these people enough to get them leaving."

"They did a little more than scare them." Did Cole let rip when he talked to other guys around town? Was a bigger part of the city than he knew as wrathful as his neighbour Hansen? The hate was sickening.

"That's what it took." Cole's face was set in stubborn defiance. "It had to end."

"Look," said Jason. "I don't like them. I think they're all hypocrites and dreamers. They have no idea of the harm they're doing. But I don't get the rage."

Cole said, "I know you don't. But believe me, I'm not alone. I'm with the majority here. Look what they've done to the economy. It's you guys who are the idiots for trying to be objective. I better go. Before I say something I shouldn't."

And he was gone, stomping out, shoulders hunched forward, off to join the battle, if only a verbal one, with his fellow warriors.

"Okay," Tim asked Jason, "what's your theory? Where's all that coming from?"

"You'd think he'd be bitter; you'd think he'd no longer care. He's fifty years old and he's got nothing to show for it. If it weren't for Lori's job and her teacher's pension they'd be in real trouble for later on. Nothing's ever worked out for him. Other people hit it rich, never him. He still thinks the next play is going to be the big one. He's still in the game up to his eyeballs. Any threat to the system terrifies him." This to Jason was dangerous. Always stand apart.

"He seems worse. Like something else is going on. If all this hadn't happened I would never have known him capable of this kind of anger. I think of him more as the patiently hitting-himself-over-the-head type."

"You're not in the game. The city is full of guys still hoping to be players. One stock tip, one 'in' on a start-up that's going places, and they'll be at the table. They forget it's a game. It becomes their whole meaning."

"I thought for a while there that you'd lost track. You were coming across as something of a believer yourself."

"Maybe a little. You get sucked into taking it seriously. Living with Alysha has made me forget it's all a game. She takes it pretty seriously. This movement has been a correction for me. To tell the truth I was a little worried you'd go the whole way with the squishy stuff. Your brother would pull you over into la-la land."

"I'm not following Deke anywhere. Though sometimes I wonder if my old resistance to him has blinded me to the reality of his message."

"Oh there's no doubt: global warming's coming. Whatever Alysha wants to think. All kinds of crap is coming. We'll cope. People will suffer, lots will die, but we'll come through. The old story."

"Wow, now that's cynical."

"We have no choice but to keep going. We can't

afford to get cautious and slow down. Then there'd be no innovation, no betterment, no excitement. Back to the Dark Ages. I'd rather deal with what comes up than start shutting down. Because you know we'd take backtracking too far if it were to happen. That's what we're like." Jason paused. "This is getting depressing. Let's talk about sports or something. Jesus. No matter what the fuck's going on you have to go on living."

"It's only been two weeks. What happens to you if you're caught up in a war or something like this that goes on for six years without a break, like the world wars, or for thirty years? What would happen to everyone psychologically? Maybe you'd get so ground down you'd no longer care. I guess we've been lucky."

"Oh this thing's not over. It's breaking up for now but it'll be back. With luck not on our doorstep but it'll erupt again."

"Now you're sounding like Shannon. The natural state of humankind is in conflict and mayhem."

"And that's why we need entertainment and distraction. Just please not dance performances. I'll be forever grateful to your wife for letting me off the hook with Alysha. Jesus I hated those things."

Tim had to laugh and nod.

●

A seat in a theatre or auditorium might be where Shannon felt most comfortable in the world, especially to watch dance, any kind of dance. To stop thinking, to escape into movement and beauty and sign. These days she especially liked being in a theatre with Alysha. Tim had never been interested in dance, nor Jason. The men liked to joke about it in a boorish way, Jason doing ridiculous poses with his big cumbersome body. She and Alysha agreed that the men were then at their least appealing.

Tonight, it was a modern troupe out of Montreal. They'd come to town and put on their performances despite the Tarstoppers, which gave Shannon huge hope. The Stampede too would go on.

Each dancer in the major piece that began the evening wore a leotard that was black on one side, white on the other, some with black on the left, others white. Although the design and the choreography had to have been set months ago, long before the Tarstoppers and Wildcatters, it was easy to impose the drama on it as the dancers twisted around one another. The dancers could quickly change from black to white and back again with a single movement. A whole line could turn.

But then it became more personal to her, the two sides of an individual, of herself. How she tried to keep a strict line on herself like the vertical line down the middle of the dancers' bodies between the black and the white. But as they moved, as they interacted, the definition was obscured and lost. For a while she saw Matt as the black, Tim and home as the white, battling for dominance over her and within her until she couldn't keep them straight. She stopped thinking.

In the intermission, out in the lobby, Alysha looked as dazed as Shannon felt. "What just happened there?" she asked.

Everyone else had the same look, seemed to be asking the same question. "Whatever it was saying, it seemed like you could apply anything you might think of to it. Tarstoppers and Wildcatters. Men and women. Left and right. I feel like I lived through something that changed me but I couldn't tell you how."

"It had to be about turning your mind off," Alysha said. "To stop making distinctions for a while. We've all been trying so hard to understand what's going on that our heads hurt."

Shannon wanted to tell Alysha about Matt, about what had happened to her. It seemed to lead directly out of what they'd just experienced. And she would have, she trusted Alysha's discretion, except when it came to Jason. Her intimacy with him, her need to share, would override any other loyalty. Shannon knew that about women. She knew that her daughter told her boyfriend family stories and complained to him about her parents, her loyalties shifted. And while Shannon understood the necessity of this shift, it had been a loss to realize it.

"How much," she asked Alysha, "should we listen to our bodies and emotions? Does the body have wisdom our minds don't? Someone like my friend Gizelle pays total attention. I sometimes worry I've gone too far the other way."

It was not the place for such a conversation. There was too much colour and noise around them, the younger dance-followers in full costume for each other, many of them wearing strange feathered and beribboned concoctions on their heads.

Alysha laughed. "Like should we eat the chocolate mousse when our bodies are craving it? I don't think so. Or maybe the smallest spoonful. Both the Tarstoppers and the Wildcatters seem to be emotionally driven. And look where it's gotten them."

"Keeping our balance. It's been hard these last weeks."

"And I don't even really believe in global warming so the whole thing seems like this fight over something imaginary. The last thing those people have is balance. I wouldn't have realized how many unbalanced people there are in the world. It's scary."

Alysha was not the person to talk to about this issue. She was so sure of her own rationality. Shannon was no longer convinced of her own. She could no longer concentrate on the conversation. She was sure suddenly that Matt was in the room. She buzzed with certainty and hyper-awareness like when he'd come into the restaurant. Her body seemed to want him so badly it would convince her rational mind that he was around here somewhere. It would conjure him up out of the air, out of random molecules coalescing. She tried not to look around. She stopped herself from leading Alysha to the other side of the room just to check. He did not have time to follow her to a dance performance. It was unimaginable for him to be here in this crowd of mostly women. Please be sensible. He'd stick out no matter how good he was at blending.

She said to Alysha, "I have to go back to my seat. I'm in a strange space. I just want to sit there for a while and absorb what happened."

Alysha was easy, never looking for ulterior meanings or taking offense. You didn't have to worry about Alysha. She put her hand on Shannon's shoulder and said, "I'll go see if the washroom line-up is any smaller."

Back in her seat, the lights up, the feel of the dance was gone. The sense of Matt being around also faded. She was stranded in an auditorium, bereft, washed up on a shore. It was a ridiculous way to feel. Her own loss seemed to fill the cavernous space like it had escaped her bodily limits and expanded so that it was a whole atmosphere. Which was ridiculous. Which Alysha, coming along the row, would never believe of her, never imagine.

●

THE WHOLLY GREEN GIANT
9:47 PM
Now that we've held the memorial, everyone seems to be getting ready to leave in the morning. What a sad end. We're up against forces we didn't even know existed. Even people I would have said were committed to sticking this thing out to the bitter end are getting ready to leave. It's discouraging. I'm trying not to despair or blame anyone but it's hard. I'm willing to take a bullet. I know I'm a marked man. I'm willing to sacrifice myself – that's how strongly I feel. Until then, I repeat my vow that I will remain here to report on this great rally of people who love this earth.

●

As Tim got into bed, Shannon reached for him, her hand warm on his chest. And in the midst of life – of work and family and the intrusion of tensions from the outside world – just the two of them could break into this other place of sensation and crescendo. Lust could invade both of them like a shared infection. It infused his whole body as Shannon used her hands and her mouth on him, knowing how to grow it in him. Lust took him over as she opened up, spreading her legs. The smell and the taste of her pumped the intensity of his bodily fervour, just the sight of a hard nipple. And then it was over and only traces of it were left in his body, a scent on his fingers. It had engulfed them and now Shannon was asleep again with her back to him.

He hoped her midnight desire hadn't been displaced from Matt onto him. If he alone wasn't enough to turn her on, he preferred to hope her passion had been aroused by something in the dance she'd seen tonight. He couldn't know, he would never ask, which seemed very sad to him, his guard against self-pity down as he too slipped into sleep.

SUNDAY
JUNE 10 2012

Armie didn't hear the shot, in his basement room with buds in his ears. It wasn't until he caught the flash from a strobe light in the bathroom window and went upstairs to investigate that he knew anything was going on. Police cars were all over the place. An ambulance was just pulling away.

As he watched, two police officers headed toward him out of the jumble of people and vehicles in the park. He watched without being able to move. It had to be Deke. Someone must have pointed out where Deke had been staying, his brother's house. The police were talking to one another as they approached and only glanced at him, standing there in the window in his pajama bottoms.

No one else seemed to be home. He called out for his parents but no one answered. Sunday morning. Where were they? He didn't move until the doorbell rang. Leaving the window was like leaving the theatre at the end of a screening. He half-expected there to be no one at the door, the whole thing his imagination, but the police were very real, huge and dark in their uniforms on his front porch.

"Who are you?" the police asked him. His uncle had been shot. The ambulance had taken him to Rockyview. He was alive, condition unknown. Could Armie get a hold of his dad?

They waited, bulky and expressionless in the hallway, while Armie found a phone and called his dad's cell phone. When it only went to message, Armie said, "Dad? Where are you? Call me as soon as you get this. Deke's been shot. The police are here."

Now what? Were they going to wait? Did he not seem old enough to be left to handle this? "He and my mom must have gone somewhere. They must be in the car. He'll check his messages soon as he's wherever they're going. I can tell him what's happened. He'll probably go straight to the hospital. Someone can talk to him there."

They wanted to see his identification. Which meant going down to the basement for his passport. He felt like such a kid, still in his jammies at eleven-thirty on a Sunday morning. In his room he pulled on a t-shirt and jeans before going back upstairs.

His passport seemed to satisfy them as to his identity and reliability. They left, turning around in the narrow entranceway and knocking his mom's oil painting askew – the one that already had white chips in it from the comings and goings during the afternoon of the triangle park melee.

His first thought was to text Katie, his old habit. Why would he ever have done that? What help could she ever have been? It was the sex he missed, not anything she ever said, not any understanding. He had to admit it to himself.

He tried his Mom's phone.

●

Shannon had been at work for a couple of hours, catching up. Eventually life reverted to some kind of norm, if only a lull. Another law. Even if it took years, crises and conflicts played out in the end. Really they'd been very lucky. It had only been two weeks. And while it wasn't over yet, it was safe to assume that everyone would dissipate over the next few days. Not that the conflict wouldn't take a different form and return again.

Then Armie called. "Mom? Deke's been shot. An ambulance just took him to Rockyview. The police were here. Where's Dad? He's not answering his phone. He's not here."

"Oh, my God, oh no. In the park? Where were you?"

"In the basement. I didn't hear it. But somebody with a gun must have been right outside our house waiting to shoot someone."

"Have they caught anyone?"

"I don't know. I don't think so. I guess he could still be around."

"Not with all the police. You're safe for now. We'll find your dad. Did you leave a message? He probably went to get his hair cut or to the liquor store or something. He's around. You'll hear from him soon. I'll keep trying him too. Okay, we better get off the line. Call me back if you hear from him. Are you okay?"

"It was a shock. It's hard to imagine Deke down and silenced. But yeah, I'm okay."

It was all balled up in her head. Matt with a gun on her front lawn. Matt in her house wandering around, no one there, then finding Armie in the basement. Not Matt. Don't be stupid, not Matt. Just some deranged Wildcatter. She'd wanted to think the worst was over. That the massacre at Windsor Park had ended the violence. It was that stupid human hopefulness, she as guilty of it as anyone else.

She phoned Tim and got him in his car. He'd gotten Armie's message. "I'll go straight to the hospital. I'll get back to you as soon as I know more."

It had to have something to do with Matt, Shannon reasoned. This didn't seem as far-fetched as she wanted to believe. Matt had had Deke targeted. An undercover agent, disguised as a Wildcatter, had taken advantage of the situation to try and kill Derek. Matt would come around now, probing her to see how it was playing out. He was on his way towards her now. He'd reveal that nothing was as she thought it was.

She had to stop this kind of hysterical thinking. Derek was a loudmouth buffoon whom no one would single out. The CIA did not go around killing environmentalists. She didn't know anything about Matt. But her body and her ancient brain stem were again not listening to her. Fear was all through her body, as pervasive as lust. Her equanimity had been as flimsy as paper.

Another call. She had to answer, although the number was unknown. It could be the police. It could be anyone. "Shannon Armstrong."

"Hello, Shannon Armstrong. Don't hang up. I just wanted to say good-bye. I'm leaving town. I won't bother you again. I'm sorry about your brother-in-law. I hope he'll be okay."

"What do you know about it? It just happened."

"It's my business to be informed. I'm sorry if I frightened you. You're much too suspicious, you know. I just wanted to talk to you."

"I don't believe you are who you say you are but I don't even care anymore. Good-bye."

The feeling was still there, all the lures of the foreign and transformative in his voice. Come with me into raw feeling and revolution, her body seemed to hear. She didn't believe in escapism, the romanticism of it. You could do quite thrilling, substantive things by confronting a fear on your own doorstep; take a big chance just by inviting someone you didn't know very well to dinner. She didn't at all feel her life was safe. Her brother-in-law had just been shot outside her front window. She didn't feel deadened by the routine and normality of her life but freed by it to venture out.

Why was she defending herself? He was still in her head; she was still in dialogue with him. Had she responded to him because of a need in her or had it been random, chemical? A thousand tangled explanations. She'd learned something and had been changed just by his appearance in her life but there was no lesson, no meaning, nothing to act on.

There'd been another call while she'd been talking to him. Armie. "Did you talk to Dad?"

"I was just going to call you." No need to tell him she was delayed by talking to her stalker, although she hated Armie thinking she'd ignored him, even for a second. "I talked to him. Did you?"

"Yeah. I think I'll head down to the hospital to keep Dad company. I'll take the bus. They're running again on Elbow Drive."

"There's part of me that wants you down in the basement for weeks, until every little bit of this is over and gone. Too much to ask, I know."

"Mom. I'll be fine."

"Stay away from the park."

"It's crawling with cops. It's probably the safest place in the city right now."

She had to let him go. But it struck her that if Matt really wanted to get her attention, all he had to do was strike up a conversation with Armie somewhere.

●

In the hospital waiting room Tim sat, making calls, grateful that everyone was accessible with their cell phones. Even though he'd lived through it, it was hard now to imagine the time before you could even leave a message, when long distance was a luxury, when you had to have a lot more patience, trying again and again to connect to people.

"Mom?" he said when she answered. "I'm afraid I have bad news. Where are you? Can you sit down for a sec?"

"What is it? Who's hurt? Derek. It's Derek, isn't it? I've been so worried, with the killings out there."

"He was shot. He's being operated on. He's going to be okay. I'm at the hospital."

She shrieked. "Oh, I was so afraid of this. Oh my God. I've been waiting for this call. Dreading it. Oh my God. I'll get a flight. I'll get there as soon as I can. Oh my God. Where was he shot?"

"Close to his heart. But it missed major organs. He lost a lot of blood. What I need from you is his health care number. He doesn't have the card with him. We've looked. The hospital needs it. Do you have it? Can you find it?"

"I can't think right now. I've got to absorb this shock. I'll call you back."

"He's going to be all right. In the end."

He didn't want his mother to come, although he knew that she had to. He imagined her arrival, her surge down a corridor, all her loose clothing flying – layers and capes and dangling triangles of gauzy fabric – and her emotion that was like another layer around her, huge and engulfing. Of course she had to come.

He called his dad.

"Yeah." That was how he always answered – don't waste my time.

"It's Tim. It's about Deke. He's been shot. They're operating on him now. He should come through it okay."

"By one of those fucking Wildcatters? What in hell did he expect? Putting himself in their line of fire. He asked for this. You can't stick your finger up people's noses and not get a retaliation. Fuck. What, was it another one of those mass murder things? I haven't seen the news. The world's gone to hell, especially your part of it. Fuck. The idiot. Out to save the world."

"Only him. A random thing. I'll call you back as soon as I know more. I think Mom's coming out." It was unlikely that his dad would have come anyway, but hearing that his ex-wife Marilyn would be there settled it.

"Poor you," he said about her, sarcastic. "Let me know."

Sometimes his dad was almost a caricature of a male: abrupt, dismissive of niceties, self-absorbed, gruff. Garth would say you had to be like that to get ahead in business, something neither of his sons would appreciate. Something neither of them had the balls for. Now Garth spent most of his time playing golf, in Florida in the winter, golf another occasion for anger and frustration, another reason for disappointment with his sons, who wouldn't ever even try it.

Tim phoned Ardith to tell her but she was unavailable. He left a message about her Uncle Derek but really she hardly knew him. And had little interest in her weird greenpeacer uncle.

A woman sat down beside him, a nurse who introduced herself as Patti, one of the Tarstoppers. She had come with

Deke in the ambulance. Tim remembered her from when they were bandaging people up after the triangle park. A nice, ordinary, plump woman around his and Deke's age. "Tell me if I'm bothering you," she said. She meant it. It was not a cover for insecurity or pro forma.

"No, it's okay. I had to call our parents. There should be somebody else but I don't know his friends. He's not romantically involved with anyone at the moment as far as I know. Were you there? Did you see it?"

"I heard the shot. I don't think anyone saw the gunman. It wasn't a raid. Just a lone psycho. Maybe Deke was just the biggest target around."

"He thought the CIA was after him. Or the Mounties."

Patti let this go by. "He talked about you a lot. You're huge in his mind."

"He talks about me too much. On that blog of his. We had a falling out over it."

"He told me. Thanks for taking in the people in the storm Wednesday night."

"Was it that recent?"

"It'll be the end now. At least for your park. We'll all be gone soon. You'll be free of us. Well, not of Deke, for a while, I guess."

"Are you leaving too? Where are you from?"

"Ottawa. Yeah, I'm going home. I know better than to get involved with your brother. I'm not going to do the nurse thing and look after him. I've learned the hard way not to give myself away. I know there's been a long line of women in his life like that. You don't even have to say."

Again she meant it. He felt badly for her, for the long line of men who'd used her, too. He would have warned her away from Deke but was glad that he didn't have to.

She stood up. "I hope it all goes well. Say good-bye to him for me."

Tim sat there thinking that there had to be somebody else, somebody besides his parents and a woman Deke had met a week ago who cared what happened to him. There was Glynnis, his longest-lasting girlfriend, but that was more than five years ago now. His friends seemed to come and go the way the women did. Deke would say that he had lots of friends, thousands of them, but he didn't have the time and energy for a deep relationship because the cause was too urgent.

Tim texted Jason. *Bro shot. At Rockyview. Ill be here for duration.*

A text right back. *come as soon as i can.*

Shannon wouldn't come. It wouldn't occur to her. She wouldn't expect him to do so in similar circumstances either. She hated hospitals.

Tim waited, blank-minded. It was Armie who showed up next. Tall, skinny Armie looking around like an imperturbable giraffe, backpack over his shoulder like a permanent hump. Tim leapt up and hugged him, catching Armie a little off guard.

"Any news?"

"It's going to take hours apparently. He's a mess."

Armie sat down next to him, Armie so reassuring because he was the opposite of restless.

"Marilyn's coming as soon as she can get a flight."

Armie looked momentarily alarmed. His grandmother, who insisted on being called by her name, was such a force. Tim could almost see him grip himself as if she were already approaching, ready to hold on in the gale. "That's good," he said.

Tim's phone rang. His mother. She said, "First, any news?"

"No."

"Okay. I've got a flight. I arrive at eight tonight. Air Canada. And I'll have to get back to you on the health number."

"Okay. I'll pick you up. But I'll talk to you before that I'm sure." His mother was incredibly competent. He sometimes thought of her as someone who could move an army across a continent single-handedly. Or she and Shannon together in half the time. Add Ardith and the war would be won. The Tarstoppers could have used them, except that none of these women would have the patience for meetings and slow consensus.

He said to Armie, "What's the basement like? We never got to it yesterday."

"It's not too bad. Deke cleaned up pretty well from the storm people. It's probably not up to Mom's standards, though."

"It's times like this I wish we still had the big house. Your mom will be home soon. She'll deal with it."

"I'll help."

"Do you feel like we've somehow got out on a tangent and we keep expecting to rejoin normal life soon, but instead we just keep going out on it further and further?"

"So much has happened in such a short time. Katie, my job. Aside from the whole Tarstopper thing."

"At least you won't have to listen to Deke now for a while. Has he been at you the whole time, trying to get you involved?"

"I've learned a lot. He'll get going on something like coal and how even in Alberta we use coal to generate electricity and it's a worse carbon polluter than the oilsands. He's always telling me that everything's even worse than we know. He keeps piling on the info. I get buried under it. I don't know how he keeps all those statistics in his head and has any room left around them to even live."

"He's not above making up numbers when he forgets. But it's become his life. In some ways it simplifies life, to have a cause that always comes first. He has no long-term friends, you know. No long-lasting attachments. I don't know anyone to call for him except our parents."

"But he's not wrong. Maybe it's the rest of us who are in denial. Everybody else distracts themselves with ordinary stuff – like games and Twitter and stuff. I kind of admire him. If he weren't so annoying."

"His total commitment also suits his needs. There's always a personal angle to anyone's actions and decisions. We all have to find a comfort level. Most people just don't want to know. They think that if it's that bad, someone will do something about it. I sure don't have any answers. But I don't think we're psychologically designed to feel responsible for the fate of the whole world."

He felt for Armie, flailing around at the start of his adult life. At his age Tim had felt locked into a path he knew he didn't want, trying to please his father and avoid the murky, lofty dreams of his mother. Was it better to be adrift, all options open? Armie, no doubt, would say it was best to be Ardith, on a path she was sure was the right one. Armie just couldn't imagine wanting the one she'd chosen.

Armie changed the subject. "Do you think it was a random Wildcatter? Deke thought he was being targeted. It's starting to look like it now. With him the only one hit."

"I don't know. We may never know. But when you've got a huge agenda and you start thinking you're one of the few who really gets the big picture, paranoia and self-inflation usually aren't too far behind."

"What about that guy stalking Mom? Deke thought he was after him."

"On little evidence. Deke writes a blog. He's nobody. Unless he's involved in ways we don't know about – although everything I know about him tells me he'd never be able to keep quiet about it. Maybe it'll turn out he was a leader of this whole thing with Wendy. Or maybe he's a counterspy. Maybe he got recruited when he was deep in debt or they had something on him. I can think of all kinds of possibilities, none of them at all likely. But then two weeks ago I would have said none of this was remotely possible."

There were two detectives at the hospital, waiting to interview Deke when they could. Tim had spoken with them when he'd come in but only briefly, since he hadn't been at the scene.

One of them, a man of around forty, with the rangy hard look of an extreme athlete, sat down next to him now. Tim introduced Armie.

"Do you think it was a Wildcatter?" Armie asked him, curiosity overcoming his shyness.

The detective, Adam, took an interest. "Who else?"

Of all the times for Armie to speak up, this was not a good one. Armie now looked shocked at himself. But he thought that he had to continue, now that he'd made his mistake. "He thought he was being targeted by the CIA. My mom is being stalked by this guy who might be CIA. This guy wanted to know all about my uncle."

Adam looked to Tim.

"I think it was my brother over-estimating his own importance. The guy's name is Matt Brown. He said he was with ABC News. He took a shine to my wife, that's all."

"But he brought up Derek? He knew she was his sister-in-law?"

"He seemed to know everything about her. That was just one thing."

"Okay, from the beginning."

Tim told the story as succinctly as he could, although Adam interrupted him often with questions. Tim was aware of Armie's big ears almost flapping as he listened. He wondered if Shannon's ears were burning as she was talked about in such detail. There was no way to protect her privacy in this situation.

Adam was not going to give anything away, answer any

questions himself. Eventually he abruptly got up and left without looking back. Across the room an elderly woman was crying, sitting there alone in the hospital waiting room on a plastic chair, head up, sobbing. Tim hadn't seen her come in.

Armie said, "Dad? What's going on? This is creeping me out."

"We may never know. For now I'm sticking with the idea that the shooting was a random Wildcatter and the Matt guy's interest in your mom was nothing. Don't tell her about this. She wouldn't want to know."

"I'm sorry I opened my big mouth."

"It was only a matter of time till it came out. The moment Deke can talk he'll be full of information and theories for the police. You don't have to stay. Go home. I'll call you as soon as I hear anything. Put in some laundry."

Armie was reluctant, but it was not too hard to persuade him.

It was a long afternoon. People came and went. Abe, the nuclear scientist Tarstopper, showed up for a while. By the end of the afternoon quite a few Tarstoppers had stopped in, a surprising number given how many of them had to take the bus in an unfamiliar city as they were preparing to pack up and return home. They all spoke warmly of Deke. The big guy. The Wholly Green Giant. So good at keeping their spirits up. So helpful. Tim had to think he might have misjudged his brother, although these Tarstoppers were not a representative sample.

He talked to his mother again, to Shannon on her way

home, who panicked at the thought of Marilyn in the basement in the state it might be in.

Tim sat there and waited to see what else would happen. He had stopped analyzing. He knew he knew too little for any conjecture.

●

What a mess, Armie thought, approaching the park from the bus stop. Garbage, abandoned and collapsed tents, wet bedding hanging on whatever would get it up off the ground, mud, and this whole end of the park surrounded by yellow plastic police tape. Armie stopped and watched. The Tarstoppers were still being interviewed by the police. Maybe twenty of them sat on the lowest levels of the baseball bleacher, waiting their turn in a tent the police had set up as more storms threatened. Everyone else was getting ready to leave. Already there were only maybe a third of the people in the park there once had been.

Another day or two and all of this mess in the park would be gone as though it had never happened. There wouldn't even be a memorial to Deke at the site, with teddy bears and flowers, since he hadn't died. The city would clean it all up, although there were bands of people – these were environmentalists after all – who were already sorting and stacking and hauling the unredeemable garbage to the curb. It must have dismayed them, how much crap and junk a small group of people could produce in such a short time. The police had probably already rummaged through it all.

His mom was home, in the kitchen, making tea. She was pale, drained-looking, so he could almost see what she'd look like when she was old. He wrapped his arms around her head the way he did, still amazed at how much taller he was than her, and she leaned against him for a second. His mom never looked to him for anything emotional, the way some of his friends' mothers did their sons, wanting them to listen to their problems, so he knew how depleted she had to be.

"No more of the stalker guy?" he asked her, moving away, getting out a cup for himself.

She shook her head. His mom could be very articulate and out there and then go quiet and remote. She tried not to be like that with him. She knew that it used to scare him as a kid, but she didn't seem to have the energy now to even try.

He said, "I can't get over how in another couple of days all evidence of this movement will be gone. No sign that it was ever there. All of the stuff that happens and then we forget. Like in five years someone will mention the Occupy movement and we'll have to try and remember what it even was and what they wanted. Even 9/11. We'll think: when was that? 2000? 2001?" He knew this subject would pull her out. He still had the little-kid need to engage her. He used to pepper her with questions, trying to find the one that would attract her attention.

She pulled herself away from her preoccupation. "Let me tell you, much much worse than this uprising gets buried and forgotten. Look up Babi Yar. I was in such shock when I was your age and first heard of it. That was the start. It became a hunt to find what else in the twentieth century I'd never heard of. I wanted to know it all, although that turned out to be impossible, there was much too much. My first time in Europe I was very aware that all of the soil was blood-soaked and yet it was very beautiful on the surface." She stopped and smiled weakly at him. "Probably not the best topic right now. But I more than know what you mean about our shocking ability to cover over and keep moving on. I'm sorry about Katie. Even though it's time, I know it's hard."

"That's it though. She doesn't want to know. She's sealed off and that's the way she likes it."

"Maybe her parents protecting her so well made the outside world seem too threatening to even think about."

"So why were you so different from her? Wanting to know."

"My parents kept a façade going about our kind of nice people which I knew was false. They were really scared of something; I could feel it even as a kid. It was like they were scared they didn't really belong or they didn't deserve what they had or they wouldn't be able to hold onto it. They were sickeningly smug about life in that horrible town and yet insecure, really nasty about other people. I never wanted to spend much time at home. And those were different times. I was never hovered over the way Katie is. They didn't pay that much attention to me, as long as I dressed well and got good marks and had the right friends. Made them look good. But then there's your Aunt Cara who grew up in the same house as me and believed the whole thing about appearances. The right fork and the best golf course are what really matter. All of that talk about standards. Not that I don't have my own obsessions with appearances. But I know what's underneath and Cara, like Katie, doesn't want to know. Mostly I choose the surface now, but knowing that that's what it is."

It was not often that his mom was this self-revealing. Maybe it was because she was tired and anxious, though that usually made her quieter. She shook her head again. She was doing that a lot, like trying to clear it. "I know you're having trouble figuring out how to live with all Derek's told you. We can't live day-to-day with too much knowledge. There's always another perspective on any issue anyway. And meanwhile we have Marilyn arriving in a couple of hours. I'm gearing up to take a look downstairs. At least Derek's not going to show up again for a while." She paused. "Sorry, that's not very nice," she added.

After they finished their tea, they descended into the basement, which thankfully wasn't as bad as she'd feared. Armie remembered what it was like to try and do something like this with her, with her going so fast at changing beds and dusting and rearranging that he just felt in the way. When her phone rang she jumped. She pulled it out of her pocket and looked for the caller like the wrong name alone could cause the device to explode in her hand. She slumped, seeing who it was. He knew it was his dad by the way she said, "Hi."

"Deke's out of surgery," she repeated for his sake, "in ICU, prognosis good, lucky." Then she said into the phone, after his dad must have told her his plans, "Armie and I will have everything ready."

After she hung up she said to him, "He'll pick up Marilyn at the airport and then take her to the hospital. They'll be late so we have lots of time."

But that didn't stop her from headlong cleaning, now the bathroom. Armie retreated to his room.

Babi Yar. He looked it up and read about it but there was no way to take it in. He pictured ancient earthworms burrowing through the soil eating anything organic they came across. He pictured bacteria, microbes, beetles, all kinds of black shiny crawly things feeding off of death. Making it all disappear. Until they came across a nugget of metal, which they would have veered right around.

He was going to play a video game now. Something completely imaginary except for the pixels on the screen and they weren't really a substance either. Just the electricity was real, although he had to take that on faith. Coal-generated electricity. Coal was the result of more death, this time in ancient oceans, and now powering the screens in front of him.

There was so much of Deke on the bed. One enormous bare foot protruded from the end while his arms fell off both sides. His blanket was twisted on him like a loin cloth. The people in the other beds seemed shrunken in comparison, barely disturbing their tight covers.

Deke gripped his arm with surprising strength although his eyes were barely open. "I told you."

"Put that out of your mind for now. We may never know who it was. Concentrate on getting better. Mom's on her way. I'll bring her here for a few minutes after I pick her up."

"I'm a marked man."

He shouldn't let Deke's self-dramatization irritate him now. Give him some slack: he'd been shot, almost killed. But Tim was relieved that he didn't have to stay, that he'd only been given a few minutes with him. It was the usual mash of emotion that he felt around his brother.

It was six-thirty. He needed to go home in between the hospital and the airport, re-establish himself, as well as eat dinner. He wanted normalcy, routine, boring ordinary life back. He wanted to drink a little red wine in the kitchen with Shannon while they put together their dinner. No one had been grocery shopping for a while now. He texted Shannon for what he could pick up.

●

Tim had left for the airport to pick up his mother, Armie had disappeared downstairs, and Shannon could plunge into her garden, the lush greenery still a recent miracle to her after the stark winter. She would finish putting it back to rights after the storms of the week. The front yard would have to wait until every single Tarstopper was gone. Which would be soon, she fervently hoped.

As she tied up the verdant new growth on the perennials, she was picturing Tim and his mother, by now probably on their way to the hospital from the airport. Marilyn always flattened Tim down, which made Marilyn impatient, to have that effect on him, as if Tim should really be made of stiffer stuff. Marilyn's emotion, her great distress and worry over Derek, would be filling the car like a balloon, squeezing Tim against his car door. Her emotion was legitimate, of course, but Shannon thought of her mother-in-law as always consumed, burning feverishly over injustice in the world. Shannon was not looking forward to having Marilyn in the house.

At least it was Sunday night and she could escape into work tomorrow. Maybe Marilyn would spend all of her time at the hospital. And then once Derek was released she'd be able to airlift him back to Toronto. Shannon would be rid of them all. This thinking wasn't very gracious of her, she knew, but it was what she felt, extended as she was beyond all emotional reserves.

Her garden wouldn't stay as perfect as it was right now. Bugs were already munching the plants, hail could shred the leaves, mildew and fungi would spread. But for now she was trying to breathe and relax into this green moment.

Instead, out of nowhere, the busyness and potency and grease of life dispersed. She was alone in a clear patch where she knew her own isolation and the basic ruthlessness of the universe. It was back. The void. When not inside it, she was never able to imagine the sensation, the desolation of it, not really. She'd learned tricks to avoid it, keeping busy, meditation and yoga, all the distractions, but sometimes this extreme alienation from everything descended without warning, scattering any atmosphere she'd been able to surround herself with. Then she was convinced that isolation was the reality and all her means of avoidance and denial seemed fake and obvious. At times like this, civilization itself seemed like just another cover-up.

When she was ten in the small Manitoba city where she grew up, a bridge collapsed, killing three people. No one was ever held responsible. And yet her best friend Karen was terrified that her father, who'd supplied the concrete for the bridge, would go to prison. Shannon hadn't understood until Karen, having to tell someone, cried that her father had owed money to mean people and that he'd had to cut corners. Her father, drunk and crying, had confessed to her and now she was telling Shannon. It was a shock. A drunk father who cried? Who cheated? Mr. Evans? Shannon knew better than to ask her parents about their good friend Jerry Evans. She was forever alone with the information. Even Karen found ways to live with it, one of which was to no longer be friends with Shannon.

The rest of her life sometimes seemed like a confirmation. Everything she'd learned since then about the prevalence of corruption and paybacks in legitimate businesses had been no surprise to her. And that wasn't even counting the enormous underworld of drugs and prostitution and gangs, which she'd known nothing about as a ten-year-old. Or the whole ugly dark world of counterintelligence and security. People like Matt, if he was in fact an undercover agent of some kind, lived down there, doing his best to not let the malignancy break through to the surface. Was that the attraction of someone like Matt? No pretending the world was other than the dark place it was. Maybe that was what had appealed to her.

She knew she'd eventually move on from this stark view of life, although her awareness would stay with her for a while. It would create a distance between her and the others. Tim would worry at the edges of the gap and Armie would give her that kid-look of reproach that he still did and Marilyn would again think her a little too cool. By tomorrow, at work, her stark alienation would soften and in the press of business she'd start to forget this clarity. She'd be able to go on as if calamity were not beneath her feet, as if somehow the bridges would hold.

●

Armie didn't feel up to his grandmother. When he heard her and his dad come in the back door, he wanted to stay with what he was reading. He was hopeless with people. He was happiest with words and ideas. He wanted other people's thoughts and research piped straight into his brain without having to interact with them. As he climbed the stairs her voice in the kitchen came at him in undulations, in waves he could almost see.

His grandmother took up a lot of room in the kitchen. His dad seemed squeezed into a corner, arms folded, just like when

Deke was around. Marilyn seemed to have no edges, all of her in waves, her clothes in layers of grey and off-white and black that ended at different levels so that he thought of her as being like a Christmas tree with her big face up top like a sunburst. Her long grey hair fell in swoops out of the comb-things she was always shoving it back up with. Her vitality surprised him every time. She was seventy-five but nothing like the little old lady image he associated with that age.

"Armstrong," she cried and came at him, arms flung wide, sleeves drooping. She had a large iron jagged object on a chain around her neck and for a moment he felt he might be stabbed by it.

"Oh, Armie," she said from within his arms – what could he do but put his arms around her? – "this is such a nightmare. Thank God you're safe. Thank God you weren't with him."

He patted her and waited for her to release him. She smelled a little, of heated skin and the mustiness of travel. But she seemed to like being pressed against him.

"Who would do something like this?" she cried, leaning back to look up at his face, searching like always for something she needed from other people. "Derek would never hurt any-one. My gentle giant. The only thing he does is care too much about the world. What kind of monsters are loose in it now?"

Finally she moved back a bit. Now she was in tears, the back of her hand pressed under an eye. Armie asked, "How is he doing? Is he conscious yet?"

His dad said, "He's out of danger. They'll have him on his feet by tomorrow. You know what hospitals are like now.

There was a big change in him even between when I left to pick up your grandmother and when we got back." He smiled. "He's getting his voice back."

"All my life," said Marilyn, "I've fought against the patriarchy. This is one of its ugliest, most ignorant sides. I have to believe this is the desperation of a dying system. I have to believe that, even when I despair that it seems to have more power than ever. I knew it would get more vicious but I wasn't prepared for my own son, right here in Canada, to be a victim."

His grandmother talked like that, about big historical forces that tossed humanity around. He pictured her as one of those ancient warrior goddesses, up on a bluff, sword raised, except that she hated violence, so maybe a lamp lit and held high like the Statue of Liberty.

Marilyn wanted a glass of wine. His grandmother drank a lot of wine, her voice getting louder and more belligerent as she did so. Or she could get sappy, in tears over some injustice or suffering. His dad seemed like someone standing around just waiting to be of use to her. She said, "Oh, don't open a new bottle just for me," but of course he would.

"Where's your mom?" his dad asked him.

"She went to bed. She said she'd see everyone in the morning. She was pretty tired. She said everything was ready in the basement."

Marilyn looked a little put out with this fact, that Shannon was not up to greet her, but Armie knew that she was also a little intimidated by his mom. In Toronto, Marilyn had tried to talk to him about his parents' marriage, how it worked, what he thought, but Armie had been almost rude in avoiding the subject. He wasn't going there with her. Just like he wouldn't talk about them with Deke.

His dad kind of laughed and said, "You know Shannon," but he sounded funny, like he was performing, like he was keeping his feelings tucked away inside, out of reach of his mother's keen eye.

Marilyn surged out into the living room with her glass of wine. "Let's see where it happened. I want to look at the infamous park. The place where my son was shot."

Armie and his dad followed her. His dad pulled the blinds all the way up, not just opening the slats. There were still tents here and there and the water tower had still not been dismantled. He didn't think it had ever worked. The grass was a mess of muddy pathways but the garbage had been picked up from the curb, the city returning everything to normal as quickly as possible. The yellow police tape made it look like a crime scene on a vacant lot and for a second he imagined bulldozers pushing dirt to fill up trenches. In a few days it would be hard to even remember the park had ever been a campground.

Marilyn said, "This is all so unbelievable. The whole thing, start to finish. I was so worried when he set off. I watched the clips on the news of all those innocent environmentalists wending their way to Calgary to save the world and I knew it would end badly. They were so naïve. Derek likes to talk about the power of the system and the vested interests but he really has no idea of their power. Now there'll be such a backlash. We'll all end up profiled. You wait, in the end we'll all have security devices implanted under our skin so no one's ever able to get out of control again. We haven't seen anything yet. He was so brave and so doomed." She started to cry again and his dad put his arm around her. They were about the same height.

His dad had once said that Marilyn had been like a witch in his childhood, stirring her cauldron and shaking her head and prophesying doom. Nuclear proliferation, pesticides in breast milk, over-population. He said it was like she was on a search for confirmation that some horrible end was in store for us all. It could come from a thousand sources, it was that pernicious, and the authorities didn't want you to know about any of it. She was always on the hunt, on the dig.

Sure enough, she now said, "Did you know that the US will spend fifty-one billion dollars on the black world of security this year, with almost no accountability? All of it is by definition undercover. Drones over their own territory looking for terrorists. It's going to be a scary world. We're in much more danger from covert security than from any real terrorists or rogue governments out there."

Armie found her hard to follow. "Are you saying that people shouldn't protest because they'll only make things worse, make the government even more paranoid?"

She took offence. "I'll have you know I've spent my life on picket lines. I had people spit on me in the great access to abortion fight in the seventies. I'm saying we should never underestimate the ferocity with which the state will protect the status quo."

"But it was Wildcatters who were killing people and they

hate the government." He really didn't want to argue with his grandmother, but sometimes he was just too perplexed by inconsistency to remember to keep quiet.

Now she did that adult thing where he was just too young to understand the deviousness of the world. "Always get somebody else to do your dirty work for you if you can."

His dad said, "We're all tired. It's after midnight your time, Mom. We should all turn in. There's lots of time to talk."

Tomorrow was Monday, but Armie had nowhere to go. No Katie. And no work to go to. Marilyn couldn't spend all day every day at the hospital so she'd be around a lot, expecting him to interact. Tonight he'd be sharing the basement and a bathroom with her. It would be like with Deke all over again, being waylaid as he tried to read or just get breakfast. Deke and Marilyn shared a need to talk, to constantly engage and argue and deliver opinions as information. And he'd have to be a lot more polite with his grandmother.

She said, "I need to finish my wine," swirling it.

A slight nod from his dad said he could go. Armie leaned in and kissed his grandmother's cheek, quickly, in case she fell to weeping on him. He should probably be more generous toward her. She had fed him many a memorable meal when he was in school in Toronto and sent him back to residence with enough food to last a week, if the whole floor hadn't gobbled it all down as soon as he got back with it. He'd say he loved his grandmother, just not from too close. He was grateful to get away.

MONDAY
JUNE 11 2012

If only Connor would go away like the Tarstoppers, without Tim having to shoot anyone. There'd been another complaint this morning from one of his staff, Sean, obviously exasperated beyond endurance by Connor's high-handedness. It meant he'd have to have yet another conversation with Connor about his managerial skills.

There was no point asking Shannon her opinion, to her it was clear. Or his mother. Or Deke. Jump, jump, jump, they all yelled in his mind, sure any action was better than none. Which was the difference between him and them.

"You wanted to see me?" Connor was at his most arrogant, lip curled, eyelids slightly lowered, irked at having to justify himself to Tim. He leaned against the doorjamb, smirking. "How's your brother?" he asked, just to remind Tim how much he knew about him.

"On the mend."

"Are you starting to see the forces at work?"

"I get enough of that kind of talk from my brother himself. That's not why I wanted to see you. Look, I'm going to be frank. If you're waiting around to take over from me, I have to tell you that I have no plans to leave and the Board is not unhappy with me. And even if I were to go, they wouldn't choose you. Whatever your fundraising and organizations talents, you alienate people and this is above all a people business."

He had Connor's surprised attention. He was like an animal, advancing, sniffing this change in him, evaluating, calculating. He might even circle him. "What's got into you?"

"I'm tired of you pissing staff off."

"I should be more like you. Hold everyone's hand and mildly suggest improvements."

Which, Tim had to admit, was pretty much what he'd used on Connor these last few months. Connor viewed donors as having money he could smooth-talk and wheedle out of them, his staff as minions to facilitate his wins. It was all about results. For Connor, not unlike Deke, come to think of it, it was about single-mindedness and taking control. Winning.

"Next complaint I get, you're gone. And don't try and intimidate Sean into keeping quiet. You know it was Sean. Following in the steps of Terri before him and Luke before her. If Sean quits, you're gone." Speaking this freely was addictive. "Why are you even still here? Your talents could be used to better advantage, and be so much better rewarded, elsewhere."

Connor had widened his eyes and then Tim could see the fun go out of it for him, like Tim had finally called the game, a whistle had blown. Did Connor have a brother he once tormented? Had he been as helpless in their interactions as Tim?

"You may be right," Connor said. "I'm starting to see that the people who get into non-profit are mostly wimps hiding out from the real world. I've tried my best to introduce some rigour into it but it's hopeless. If I go I need a top reference."

Tim could only nod. Was it going to be this easy? A tone of voice that had eluded him for months and months? If he could keep it up, maybe he wouldn't have to let Connor go and lose his amazing ability to raise huge amounts of money. Maybe he could have it both ways.

"I'll get back to you," Connor said and he was gone.

Tim had to laugh at himself, being a kid again and thinking he'd found the right approach to Deke. Playing out a private story in his work life. Catering to Connor, trying to get along with him despite the bullying. If he was guilty of anything it was that. The fact was that the agency couldn't afford Connor. The complaint from Sean had tipped the balance. The personal stuff, the sense of pulling free from something, was just a bonus.

●

THE WHOLLY GREEN GIANT
2:13 PM
I've been blown away by all the posted best wishes. Thank you

thank you everyone. I'm dictating this – slowly – to my mom, who's here at my bedside entering it. I feel like a kid again being looked after by my mommy. She flew in last night. You know what's great about my mom? She doesn't shush me and tell me not to get agitated. She knows I've got to get this out. And she promises not to edit a word.

I never saw him. I assume it was a him. I'm in the park yesterday morning – it seems like years ago – helping people dismantle tents and pack up. I'm collecting garbage. I've just stood up and – this is weird – I hear the shot before I feel it. Then I know something has entered me but I can't feel it. Everybody starts screaming and only then do I fall to the ground. That's all I remember until I'm being off-loaded from the ambulance at the hospital. Not to be melodramatic but I knew I was a marked man. It could have been a lone Wildcat sniper or it could have been one of the security forces masquerading. Or one in the pay of the other. I have to think that if it was a real hit man, I'd be dead. They say my bulk might have saved me. It's easier to kill a skinny man – less flesh in the way. Or maybe they were just warning me to shut up.

It's really put an end to the park, I guess. Mom tells me almost no one's left now. Some hardcore protesters have moved to another park, but now that there's so few of us in the city, the police can clear the parks more easily. The schools have reopened in the area and the playgrounds have been cleaned up. It's over for now, folks. What we have to remember is how powerful our movement became. We know that now. And we know the power of those against us. The Tarstoppers who are camped at the border are all heading back home now and the jackals and other scum predators that preyed on them are leaving too.

I know I have to go home to TO but my dilemma is over how to get there. I know, fly, baby, fly. Make an exception. I won't be able to drive myself and I can't ask my mom to rent a car and drive me. I thought of the neph but it turns out he doesn't even have a driver's license, which otherwise I have to admire, though he's got a learners and we could get by. Good practice for him. I don't know if two people driving for three twelve hour days would be better than one person on a three and a half hour flight in a full plane. Anyone know? That kind of information should be readily available so we can weigh decisions.

I've got to stop here. Just this much has taken me all day. My mom's tired. Thanks Mom. Tomorrow I hope to be able to come at you direct.

●

In the hospital it took Armie a while to find Deke, who'd been moved out of intensive care. Now he was in a private room, an upgrade paid for by Marilyn, he had to think. Had Deke protested his removal from the common herd? Armie had come to the hospital on his bike because he didn't know what to do with himself in his acute state of sexual deprivation. He'd needed distraction and vigorous exercise. In just the way that he'd gone on listening to Katie, easing her way, he wanted badly to have just one more transitional fuck. He knew it would be wrong to take advantage of her that way, even if she too wanted it. He also knew his hyper-arousal would fade in time. After all, somehow he'd made it through months without Katie when he'd been in Toronto in school. He could do it again.

Marilyn for the moment was not in the room. Deke seemed to be asleep. Armie sat down in a chair to wait for either Deke or his grandmother. Today he'd been online looking at jobs, when he wasn't sidetracked onto porn sites. He wasn't qualified for much and this time of year he was competing with all the university and high school kids. He had rules. No retail: he'd almost died of boredom the one time he'd tried it. He really didn't want restaurant work but there didn't seem to be too much else available. The temptation was to go back to the brewery. He'd been talking to Carly, the office manager. They wanted him back. Carly said they'd put his outburst down as a stress leave. Everyone understood he'd been rattled that day; everyone had been.

Take off. That was another option. He had money saved, living at home. Thailand, Australia, maybe working an organic farm in Italy or building schools in Haiti. The opportunities on the Net were almost endless. Teach English in China.

"Dude," said Deke.

One of the guys at work called everyone dude, a generational thing, Armie had to think. He asked him, "How are you doing?"

"Never mind me," Deke said, his voice even deeper than it usually was but still urgent. "What's happening? What's the latest?" He was patting around, looking for his iPad. Someone must have found it and brought it to the hospital.

"Not much new. Everybody's gone from our park. The border war is winding down. Only three people killed overnight there. Life's getting back to normal."

"Tell me something I don't know. What's being said? What's online?"

"I don't know. I haven't looked."

"You haven't looked? This is the biggest story in history. How can you not be following it second by second?"

Armie shrugged.

"Don't go shrugging on me. Do you know how huge this is? It's like the sea, that's what I've learned. Nobody can control it. The forces are bigger than all of us. Storms come up from a thousand causes and most of the action is way below the surface. There are the populist forces like us and the fucking Wildcatters and then there's the authorities trying to direct it all. Some of the big oil companies are as big and powerful as countries and they're out there manipulating and influencing and going rogue if they have to. And meanwhile the poor planet is going absolutely haywire. And you're not that interested?"

"Somehow I don't think Exxon's covert actions are posted on the Net." Deke had closed his eyes again, like he'd strained himself with that outburst. "Maybe you shouldn't talk right now."

"Nothing's going to shut me up. Say something. Tell me what you're thinking."

"Well, I guess that it's hard to believe this all started with Wendy and her boys tweeting up some environmentalists while they were knocking on the Morrisons' front door. And then it's over and it'll be like it never happened."

"You want it all to go away so you won't have to act. We accomplished a huge amount here. We terrified the power guys with our numbers. And one good thing, the other side went so wacko and extreme that sympathy's swinging back around to us. Not that people getting killed was a good thing. The trouble is we don't have the time for this to play out. I have to fight my pessimism that we're going to be able to do fuck-all before the planet becomes unlivable."

"What about a carbon tax? From everything I've read, it seems the best solution."

"We don't have time. Anyway, can you imagine that ever becoming law in the States? Or in China? Come on." He sat up a bit. "Hey, do you have any interest in chauffeuring me home?"

"What? To our house, you mean? Now?"

"No, Dude. You and me, on the road to TO. When I get out of here. I'm against flying."

"You've been shot. What if we're in the middle of Saskatchewan and your stitches pull out or something? It takes four or five days to drive to Toronto. I don't even have a driver's license. Anyway, I'm probably going back to work at the brewery."

"You can put it off for a week. Come on, kid. Where's your sense of adventure?"

"How would I get back? Fly? Drive by myself? Wouldn't that kind of negate the whole thing?"

"Good point. Fuck. I swore I'd never fly again. It's been ten years. Fuck." He closed his eyes.

"Just out of curiosity, what did you think when you set out for here? How you'd get back, I mean. Like after you'd shut down the oilsands and changed the world."

"What? I wasn't thinking about that. I was wild to get on the road."

"Well, isn't that like somebody drilling for oil or something without thinking long-term? Isn't that the whole problem?" Every once in a while he could emerge from his shyness and hesitancy and say something straight. He had to think it meant he didn't respect his uncle much anymore, not to be afraid of challenging him.

Eyes still closed, Deke wasn't paying any attention. After a while he opened his eyes and said, "Did your mom ever hear from that guy again?"

"Her stalker? I don't know."

"He's the one. A pro. They found the bullet but it was untraceable. Mark of a pro."

Armie didn't know where to start. He really didn't want to hear Deke's theories. Why couldn't it be the obvious, a lone deranged Wildcatter randomly picking off the biggest Tarstopper around? "What difference does it make who it was? There are an awful lot of people who don't want the Tarstoppers to succeed. You'll probably never know who it was. Isn't the cause more important? Going ahead?"

"You think you know what you're up against. Ordinary stupidity and the system's reluctance to change. But you don't know. We have to learn who our real opponents are."

"Isn't it easy to become paranoid and put all your energies into tracking your enemies?" Armie gave up. "Where's Marilyn?" he asked. "Is she still here or did she go back to our place?"

"Oh, kid, you're so like your old man it's heart-breaking. So balanced and thoughtful. It's a default position, don't you see that? You gotta get out there and commit. Maybe if we took that trip by the end I'd have you convinced. Don't you understand how ruthless the system is? Don't you see that to fight it is the cause of a lifetime?"

Armie smiled. "Four solid days of you lecturing me? I think we'd both end up off a bridge somewhere in northern Ontario." He stood. "I gotta go. Glad to see you perking up."

He left, some things more easily done than others, but he could not avoid his grandmother, big dominant Marilyn, sitting in the coffee shop near the hospital entrance. She was at a small table by herself, watching the others, the people at home in the room and those sitting stiffly, not at ease, waiting. There were no other chairs at her table so he had to hunt one out and carry it over his head in the crowded room. Marilyn watched his awkwardness fondly, like he was a cute little kid, which made him even more self-conscious, the nice boy with his grandmother. Putting down the chair and sinking onto it didn't take him as far out of view as he would have liked.

"Was he awake?" Marilyn asked him.

He nodded. "He had this idea I could drive him back to Ontario so he didn't have to fly. I pointed out that he'd use twice the energy that way, since I'd have to get back somehow. Never easy being green. I guess."

"Between you and me I have to confess that with so much wrong in the world, global warming is not near the top of my list. I don't tell Derek that of course. Although it's not like I don't know the projections."

"It's so weird, the number of different tracks we're on." Here it came, one of his shifts into articulation, here with his grandmother in a crowded, very noisy coffee shop. He knew she wanted this engagement from him, but so did lots of people and usually he was incapable. It was like his thought coalesced at a certain moment and didn't care where it happened. "And the tracks don't overlap or connect. They're getting farther and farther apart. Like the whole nanotechnology, 3D printing line that's coming. It'll change the world. And yet it won't be able to do anything about climate change and wild weather and flooding and drought and stuff. It'll probably put more people out of work as more and more becomes automated and robotic, and yet the whole economy is based on the creation of jobs so people can spend. And it'll just alienate all the fundamentalists and out-of-it traditionalists around the world even more. It's hard to know which train to get on, the slow clean-up one or the one speeding into the future. And either way we take our old paleo mentality and reactions with us."

Marilyn, although a little taken aback by his sudden loquacity, quickly joined in. She loved a conversation like this one. Although she probably wanted to tell him what she thought, she was enough of a grandmother and a teacher to stifle that urge and encourage him. "It's certainly much harder for kids today than ever before. I guess that, like most of us, you have to just go with your gut. Aren't you pulled in one direction more than another? Doesn't something compel you?"

"I've tried that. You know, paleo-anthropology. But I'd rather have it as an interest and read the latest stuff rather than inch along on the ground." He didn't really want to talk about himself. He didn't want Marilyn to feel like she had to help him out and patiently nudge along his thinking. "Anyway for now I'm just as happy to work at any ordinary job and go on watching and reading." No doubt Marilyn would see this as avoidance. "Maybe it'll come to something but probably not. It's okay. It's not about me."

Marilyn understood that he didn't want to talk about himself. He could see her pick up and shift. She said, "What I see as the big crunch is the unwillingness for anyone to pay for what's going to be needed to cope with climate change. We've lost the communal spirit. Aside from the Tarstoppers, and they're still such a minority, even if they don't seem like it right here and now. Since global warming is going to happen – we can probably agree on that – we have to put protections in place. But no one will want to spend the money. Especially in some place like Bangladesh, but even in the States. Those with money won't pay their share. They'll be able to relocate."

She liked to talk about ideas as much as he did. It was a family tradition. How many other grandsons and grandmothers in the world would be talking like this? Not many. None in this coffee shop. He could have kissed her.

But then she let him down. "Now there's something you could do," she said spiritedly. "The promotion of public policy. You're a bright guy. We need you to apply yourself to the problems of the world. Although I understand the allure of ideas, in the end you have to act."

He was supposed to nod and agree, make her feel like she'd got through to him. He wasn't that good an actor. Even she, theoretically the most open-minded of people, thought that she had to come up with a packaged solution to his life. The promotion of public policy: now there was a hot prospect.

The noise and the people jostling the back of his chair and the weirdness of talking to his grandmother like this in a hospital coffee shop broke back in. He could stay and chat about hospitals and Deke and what would happen now with the Tarstoppers or he could leave. He had no choice but to leave. Either way he'd be disappointing his grandmother, and all in such a short time. He'd get back on his bike now and pedal like crazy all the way home.

●

Tim wasn't sure what he was doing it for, sitting beside Deke's bed watching him sleep, having left work early. Pleasing his mother, no doubt, who'd taken his car and gone back to the house for a rest. He was trying to feel some affection for this great crude lump of a man, his brother. The coarseness of him, his rough skin bristling with wiry hairs, his thick and cracked fingernails, the folds of fat surrounding his neck, repelled him in the way that his transformation at puberty into a hairy rough monster had. Although Tim had also felt paler and less masculine in the comparison – Deke's voice had suddenly become an octave lower than his – another part of him had been relieved that he had not become as grossly unfamiliar to himself. Now here he was again, basically waiting for Deke to shut up and go away. When it came to his relationship to his brother, he hadn't advanced much since childhood.

Lori! Suddenly she was there in the room, beaming at him. He was thrilled to see her, as he would never be at the sight of Deke, although partly it was the relief of distraction. He jumped up and hugged her, surprising her. He took her arm to lead her down to the lounge at the end of the hall.

"Thanks for the messages," he said to her on the way. "It's been a tough time. But he's really coming around."

"I'm sorry I couldn't get here until now. Poor Deke. I felt so badly. I can't tell you how much I enjoyed my time with him looking around the camp and talking to people last weekend. I had to come tell him what a difference he'd made to me."

"A convert? He'll be ecstatic to hear it."

They were dodging stretchers and nurses and pale patients wandering in their ratty old bathrobes. Lori gleamed with colour and health under the lights in the drabness. The lounge with its plastic, shiny, turquoise sofas was thankfully empty.

Lori twirled to face him. "Okay. Right up front. Just so you know. Cole and I are splitting up."

"Because of my brother?"

Lori laughed. "Indirectly. Okay. So you know how you

go along not happy with a lot of things but thinking that on balance it's not so bad, it's okay? You've got this far and you might as well keep going to the end. And then something comes along that tips it. Like his rage. He's always been an angry guy. He usually kept it under control in public. You guys never really knew. There'd be an occasional flare or maybe he'd drink too much when you were camping or something and get going but you wouldn't know how routine it was. My father was an angry guy: it's just the way I thought men were. But Cole's rage at the Tarstoppers was, is, way over the top. He starts drinking as soon as he gets home from work and then he gets vicious.

"Anyway, after I was with your brother and the Tarstoppers last weekend I drove home and it was like I'd been away for a thousand years. That house I've never liked but have stayed tied to because any day now we were going to have more money and move on up. All the time yearning for something better. The kids are grown and gone, so why was I still there, living like that? With Cole's frustration and anger. As Deke says, it's a disease, wanting stuff. It was so clear to me. Putting up with crap while you wait for some affluent future that won't be all that satisfying anyway. And all along you're doing your part to poison the earth and clog it up. Like that night at dinner at your house and you were talking about how inconsistent I was being. I was kind of pissed off at the time but it's so obvious now. So thanks for that. And for your brother."

They were still standing. "Wow. I felt badly for how irritable I was that night. Waiting for Deke to show up. Normally

I know how compromised we all are and I'm more forgiving. How's Cole taking this?"

"You know what? I don't care. I'm tired to death of carrying him and humouring him and protecting him and encouraging him. I would have said I was fond of him, you know, because of the history and surviving so much together, but then I looked at him and realized I was fooling myself. This is such a liberation. I can't tell you."

"I was just sitting beside my brother wondering why I didn't feel more. Maybe I shouldn't think of it as a failing. What are you going to do? Have you moved out?"

"I'm looking at condos. With my new eyes. It's not about what looks best – how stylish it is – it's about what suits me, what works for me, what I need. It'll take a while. We have to sell the house."

"And Cole's going along?"

"He's all hang dog now. You know – everything's always gone against him and now I'm deserting him. He's a failure because he's never been able to give me what I wanted. He doesn't get that it's not about having stuff. But this stage won't last. The anger will take over. I know this split is not going to be amicable. I'll rent a place if he gets too difficult."

"Do you think he's dangerous? I can't believe I'm asking this about Cole. Nice quiet Cole. Although I have seen the other side, of course."

"I would never have said so but now I'm not so sure. His rage at the Tarstoppers was beyond extreme. I started to think he'd get a gun and join the Wildcatters."

Tim smiled. "You're starting to think like Shannon: that anyone's capable of anything in the right conditions. Let's go see if Deke's awake. It'll aid his recovery immensely to know he's had an effect on you."

She held him back, peering. "Are you and Shannon okay? She was almost as mad as Cole at the Tarstoppers."

"We're okay. Rocking wildly but staying upright. I never doubt how I feel about Shannon. I don't get as much from her as I'd like but I can live with that. The last thing she's looking for is liberation."

The old Lori was still there, probing at him, waiting for equal revelation, assessing. He thought he'd given her enough, more than he would tell anyone else. He said, "We'd better get back, see how he's doing."

In the corridor they came across Marilyn, surging along, taking up so much room. She seemed already at home on this floor. The women hugged, having met a few times over the years. Lori had always thought Marilyn was the kind of cosmopolitan with-it mother she herself would love to have had. It meant Tim could leave. Lori and Marilyn and Deke would get along fine without him. He said to Lori, "Call me if you need me. Any time. Tell Deke I'll talk to him another time."

He didn't check for reaction, just turned for the elevators. He didn't owe Deke an audience. What more could he have done for him than deliver up a converted Lori? Marilyn frowned at him almost imperceptibly, which was all it had ever taken to keep Tim in line, and in catching it, the power of it, he could almost smile at how little it had always taken to make him second-guess himself. He didn't have to be there.

●

THE WHOLLY GREEN GIANT
6:31 PM

Hey I'm entering this myself. Slowly. Very slowly. I think I'm going to make it. When you first come out of surgery you think you're going to die for sure but a few pain-killers & a little sleep & you can start to imagine recovering. Thanks again for all the tweets & texts & e-mails. They're a big part of my bounce-back. & thanks for all the offers to drive me back to TO. Turns out this dude I knew years ago is here with a camper. He's going to wait for me to be released. He even has paramedic training.

I wish I could stay. I wish I were going to be among the loyalists who stay put to remind the city & the world what happened here. We estimate there were fifty thousand Tarstoppers in the city at the peak & another fifty thousand of us stopped at the border. Numbers that can't be ignored or forgotten. I'll keep working against the oil & coal industries & on our whole dysfunctional corporate excessive way of life. I'll go on faithfully reporting in.

Am I discouraged? Hell no. I believe in the whole tipping point thing & don't think we're that far away. The friend of the Bro's I met — the pretty nice one, not the pipeline guy — came to the hospital today to tell me she'd seen the light thanks to me & what's gone on here. There's got to be lots more like her. It's going to be too late to prevent a lot of the destruction to come but at least we're waking up to it in bigger & bigger numbers.

Everyone was gone from the park. From the head of the dining room table Shannon could look through to the living room window and out into solid greenery, no other houses visible this time of year. From here, she couldn't see the muddy pathways or the long uncut grass. The green haze hid the big black circles where campfires had burned and all the broken trees and shrubs. The sun had even come out.

She was barely listening to Tim and Marilyn, mostly Marilyn, who was asking Tim, "Have you heard this hare-brained scheme of your brother's to drive all the way back to Toronto with someone? I know he doesn't want to fly but this is ridiculous. Can you talk to him?"

"Me? I'm the last person he'd listen to. He tried to talk Armie into driving him. He seems determined."

Armie nodded in confirmation but he wasn't otherwise part of the conversation.

"What in the end has been accomplished?" Marilyn moaned. "All those people killed and injured. It was all so well-intentioned and look what it came to. We as a society have to become more adult and think ahead to consequences."

Who could argue with that? And while we're at it, Shannon thought, let's all be nicer to each other. She wanted to cover Armie's ears. She hated this kind of talk, "we as a society." Cutting Marilyn off, surprising them all, she said to Armie, "Don't go back to the brewery unless you're planning to go back to school in the fall. You don't have to know what you want to do. Life happens in the process. You can't think it out too much ahead of time. And you're even allowed to have some fun along the way."

She'd pinned Armie in their attention, something that he counted on her not to do. She was as bad as everyone else, giving him advice. Tim was squinting at her.

Marilyn, as if given permission by Shannon to voice her concern, said to Armie, "Your mother's right. You have to get going. It doesn't even matter so much any more which direction you take. You have to get going."

Shannon said, "Actually I take back what I said." She turned back to Armie. "Do it your way. I have huge faith in you. I'm sorry that if in my anxiety I made you doubt that."

She could watch Armie do his best to not shy down. "No, it's okay. I mean, I appreciate that everyone wants what's best for me. I'm just trying not to take myself too seriously." He smiled. "And anyway, weren't we just saying that running off in all directions with no plan is part of the problem?"

Marilyn wanted to argue it. She loved a good argument. Her voice would rise and she'd bully them with her size and her age and her status. She fixed Armie in her sights, almost like she'd grabbed him by the arm, and said, "No, you need to get involved. Bright kids like you have an obligation."

Tim said, "Leave him alone, Mom."

Tim speaking up to his mother; Tim knowing first-hand the pressure to better the world.

As Marilyn started to say, "No, he should," Tim said to Armie, "We're finished eating. You don't have to stay."

Shannon could have kissed him. She stood up. "If you'll excuse me, I'm going out into the front garden for a while. With the Tarstoppers gone, I can start to tidy up. That's all I care about right now." She smiled at Armie and waited for him also to rise. Then she turned away.

A little while later, Tim came out and sat on the front porch steps. "Almost back to normal," he said, looking around.

Shannon was tying up the new rampant growth on the clematis trained against the house. She turned to look at the park. "I'm starting to understand why people need to pretend and forget after a debacle. Was your mom offended? I had to get Armie off the hook. I'm sorry I left you with her and the clean-up."

"It's okay. I think she's gotten over her disappointment at not having a daughter-in-law who wants to join her on the barricades. I'm pretty much of a write-off in that regard myself. So's Ardith. Mom still has hopes for Armie. Otherwise it's just Deke. Even she realizes the problems with that."

He hesitated, wanting to ask or tell her something. Being Tim, he couldn't just come out with it. She wasn't going to help him out. Finally he said, "I forgot to tell you: Lori was at the hospital to see Deke. She's left Cole. For which she mostly credits Deke. Making her see the light and change her life."

Indirection. She answered his subtext. "Look, I'll admit I was a little deranged there for a while but there was never any danger of me leaving you. You know that. I'm not surprised by Lori though. She hung on with Cole long after she should have left and she needed something to come along and release her. I just hope she doesn't become all righteous with it. You know, become a vegan, bike to work, and then be no longer able to be friends with me because of what I do for a living."

"None of this has made you doubt that?"

Not said earnestly, thank God. Instead, wryly, half-smiling. In full understanding of the complexities. She could give him the same kind of smile right back. "Better go in to your mom. I'll be in in a little while."

For a few minutes more she'd wrestle with the clematis, tame it to her will, rejoice in the green surge of it, without thinking about anything else.

●

Armie, in the basement on his bed, was playing a video game. He was going to play games until something else came to him. Thinking was getting him nowhere. Back to the brewery, back into aimlessness. He'd hold out against going back to Katie. That would probably take all of his strength right now. He was just holding on, trying not to lose the ground he'd gained.

But then he remembered something he'd read. A theory. It was amazing how some part of his brain kept chugging along, processing all of the information he fed into it, no matter what else was going on with him. The theory was that humans had become conscious when they realized they were mortal. No other animal had that capacity. The realization that you yourself would inevitably die. It was the beginning of religion, but also of denial. In order to go on living and not give into terror or despair, humans had to learn how to block the knowledge out. And once they had that ability it was useful for being able to ignore all kinds of inconvenient facts. Like their own worst behaviour.

And these days it let those in the West ignore things like how much of their cushy lifestyle was based on misery in the Third World or how their drug use supported organized crime. They could forget, or never know, the history of human brutality, the knowledge that had so thrown his mom at a young age. And they could know the reality of global warming and at the same time go on as they were.

Deke would probably say that theorizing was as much an escape from reality as a video game. But maybe knowing ourselves, figuring out our weirdnesses – the whole paleo track he'd been on – was the only safe way forward. He could look that theory up.

TUESDAY
JUNE 12 2012

Pulled up in front of the house, Tim sat in his car beside Deke, who was staring out the side window at the empty park. Tim had taken the time off to pick Deke up from the hospital and now needed to get back to work, but Deke's bulk seemed immovably wedged into the car. He was wearing one of his enormous green T-shirts, the black painted circle on it now pocked and faded after a washing, the green X blurred. On the far side of the park a red mowing machine swung through the long trampled grass.

"Well, have you been convinced?" Deke asked him, his voice low and depleted. He didn't turn his head to look at Tim. "Are you ready to get involved?"

"Why is it so important for you to get me onside?"

"That is such a Tim answer. Let's make it personal. Let's

not get fired up about the guys leading us all into destruction, the ones who'll kill anyone in their way."

"Maybe you should go in now. You'll do damage if you get too upset. Pull a stitch or something."

Deke's whole body sagged, his head now against the side window. "You're like everybody else. You just want back to your orderly life. Back to your office where you can feel satisfaction about all the good you do. You know what it is, why you get to me so much? You're not stupid. You're not one of the ignorant. You know what's going on. Yet you can turn a blind eye. You put out your recycling and shrug in confusion about doing anything more. There's so many of you out there. It's tough knowing my own brother is one of them."

Tim put his own window down to let out the dirge-like sound of Deke's voice, the smell of him. He wanted to gulp at the cool incoming air. Catching sight of his mother in the living room window, he waved to her almost frantically. "Mom's in the window. Just so you know, she's planning to try and talk you out of driving back to Toronto. She feels pretty strongly."

Deke banged his head against the window. "Just fly this one time, right? What's one flight? Since I've been shot and all. And so Mom doesn't have to worry. I'm being selfish, having principles." He banged his forehead against the window twice more. "You'll probably fly to Europe again this fall. Right? To keep the wife happy. Easy-peasy for you to join the tourism juggernaut. Tell me: what do you say to yourself?" He swung his big shaggy head part way around, reminding Tim of a bison, the small wild eye on him. "Seriously. I want to know."

There was never going to be any getting away from Deke, Tim saw. He was in his head for good. Disliking him and his methods and motives wouldn't change the validity of his warnings, only make them a little easier to ignore. "I live uneasily with compromise. We all have to. Even you. Without a thought, you've used the park whose grass is cut by a gasoline-powered mower." He stopped himself from coming up with more examples. "Look, I'm sorry, I have to go. Do you need help getting out?"

"No. I wouldn't want to inconvenience you."

He shouldn't have asked; he should have just done it, gone around to help him out. But the thought of Deke engulfing him, loading him down, had for that moment made it seem impossible. Now he could only wait while Deke slowly got his legs out of the car and then as he hoisted his body using the top of the window. Tim thought it might crumple. As Deke heaved himself up and out, the car rocked with the transfer.

Marilyn had come out, having seen Deke emerge. She rushed down the path and across the street, reminding Tim of when he and Deke were little and she, the biggest and tallest mother around, would thunder out to stop their fighting, yelling, "Why can't you two boys get along?" Tim got out of the car. He couldn't let his mother take all of Deke's weight. Deke was now bent over, his hands on his knees, in pain or winded.

It was slow progress into the house, Deke with an arm slung over each of them as he stumbled and dragged along. Tim tried not to gag, his face in Deke's armpit. Up on the porch at the door, he had to let his mother pull away as he maneuvered Deke inside by himself. Then he had no choice, Deke's weight insupportable for long, but to let him down onto the white sofa and hope he wouldn't leak out all over it.

He said to his mother, "Don't bother trying to talk him out of driving. His ride's coming for him some time after lunch. I'll leave work early so you're not here too long on your own after he goes. But I have to get back to work now. I have a meeting, I have no choice." He took hold of her arm, she looked suddenly so old and worn out, and she leaned into him. They gazed down at the bulk of Deke, this huge green mass of a man laid out on the sofa with one arm over his eyes. Tim said to her, "Call me on my cell if you need me."

As he walked back to his car, the mower in the park powered towards him over the grass, the driver invisible behind the glare on the glass. A small grey puff of exhaust hung in the air for a second as the mower swung around a spruce tree and headed in another direction. The tree's branches, which must have been in some camper's way or needed for firewood, had been hacked off to way above head height.

Christine Rehder Horne was born in Toronto and has lived all across Canada, now making her home in Calgary. A Dalhousie University graduate, Horne is a passionate gardener and volunteer in her community. *Tarstopping* is her first novel.